Confederate Saddle
Book 2

Terry P. Collins

Editing by Chameleon
Cover by Chameleon

In Honor of Two Civil War Veterans

Union — Timothy Frogge Collins
19th Kentucky Volunteer Cavalry

Confederate — Fred House
Medal of Recognition recipient
Company K, 24th Regiment, Texas Cavalry

Table of Contents

ONE

The Southern Shenandoah Valley
Early May, 1861

The Lewis Farm

The horses were at full gallop as we raced into the courtyard, throwing up large clumps of mud in our wake. Reining in our heaving mounts, my cousin, Wilson, shouted, "Damn, Levon, you must be cheatin'. I was a couple of lengths ahead of you when we went past the big pine," he said, gesturing toward the gnarled pine that sat as a solitary sentinel on the top of the hill.

I chuckled. "Ah, quit complaining, Wilson. You Missouri boys can't compare to us Virginians when it comes to superior horseflesh and riding." My cousin's family had fled the unrest that had been roiling across the Missouri territory. The pro and anti-slavery folks were pitted against each other, eager to stake a claim to the region with beliefs that mirrored their own.

My cousin's family owned slaves, as did my family, so my uncle and father figured the family would be safer down here in the southern Shenandoah. Virginia was a decidedly slave-owning state, and nobody was gonna change that. My father owned about 40 or so and it wasn't a problem. Now, up north, there was some name-calling, I won't deny that, but my father didn't appear to be too worried.

My name is Levon Lewis and I live here with my parents and sisters, Alexandria and Quinn, in the southern Shenandoah Valley around Wytheville. While walking the horses to cool them down, Wilson asked, "How is Caleb doing up there at school? You hear from him often?"

He was referring to my brother who was a cadet at the Virginia Military Institute. "Ah, we get the occasional letter from him. He is up there with one of our neighbors. Been up there about a year. Father said he needed to grow up."

"Why aren't you up there?" he asked

"I'm the oldest male family member left at home, excepting my father, but he feels I'm still too young," I replied sheepishly. "Guess I can still play around some more. He accused Caleb of as much."

I guided my roan, Sol's Mistress, into the covered stable while Wilson took his mount into the next stall over. I unbridled her as we continued talking.

"Good thing, cause we got the races at the Wythe County Fair next week. Looks like ya got me beat, if today is any indication. Even though you're cheatin," Wilson said.

"Yeah, I am looking forward to the races. I'm thinking I'll win them all with my girl here," I said, patting the roan on her back after taking off the girth and cinch. "I've heard folks around saying this colored boy from the Stuart place in Laurel Hill can give me a run. His name is Charles Henry, and they say they don't know where he learned to ride, but can, like the wind," I said. "I'm not too concerned with no slave, though."

I didn't completely trust my own words. I knew I could ride, but the Stuart family was known for their horsemanship. One of the Stuart boys, James Ewell Brown, was already in the United States Cavalry. So maybe some of their slaves could ride too. I took the saddle off and rubbed the big roan down with straw, poured some water over her as she snorted and pranced, then dried her off again. After checking for rain rot and giving her some grain, Wilson and I headed for the house.

Before stepping into the foyer, a commotion down by the slave quarters caused me to glance there. The slaves were all milling around this one cabin, swaying and carrying on in strange sing-song voices, while the glow of the fire inside the cabin burned bright in the growing dusk. The slaves had been acting rather strangely for days now. Sometimes they were distant, never meeting your gaze, but rather looking at something far away. It wasn't peculiar that they didn't meet your gaze, for that was their obedient way. Other times, they just chuckled to themselves and spoke of the Jubilee.

Lately, it had made me uneasy. This uneasiness carried me inside and was slow to go away at the end of an otherwise perfect day. The house staff brought out dinner and we all sat down.

My father and uncle talked about how the crops were doing, and further plans, until the discussion turned slightly more ominous.

"Well, Jack, it looks like Virginia is joining the lower states in seceding after the firing on Fort Sumter," my father said, his voice heavy with resignation.

"I guess whatever is going to happen was bound to

happen anyway. We knew that when we decided to leave Missouri. But with that John Brown fellow, and with these damn politicians butting in, I guess we are all going to be dragged into the fray. Just a might sooner," Uncle Jack said.

"Perhaps being down here in the valley bought us some time, but Virginia is where this nation started. Our ancestors started their lives here, and it seems to me that Virginia is the strongest of all the states, so I believe we will be all right no matter what is to come. But, Levon, this week's Wythe County Fair may be the last one for a while. So you better win those races," Father said with a slight glint in his eye.

"I will, Father," I mumbled.

"What about your son up there at the Institute, John? What happens to him now?" my uncle asked.

"I don't rightly know," my father said. "I don't know if the cadets will continue their schooling or be released to come home. I can't really see how they will continue the school. With our state's secession, they will be a target, I assume."

I excused myself and trudged upstairs. What would I do? I don't like to fight, and I only reluctantly fire a gun. But maybe it would just be one short dust-up and then be over. Plus, I'm down here in the lower valley. But my father and uncle's discussion tonight didn't seem to me like they expected a short one.

I spent the next few days prior to the fair taking Sol's Mistress out for leisurely canters in the lush valley to keep her limber. During those times, I prayed that the beautiful Virginia countryside would always remain that way.

The day of the fair, I awoke, stepped out of my bed, and tried to ignore my nervous stomach that was threatening to jump through my skin. After quickly dressing, and an even quicker breakfast, we headed out. Wilson and I rode our mounts out ahead while our families trailed behind us in two carriages. The day broke frosty and breezy, while the sun lit the sky with its shimmering brilliance.

TWO

Virginia
May, 1861

Wythe County Fair

I was the first to glimpse the banners ringing the fair. Brightly colored streamers extended on poles snapped in the breeze. Crowds of people mingled among the stalls that held cotton gins, or any other of the newest farm machinery that could be made. I was amazed. I didn't know that this many people lived in the whole valley.

I dismounted and walked into the mass of people, leading Sol's Mistress on a short tether. We made our way through the crowd of men dressed in bright waistcoats and jackets who strolled with ladies in patterned dresses clinging to their arms, while simple farmers in their work clothes paid close attention to the farm equipment. Children with dirt-smudged cheeks shrieked and shouted as they scampered through the aisles.

In one of the aisles stood a barrel chested slave trader who looked like he had just jumped off one of the slave ships. He held a chain that was linked to six or more sullen slaves who were fastened to the chain with yokes around their necks. At another stall, a beaming round woman offered up one of her pies, proclaiming that they were sure to be this year's blue-ribbon winner, while Sol's Mistress lifted her head and sniffed at the aroma to see if the woman's proclamation was true.

"There is Master Lewis, the best horseman in the entire valley," a voice boomed. Our neighbor, Mr. Nicely, walked up, extending his hand. "Levon, you and your lady friend here ready to show all of Virginia your skill?" he said, his eyes twinkling.

"Hi, Mr. Nicely. I'm gonna do my best," I replied.

"Well, boy, I'm sure you will make your farm proud, but there are some other riders who are pretty fast too, I hear," he said, slapping me on the back, then reached his hand out to my father in greeting.

"Hello, John, good to see you. I trust your family and farm are doing well?"

"Ah, yes, Bill, and yours too?"

I continued into the milling crowds as Mr. Nicely and my father continued to chat. I came upon an oval area clear of foliage and bracketed by fence rails that seemed to stretch the length of one whole field. Someone in the crowd made a reference to "the track" and I figured that this was where the races would take place.

Some of the crowd milled around the track talking and gesturing at the ground, while a small group gathered around three men clad in strange gray uniforms, talking excitedly. I remembered that my brother had worn the same uniform on his one trip home from school. So they were cadets. What were they doing here?

I didn't get too much time to ponder it because a rather large fat man, struggling as he climbed upon two overturned buckets, shouted, "Racers, kindly step forward."

Gesturing at the two men with him, he continued, "Simpson and Dill here will be handing out three different colors of cloth, one for each participant. Three initial races will be held with the color of your strip signifying in what race you will be placed. The three winners of each race will move on to the fourth and final race to determine the best horseman in the valley. Simpson and Dill will be at the finish line to determine the winners. The riders will race two laps around the oval and that will be it. So you all come here to get your strip."

I looked around for Wilson and grabbed his arm so we could get our strips.

"Uh, no, Levon, I'm not from Virginia, I can't race," Wilson stammered.

"You are living here right now. Come on," I pressed, and he followed me.

The riders began to crowd the three men, when suddenly, I heard a low grumbling. Looking around at the crowd, they all seemed to be staring with mouths agape at the sight. Charles Henry, the strapping slave from the Stuart place, was making his way to the men. He was huge, with muscles that glistened with sweat, dressed in trousers and an undershirt; reaching for a strip. Someone in the crowd shouted out, "What's that stupid nigger doing? He can't race with us."

"Yeah, this is for us white folks, not no coloreds," another yelled.

Then a calmer voice spoke, "What's the harm of letting the boy race? These races are to prove who the best horseman in the valley is, aren't they? Besides, how well can he ride anyhow?"

There was some further grumbling on what the South was becoming and how blacks shouldn't be allowed to participate, but it seemed to me that the calmer voice prevailed because Charles grabbed a green strip and melted into the crowd.

Wilson and I both grabbed red strips and went looking for our mounts. Teamed up with about 10 other riders we were placed in the first race. I found Sol's Mistress being tended to by my sister Alexandria, while my other sister, Quinn, held the reins to Wilson's horse, Mitch, and we walked them out to the start.

Mounting up, we waited for the signal to start the race. I patted Sol's Mistress's neck and reassured her, "Run just like you do on our daily rides girl and we will be fine." Next to me, Wilson good-naturedly chided me to be sure not to cheat. I just smiled and wished him luck.

The signal was a pistol shot that caught Sol's Mistress and I both off guard. I never carried a weapon, so she was not accustomed to the report of a weapon so close. She promptly reared, nearly bucking me off. I dug in my heels to keep mounted and kicked her flanks to make a charge after the other riders, who now stretched several strides ahead of us.

"C'mon, girl. C'mon, girl," I urged her as we started to inch up on the pack and passed maybe one or two of the others. We rounded the first turn, and pressing my body close to the mare, kept edging up on the pack. Running in the middle, we bumped into one rider on a bay who cursed at us and kicked at her. She didn't even flinch, and with ears pinned back, just ran harder.

We were still in the pack but closer to the front as we completed one whole turn. Out of the corner of my eye, I saw Wilson as we passed him by. Sol's Mistress just seemed to summon up more strength and speed, and suddenly, we was in the lead.

We kept our place and finished first, while Wilson finished third. I slowly reined Sol's Mistress up, allowing her to trot around the ring one more time.

"Nice run, Levon, nice run," my father remarked as I jumped down and handed him the reins. I told him how angry I was at the pistol shot, and how I was going to confront either Mr. Simpson or Dill, whoever had fired the shot.

I stomped over to the men at the starting point and yelled, "Hey, what was the meaning of firing off the pistol to start the race? My horse isn't used to it and so we got started late."

One of the men, I believe it was Mr. Simpson, said laughingly, "Hell, boy, your horse better damn get used to the shooting. You don't know what may come up with you two."

"What do you mean by that?" I sneered.

"Well, now hold on, boy. You best show some respect. Don't tell me that you're so young that you don't understand that Virginia has seceded and there may be some fighting to come about? You may find yourself riding that skittish mare of yours in some pretty hot places. You think these recent events aren't going to spread to the lower part of this valley? Least ways, you may become involuntarily involved, but you must learn to control that temper of yours."

I flushed hot and said, "What you say may be true. But just for today, can't one of you just raise and then drop your arm as the starting signal?"

"We will take that under consideration, son." Not only did they take it under consideration, but used it for the rest of the races.

Wilson and I leaned on one of the rough railings that ringed the track and watched the following races. The race after ours was uneventful, but the third race, oh boy, the third race!

The colored boy, Charles Henry, came in second, meaning he was going to be racing in the final and the muttering began again. "Doesn't that beat all? That damned slave is going to be racing in the final."

"I never would have believed it if I hadn't seen it with my own eyes. What if he wins?"

"It won't happen, Jubal. He is colored."

Wilson and I just looked at each other, shrugged, and mounting up, made our way to the start once more. All nine of us were lined up side by side. Wilson was to my left and Charles Henry to my right.

"Ready," Dill shouted. "Set, and go!" And with that, he dropped his arm and we all charged off. Off to my right, I saw Charles Henry break ahead, followed closely by two to three others. On the left, Wilson bumped me and Sol's Mistress. The bump caused Sol's Mistress to momentarily break stride so it took almost a full go around to get back to an even gallop. Henry was clearly in the lead and the crowd grew restless and noisy. I leaned next to Sol's Mistress's ear, and once again, urged her on.

"C'mon, girl, you can do it. Let's catch that boy." Hearing me, she snorted and began once more to run her heart out. Slowly, we began inching up on him, and all the other riders seemed to disappear from my sight as I focused on Charles.

Charles must have heard us approaching because he cast a quick backward glance and began kicking his horse's flanks even more violently. In a flash, we were alongside him and he said, "Ain't no puny white massa going to beat me today."

I was shocked by his disrespect, and kicked at my girl's flanks a little harder to prove his words wrong. We rode side by side, each urging his own mount on, and the crowd screamed as we neared the finish.

Sol's Mistress's muzzle, then her entire head, pulled ahead of Charles and his horse. When we crossed the finish, Sol's Mistress had more than a shoulder's length ahead of Charles. I quickly exhaled in a sigh of relief.

I slowly trotted Sol's Mistress around the oval one final time as the people clapped and cheered. I abruptly reined her in at the feet of the trio of men who had conducted the races. The fat man asked me my name, and after I answered, he shouted to the crowd who had bunched around us.

"We have all witnessed it. Mr. Levon Lewis here is the finest horseman in the entire great state of Virginia."

After receiving our winning ribbon, I led Sol's Mistress to the carriages. Wilson and I brushed down our horses, laid blankets over their backs, left them contentedly munching from buckets of oats, and went to enjoy the rest of the fair's festivities.

"Well, Levon, I guess that proves it. You are the best damn rider in all of Virginia," Wilson said as he slapped me on the back and hooked his arm around my shoulder.

"Ah, shit, Wilson. That damned Stuart's nigger, Charles, almost beat me. I didn't even think it would be close," I growled.

"I'm sorry, Levon. Maybe if me and Mitch hadn't bumped you it wouldn't have been that close."

"What the hell, Wilson, it's over now. Let's go enjoy ourselves."

We walked along, coming to a shed filled with buckets of apples, and flipped the man a coin. Wilson and I each grabbed one and bit in. We continued our walk, munching on the apples, savoring the sweetness of the juice. Presently, we came upon the small crowd that still stood with the three men in cadet uniforms.

"Gents, we are at war, plain and simple. You mean to

tell us that you would shirk from what is your duty? You all should be honored and emboldened to defend our great state from what we consider to be foreign influence," one of the cadets shouted.

"I don't mind defending what's mine. But I don't feel so almighty fierce to defend Tennessee or Georgia, or any of the other states in this—what are they calling it, Confederacy?" one of those in the crowd shouted back.

Another of the cadets piped up, "We are not asking you to do that at all. Virginia sits smack dab across the Potomac from Maryland, the rest of the north, and the capitol, Washington. Do you not realize that our state is the focal point of what is to come? While the state of South Carolina may have started what is now seemingly growing by leaps and bounds, make no mistake, Virginia will be heard!"

Another one of the cadets continued. "I come from the plantations, as do most of you. This is my second visit home since being enrolled in the Institute so I may not be privy to what is going on down here in the valley. My father has said that the slaves are acting unnaturally. He said that our slaves have a gleam in their eyes that he has not seen before. They go to their quarters at night and engage in who knows what and get all riled up. Have none of you seen it at your own places?"

There were some murmurs among the crowd. "You know, I have seen that, come to think of it."

"It is strange, and I haven't seen that kind of behavior before excepting when a couple of mine ran off."

I was thinking of the odd behavior of our slaves when my thoughts were broken by one of the cadets. Upon seeing me among the crowd, he yelled out, "There is the best horseman in the valley! Come here, young man."

I shouldered my way through the crowd until I was in

front of the three. "Tell me, boy, what is your name?" he asked.

"Levon Lewis, sir. I live here in the county," I said.

"Well, you may be young, but surely you would agree with us about the need to defend this state. Frankly, I'm somewhat surprised you're not with us up at VMI."

"Well, sir, my brother is up there with you. His name is Caleb Lewis. Do you know him?" I asked.

They looked at each other trying to place him. "I don't think I do," one said. "How about you, gents?"

"No, we don't think we do either," they both replied.

"Well, no matter. But, boy, you can ride that horse like no other. I bet you could be pretty valuable in the cavalry."

"Uh, no, sir, not me," I stammered. "I can ride, sure, but I don't want to carry any guns. I reluctantly carry a musket but that is only when I'm forced to, like hunting."

"How well do you know the countryside then?" he questioned further.

"As good as most around here, I figure. I've done some riding all over Virginia."

"Well, how about working as a scout? You could tell us fightin' boys where the enemy is. Since you ride so fast, the chances you'd be caught seem to be very little to me."

I was about to answer when my father stormed up. "What's going on here? What are you boys up to?" he said while glaring at the cadets.

"I beg your pardon, sir. We thought your son, as fine a rider as he is, could be really valuable to the Confederate cause," one cadet said, pulling himself erect.

"Who gave you this official authority to question our desires? Or ask for our support?" father bellowed.

Taken aback, the young cadet said, "Well, no one gives us the authority, but the Virginia Military Institute is falling out to follow one of our teachers. A swift victory would allow us to continue as we always have. Our duties are clear. We must rally all of you to join us."

"You say the cadets are falling out? I guess that's to be expected. Listen, I have a son up there with you and so I acknowledge that he will probably fight. But, gentleman, Levon here is a mere boy and needed at home."

"Sir, I understand your concern," the cadet replied. "But make no mistake, if this thing explodes, or should continue for any length of time, he may be drawn into it, and you as well."

"Thank you for the warning but we will manage. Levon, it's time to go home," and with that said, my father hurried me away.

The ride home was mostly quiet until I mentioned to Wilson what the colored boy from the Stuart plantation had said to me during the race.

"He called you a puny white master?" Wilson laughed. "Doesn't that beat all, but jeez, that is disrespectful. Maybe obedience isn't big over at the Stuart place."

"I don't know, but strange things are certainly happening around here. You heard the talk at the fair. We're not the only ones noticing that odd things are occurring."

We arrived back at the farm in the early evening and both Wilson and I noticed the eerie, and now almost nightly, glow of fire from the slave's quarters that lay close to the pines. Their chants slithered along the ground like snakes, seeming to run up my pant legs and into my shirt until it felt like they coiled around my heart, squeezing all the warmth from my body. I noticed Wilson shivering as we dismounted. We stabled the horses, brought in the carriages, and went inside the house for the night.

Lying in bed, with Wilson in the next bunk, we talked about the races and the fair, but mostly we talked about the mood of the slaves that everyone in the valley was noticing most vividly.

"Wilson, are you scared?" He knew I was talking about the slaves.

"Yes, I am. You know, while walking around the fair today, I passed two men who were whispering between themselves about some kind of magic the slaves are practicing. I think they called it Hoodoo."

"You know, maybe we need to find out more about this Hoodoo. What do you say about us sneaking down there tomorrow night and seeing it with our own eyes? It may do us some good. Calm our fears."

"Good idea, Levon. I'm game."

I curled up into the down quilt and fell asleep with a smile on my face.

The next day, I lazed around, keeping my eyes fixed on the slaves while eagerly awaiting the evening. That evening, with dinner and the chores done, Wilson and I waited upstairs for the evening to settle into darkness. We crept slowly downstairs, and stealing out a side door, headed to the slave quarters that sat on the edge of the pines.

Wilson and I decided the best way to approach the slave quarters was from the extreme west, just a ways from the furthest cabin. We could then make our way to about the middle of the cabins, to the one that most always seemed to be afire where the slaves congregated.

We slinked along the back of the cabins, keeping close to the tree line until we got close to the glowing cabin. We peered through a crack in the wooden slats of the cabin, keeping close to the back of the structure, lest we be seen.

Inside, a fire glowed, encircled by burning candles, while the slaves crowded around it. Seemingly holding court,, sat Mama Ella, who I immediately recognized. Mama sat in a rocking chair, and through slightly closed eyes, was speaking in a low voice. Wearing a loose blue polka-dotted blouse, pink gingham skirt, a necklace that held some bird claws and other trinkets, and with a red kerchief wrapped around her head, she held the other slaves enthralled.

The slaves were lightly drumming on makeshift tom-toms, when suddenly, a young woman who I didn't recognize, stepped from the crowd, squatted over the fire and hiked her skirt. The fluid flowed from between her legs, spattering and sizzling on the rocks in the fire, and both Wilson and the slaves gasped. I was mute from shock.

Wilson muttered, "Oh, my God. What is she doing? This is crazy. It looks red not like she's wetting herself."

I struggled to speak, but my voice just caught in a strangled gurgle, so I just kept watching. Like the slaves, I had become enthralled. The crude tom-toms stopped and Mama Ella's voice became clear.

"As this chile's blood has spilled, let ours spill no more. Neither by the massa's hand, nor by the toil of our wracked bodies. The day of release is coming to us," she intoned while gently swaying from side to side.

She stood, and holding the Bible upright, said, "The salvation of righteousness is from the Lord. He is their strength, lo, our strength, in this time of trouble. And the Lord shall help them and deliver them. He shall deliver them from the wicked, and save them because they trust in Him. I don't know children from what shape of man our Lord will come, but he surely will. As the Lord spoke to Moses to lead the people of Israel out of the bondage of the Pharaoh, so shall we be led. I have seen it in a hundred dreams."

Rubbing a red stone that hung from her necklace, she continued. "As that Exodus occurred so long ago, so will ours begin, and soon, soon. The Jubilee has come. We, and yes, our ancestors, have been here over 40 years. As the Israelites celebrated their year of restitution, so do we. The land will become uncultivated and we will escape the yoke of slavery. Jubilee and emancipation are the same, and it's fast approachin."

The slaves around her began to sway and chant, "Jubilee, jubilee," over and over.

"Let's get out of here, Levon. I've seen enough," Wilson said.

"Yeah, me too. That's not magic we saw, no sir. Mama Ella was using the Bible in her speaking. We came to calm our fears, but I don't know if I'm any less afraid," I said as we stumbled away, still following alongside the trees until we got to the end of the line of cabins.

Leaning against the wall of the last cabin, Wilson said, his voice raspy, "Hold on, Levon. Let me catch my breath. It's true what everybody has been saying! The slaves see changes coming that we don't see. Jesus, Levon, it was like your father and mine discussed just days ago. My family coming here from the Missouri territory may have only forestalled the inevitable. Maybe this situation of who is free and who is not, what is property and what is not, and what region will hold sway and control over another is just plain crazy, it's just not right. I think it may just explode."

"You may be right, Cousin, but Virginia is strong, maybe the strongest state in the whole country. Maybe we can do our part and not have to use a gun against another. C'mon, man, let's get out of here."

For days, I did nothing, but night after night I watched the glow from the slave quarters and heard their unearthly chants from my upstairs window.

Early one morning, my father asked me to hitch up the wagon and go into Wytheville for supplies. Wilson would, of course, come along, and we hitched up a team and headed for town. As we drove the team through the center of town, we spied a throng of men at the courthouse. In front of the throng were four cadets imploring men to join up.

Wilson and I jumped down from the buckboard and tied the team to some posts in front of the general store a little ways from the throng and listened. The newest cadet was holding a handbill and shouting, "Men of Virginia to the rescue! Your soil has been invaded by our abolitionist foes and we call upon you to rally at once and drive them back. Let us, all sons of the Old Dominion, drive back the invading foot of our desperate foes or leave it to eternity that we died bravely defending our homes, the honor of our wives and daughters, and the sacred graves of our ancestors."

One of the other cadets recognized me from the fair and bolted from the throng to approach me. "So, you see young horseman, every one that is true to this state must join. My fellow cadet there came down from Staunton on the Virginia and Tennessee Railroad to rally all of your brethren here," he said, gesturing toward the throng.

"You would partake of the bounty of Virginia, yet do nothing to defend her? Fleet of foot you may be but you lack bravery, I fear. We will be staying at the Hotel Boyd for a few more days. Think long and hard."

"Now hold on just one damn minute, young buck. I want to have a word with you," said a booming voice from just over my shoulder. I recognized one of our neighbors, Josiah Wheeler, a burly tree trunk of a man, storming up.

"Before you start calling us cowards for not jumping

up and going to northern Virginia to fight off the damned abolitionists, you seem to be forgetting something," Josiah said from beneath his bushy red beard.

"What's that you say?" the cadet said. "Wait a minute, I remember you. Back there," he said jabbing his thumb at the crowd. "You were complaining that you couldn't go because you are infirmed. Good God, man, you are the size of a bear with the temperament of a timid field mouse caught in a bale of hay. You ought to be ashamed of yourself."

"I'll show you how timid I am," Josiah said, glowering, and with his fists rose, started toward the cadet.

"Hold on, Josiah, don't," I said as Wilson and I struggled to hold him back.

"Listen, you scrawny son of a bitch. Let's say all of us go up there, and by some unfathomable miracle, get defeated. What happens then? The northerners come storming down here and there isn't no one to defend the women and children. Who will be left to keep an eye on our property?" Josiah spat back.

"Oh, the lion of the baled hay roars," the cadet said mockingly. "This unfathomable miracle you speak of..." he continued raising his hands, wriggling his fingers and rolling his eyes, "won't dare happen against the best of the South, so your point is mute. You can choose to charge with the lions or prance with the mouse, but, Levon, to you and your friend there," meaning Wilson, "the offer stands. We will be here a few more days." He stormed off, his boot heels grinding in the dirt. Josiah walked away grumbling, while Wilson and I went in the store to gather the supplies that had caused us to come to town in the first place.

For days after, I considered what to do. I kept away from town so I wouldn't run into the cadets and their recruiting and be forced to explain myself again. They claimed I was a coward to not defend my home. I didn't feel like a coward just because I didn't carry a gun. Lots of folks didn't. As far as defending our homes, it seemed the fighting would always be up north, not here. But Josiah had made a point that day in town.

If the lines of war were drawn along the Potomac and they were broken, who would be left to defend my mother and sisters? My father is a strong man, as is my uncle, but they are only two men. What chance would they have against a troop of men intent on crushing what I guess they would feel to be disobedience? That, coupled with the lack of authority and control of their masters, what would the slaves do? They would run for sure and no one would be able to stop them.

One morning, while standing on the porch, a group of riders came trotting down the lane. There were eight or so of our neighbors being led by Josiah Wheeler. The group pulled up in front of me. They were all armed. Josiah, wrapped in a heavy coat, spoke while cradling a carbine across his lap.

"Hello, Levon. How are you this fine morning? I got an idea in town a few days back that you might be agreeing with me. That about it?"

"Good morning, Josiah. That is about right. Whatcha got in mind exactly?" I said.

"I was thinking you and I and the others here could form what you might call a home guard."

"Home guard?"

"That's right, home guard. We would protect this area, fight some if needed, and also be slave-catchers if any of those devils should try to escape," he said gruffly.

"Well, Josiah, you know I don't like guns, and you are all armed."

Leaning back in his saddle, he said, "I understand,

Levon, I really do. But I'm inclined to let circumstances dictate your choice on whether to carry a gun or not. But if all we're doing generally is rounding up slaves, you wouldn't be needing no gun. A slave can be brought to heel with a rope just like an unruly horse, and I know you certainly know how to use a rope. You've lived here on this farm all your life. Give us a try."

I stood there rubbing my chin and thinking about his offer when Father walked up. "Hello, Josiah. What brings you up this way?" he asked.

"Good morning, Mr. Lewis. We were asking Levon here to join us as a kind of home guard."

My father asked the same question I had, "Home guard? The Wythe Grays have always protected us, so we don't really need any extra protection, Josiah."

"No disrespect, Mr. Lewis, but the Wythe Grays have left. When the Harpers Ferry incident happened, they formed rank and are now Company A of the 4th Regiment, Confederate infantry. They have been serving in the war, so now it seems right that we should take over where they have ably served."

Josiah continued explaining his plan while my father nodded his head in understanding, and seemingly in agreement. After listening to Josiah, my father asked me, "Levon, what do you want to do? I guess you have figured it out, as I have, that your brother will no doubt become involved, if he hasn't already."

Gesturing with his hand at the band of men, Father continued, "What Mr. Wheeler says does make sense to me. You can stay around here as needed and still be of service during this conflict. I understand that you may be away for a day or two so we can manage. What about your cousin, Wilson?"

"What about me, Uncle?" Wilson said as he sauntered out onto the porch.

"I'll spare you, Josiah, from describing your plan again," my father said, and briefly explained the plans to Wilson.

"Heck, I'm good with that. Keep me from being bored if Levon wasn't around. But I'm going to carry a gun. I want to be careful," Wilson said, pulling himself erect.

"Okay, son, if these gentlemen's plans meet your father's approval, then you're set. What's the next step then?"

Josiah replied, "I was hoping Levon and Wilson there would ride out with us to gather a few others, then we will meet at my parent's place in the early evening. They should be back tonight."

"Very good then," Father said. "Wilson, why don't you check with your father and I'll get the horses saddled. Don't want to leave these boys waiting long. James, help me saddle up Sol's Mistress and Mitch. The boys are heading out."

"Yes, massa, right away," James said from across the courtyard.

Wilson came back out not too much later and tucked an old Colt revolver into his waistband, smiling all the while. We mounted up and rode out with the rest of the group.

 THREE

Late May, 1861

The Wheeler Place

All told, there were 12 of us gathered in the Wheeler parlor that evening. All were fairly young like me, with the exception of Josiah, who was five or so years older than us.

"Well, gents, it looks like us here are gonna constitute what I suggest we call the Wythe County Home Guard," Josiah said, his feet propped up on an old pine barrel.

Henry, a neighbor of Josiah's, asked, "Josiah, I'm still not really clear on what we are supposed to do. Are we now considered part of the Confederate army or what?"

"Well, we don't have no official orders as such, but I think if we protect our homes, and more importantly, our property, which naturally means the coloreds, then that is what we should do. I don't expect no Yanks down here, but if they come, we should act like the Confederate army and fight with them. We won't have no uniforms initially, probably won't need them, but I believe we need some kind of command structure."

Another one of the group everyone called Lo spoke up. "Mr. Wheeler, sir. You got us all here. I'm thinking you should be the leader, plus, you're the oldest."

"I appreciate that, boy. All the rest of you okay with that?" Josiah said, spitting a stream of tobacco juice into a bronze spittoon.

"We are," we answered in unison.

"Okay, boys, that's right good. Now, let's lay down some plans. I think we should split into two groups. We can cover more area that way. We will just roam, or patrol, this entire county," he said, tapping his cane on the floor for emphasis.

"If we have to chase down runaways and leave the county, that will be on my orders only. To keep in contact, we will meet every third day at the old Graham place at Cedar Run. "You boys all know where that is?"

We all nodded in agreement.

"First order of business, then. Some young buck took off from the Larkey farm last night. They don't figure he went too far, though. Seems he has a wife and a couple of children, so he could be lurking around. We are gonna check that out tomorrow. I intend to catch them all. Remember that is our duty. Tomorrow, me, Levon, his cousin, and you there, and there," he said, pointing at two others, "We'll ride over there tomorrow morn to assess the situation. We will meet here first. The rest of you start patrolling next to the peaks on Little Walker Mountain and keep your eyes open. That's it."

As we exited the Wheeler parlor, I spied Josiah gleefully rubbing his carbine and bullwhip with an oilcloth.

FOUR

Summer and Autumn, 1861

Slave Catching

The next morning broke overcast and dreary. Purplish clouds heavy with rain hung low to the ground. Exhaling caused our throats to tighten with the cold, and our breaths to burst forth like puffs of steam from a locomotive.

Wilson and I were both bundled up with mufflers bunched around our necks, heavy coat collars pulled tight, and our felt hats pulled down low. I was wearing gloves to keep warm, but Wilson didn't, and I'm sure that was because it was near impossible to shoot a revolver with gloves on. Although I didn't see his Colt, I knew it was on him. Our group was gathered in front of the Wheeler house when Wilson and I rode up, but Josiah hadn't come out yet.

Josiah came limping out in a sour mood and went

right into complaining. "Damn cold makes my bad leg hurt like hell." He slung his wound up bullwhip over the pommel of his saddle and slipped the carbine into its sheath which clung to the side.

"Those damn niggers can't take off on a warm and sunny day? This weather isn't too good for traveling, but hey, we live in Virginia, so what are you going to do?" he asked to no one in particular.

"Let's ride out to Larkey's and see what's taken place." He kicked his horse's flanks and we galloped off. We arrived at the Larkey place, and Mr. Larkey bounded out of his house screaming and hollering.

"Jojo, he came back, sure as hell did. Took one of my wagons, his missus and children, two of my horses, and took off. He was mighty quiet too. I didn't hear a thing, and I'm a light sleeper," Mr. Larkey howled.

Mr. Larkey was a small slight man who dressed and acted more like a shopkeeper than the farmer he was. A few strands of hair swept back over his pallet and his round spectacles made his face look like an owl. His trousers were held by suspenders and his long-sleeved shirt was held by garters. Hence, he looked more like a timid shopkeeper I often saw in town.

"Now, now, Mr. Larkey, calm down a bit here," Josiah said, trying to stifle a chuckle.

"Calm down, you say? Hell, Josiah, I don't have as many slaves as most folks around here, and Jojo's a good worker. I really can't spare him, and plus, I treat 'em nice. Never used no whip on him. Not at all."

"Then maybe that's your problem right there. I find that both man and beast respond real well to the taste of the whip. Keeps them in line and real obedient," Josiah said, smilingly as he caressed his coiled whip.

Mr. Larkey whimpered as he wrung his hands. "Oh, I don't know, I just don't know. What am I going to do?"

"Don't worry, Mr. Larkey. We're going to catch him, don't you fear. I figure he is going to head straight to the Potomac, and then Washington. To freedom, you know? But he is your property, and your property he will remain."

"But, how will you catch him? I don't know when he left. He could be miles away. That Jojo is pretty smart for a slave. I bet he won't go straight, but try to lose anybody he feels might be chasing him."

"Mr. Larkey, he is a slave," Josiah said abruptly. "You know Levon here is the fastest rider in this whole valley. If you was at the fair a week or so ago, you witnessed how fast he is. Jojo can't outrun him, not with a wagon and family in tow."

Just then, Wilson piped up, "And I can track. Back in the territory, sometimes the dust would cover just about every kind of animal track and wagons too. I'll bet I can find him, and soon."

"Don't hurt him, boys, he is needed for work here."

"Ah, we're not gonna hurt him. Unless he foolishly has what he thinks is a bit of freedom. The whip is a quick teacher. Times a wasting, Larkey. We best be on our way," Josiah said, spitting some tobacco juice which splattered on Mr. Larkey's boots.

Mr. Larkey didn't seem to notice, but asked, "Why you doing this, Josiah? Why are you helping me?"

"Just doing our job. This here is the Wythe County Home Guard. Guarding all of the good people of the valley's home and hearth. We will be back," Josiah said. With that, we trotted off.

There didn't seem to be any major hurry as we cantered off. Wilson slouched along Mitch's flanks searching the ground for any signs.

"Seems he is just following this road if these are indeed his wagon's tracks. There are a lot of tracks here, but these here," Wilson said, pointing out what looked to be new ruts in the road. "These are fresh. As cold as it was last night and this morning they haven't had time to dry and harden. I'm betting that's them."

Josiah rode up alongside us and growled. "Find anything you two? Well, Wilson?"

"I think so, Josiah. I was just telling my cousin here that this particular set of tracks here, they seem real fresh. You see the other wagon tracks are dry and worn in, real good ruts. But these got to be the runaways."

"Good job, Wilson. Real fine job. Maybe we can catch them before the day is out." Josiah kicked his horse's flanks hard and his mount bolted ahead.

Hell, I thought as I stared after him, *I would never treat Sol's Mistress to the rough treatment I saw Josiah and others give to their horses.* To me, Sol's Mistress was a trusted friend, and she always responded so well to me that there was no reason to be harsh.

After riding for several more hours with no sighting of them at all, Josiah begrudgingly ordered a stop so our horses could rest and drink from a trickling spring.

"Not a damn sight of them. Do you think Larkey was right? Maybe they got off the road, less chance of them being seen," Josiah said.

"I don't think so," Wilson said. "The grass here on the sides would have been crushed down and I don't see that."

After the horses had drank their fill, and we ours, we remounted and started again.

"We got to catch them before they get to Aquia Creek. I heard from some fellas that just came back from up north that there may be some action up that ways. I don't want to get caught up in it," Josiah added.

"Me neither," I mumbled.

After about another hour of hard riding, we saw a

wagon in the distance. "There they are, I bet. Let's bring 'em back," Josiah said, and I urged Sol's Mistress on.

Sure enough, it was Jojo and his family. We circled the wagon and I reached out and grabbed the traces to bring it to a stop. Jojo glared at us from the seat of the buckboard while his wife and children huddled together behind his seat.

"Would you look here, boys. Looks like we got our first runaways. Time to go back to your owner," Josiah said gruffly.

Jojo said blankly, "We ain't going back."

"Now see here, you damn devil. You ain't gonna be defiant with me. You don't make your choices, we do. You are your master's property and his choice is having you back to work. I think it's right nice of him to allow your little family here to stay together. If it was me, I'd sell you all apart. More money that way and make you less inclined to run. Hell, why should I be explaining myself to you? I must be getting soft in the head," Josiah said ruefully.

"Now climb down from that seat and one of us will take the reins and take you all back. Now, climb down quick!"

"No, suh, I won't," Jojo said.

Quick as a flash Josiah brought out his whip, and with an even quicker flash, it wrapped around Jojo's torso and he was jerked off the wagon. He landed in the dust with a thud, and Josiah, his face now red with rage, shouted down at him from atop his mount, "You will do as I say or I'll give you a real taste of the whip. Now, boys, you all jump down and tie this nigger up and throw him in the back. Levon, you take the reins and get this wagon going the other ways."

Jojo tensed up as we approached him. I got the sense that this wasn't going to be an easy task, and I was right.

Fists started flying and the struggle was on. Wilson got clocked by a hard right from Jojo. He stumbled and fell on his backside. I tried to wrap the rope around Jojo but he tore it away from his body while another of our group jumped onto the big buck's back. Jojo swung himself back and forth while the boy on his back legs splayed out behind him, gamely tried to hold on.

"C'mon, boys. You telling me the four of you can't control one slave?" Josiah shouted.

"Jojo, don't...please stop," his missus yelled from the wagon.

"Don't hurt my pappy," one of his children screamed.

Jojo flung the boy off his back, and the slightly hurt Wilson and another of our group grabbed hold of his flailing heavily muscled arms. I crept up in back of him and quickly looped my rope around his neck and pulled him to the ground flat on top of me. I wound two more loops around his neck and pulled it tight as Wilson landed a kick to his privates. Jojo moaned in pain and we were able to finally bind the rope around his torso and neck. With his wrists bound behind, we stood him up. I looked into his eyes, which no longer held fire, but defeat and despair.

Josiah sat back in his saddle and laughingly said, "Remind me, boys, to tell the folks around the valley to not place any bets on you in no fightin' matches. Now, fellas, lets lash this colored to that wagon wheel with his back to me."

"What do you intend to do, Josiah? We've captured him. Now let's just return him to Larkey," I said.

"Don't you show any sympathy for this colored, Levon. I might become suspicious of just what's on your mind. He must be punished. It might give him pause about thinking of running off again. Will, strip his shirt off him."

With Jojo now tied to the wagon wheel and stripped of his shirt, I would witness the ugly side of Josiah's character. The lash of the whip left a thin red welt with blood seeping from it on Jojo's back. Again, and yet again, Josiah's whip laid cruel lines on his back from which he flinched, but uttered no sound.

"Good Lord, show him mercy," Jojo's wife wailed.

"Shut up, bitch. How dare you call on our Lord. You're a spawn of the devil hisself and the color of your skin marks his stain," Josiah sneered at her.

Another lash and another welt opened up Jojo's skin. I stepped between Josiah and his whip's deadly work.

"Stop it, Josiah, that's enough. He's been punished enough," I said.

"Levon, what in the world..." Josiah stammered, momentarily stunned.

"That's enough, Josiah. It doesn't do Larkey any good if Jojo is too hurt to work."

"Okay, Levon, I'll stop," Josiah said, shrugging his shoulders. "I'm beginning to wonder about you..." he said, his voice trailing off.

The trussed up Jojo was tossed in the back of the wagon after I gave him a drink of water from my canteen. I tied Sol's Mistress' reins to the back of the wagon. She gave me a scornful look as if asking me why I wasn't riding her. Before climbing up onto the buckboard, I looked at the others. We all sported various cuts and bruises, with Wilson sporting a particularly angry swelling to his eye. Josiah was unscathed, naturally, but his face was etched in a scowl. I directed the team around and headed toward Larkey's farm.

And so it went, through all of the summer and most of autumn. Returning runaway slaves to their owners while Josiah's dual character shone through, again and again. He was brutal to the defenseless, and cowardly to his equal. But still, we had not seen any Yankees.

FIVE

The Situation at Dranesville
Mid-December, 1861

Dranesville

It was mid-December when Josiah issued a strange request while at our meeting place at Cedar Run. Josiah announced, "We are going to have a little change from the way we've been doing our business. Seems a young buck ran away from the Jason place about, oh, two days ago. Normally, I'd have us right on it, but I've waited a couple of days because I wanted to test ourselves."

Scowling, he said, "Levon, you, Wilson, and Lo are going to catch him. You don't have to be back in the usual three days because this might take a little longer. I'm sending you, Levon, because you are the fastest, Wilson's a good tracker, and I'm betting Lo here is good with the gun. Oh, another thing, leave tonight. Bring him back alive."

That said, he waived his hand to dismiss us with an odd look in his eyes. From anyone else, his look would have struck me as queer, but coming from Josiah, it had become increasingly standard. Especially when he was talking and looking at me.

Wilson and I mounted up and waited for Lo, who was talking with Josiah in a whispered conversation. When their conversation ended, Lo cocked his head quizzically, then shrugged his shoulders and mounted up.

Lo, too enthusiastically for me, shouted out, "Yeehaw, boys, let's get that nigger. Who knows, we might even meet up with some Yanks I can plug some holes in."

Wilson and I quickly looked at each other and then rode out. Now, Josiah knew I didn't carry any weapon except a recently acquired jackknife, and maybe he had forgotten about Wilson's Colt because I hadn't noticed it since we took up this business. But I think he was hoping we'd get ourselves in trouble, and sent the altogether too eager Lo along to stir the pot. Maybe he hoped that this Jason buck would be brought back alive, after all, there was a big reward, but I had a feeling me coming back in one piece was optional for him.

We rode out of the county that night, criss-crossing the many paths that we knew previous fugitive contrabands had taken. Josiah had given Lo a brief description of Hugh, the runaway slave. It became apparent to all of us that there was an awful flood of runaways, and hey, they all looked the same to me. But Hugh did have one distinction.

Somewhat cultured in his gait, he was tall, slender, and Lo said he was considered quite good looking for a darkie. Seems a master's whip had left an ugly scar that ran diagonally across his face, and I hadn't seen none of the other captures sporting whip marks. At least not noticeable ones that ran across the width of their face.

Even with that, I thought it would be nearly impossible to find him. We would charge off the road into the underbrush after sure runaways only to inspect their faces and then continue on.

As the year dragged on, the owners' desperation, and Josiah's greediness, increased the rewards. Lo confirmed that Hugh's reward was big without exactly stating an exact amount. Still, I wondered if it was Josiah's greed or my possible end that had caused Josiah to send us out. Maybe it was both.

When the star-filled night had faded into its slumber and the sun had awakened for several hours, we stopped to rest our horses.

We all dismounted, and without tying her up, I let Sol's Mistress' reins hang limp, allowing her to graze. Wilson and Lo did the same with their mounts.

Wilson and I walked down a bit away from our horses and Lo. Wilson, sensing my uneasiness, said, "Don't worry, Cousin, I got my Colt right here," patting the slight bulge under his coat.

"I know you got your pistol, Cousin, but it's not our safety I'm concerned about. How are we going to find one runaway among all that's fleeing? You and I ain't never seen him at all, and Lo says he has only one distinction, that scar across the face. We've been chasing all these runaways to get a look at their face. What has happened every damn time we have chased them down and looked at their face? We haven't seen that scar and we've let them go. It's like looking for that one weevil in a field of cotton."

"What you boys over here talking about?" Lo said as he strode up.

"Levon was just saying how this is a colossal waste of time," Wilson said. "What are the chances that we are going to happen upon this Hugh?"

"I admit it does seem slight. But I have family up there around the Potomac that say between the river and up into Maryland, there is some kind of slave smuggling going on. Smuggling them to freedom. We owe it to Mr. Wheeler to try," Lo said.

"We owe Josiah nothing," I said hotly. "He collects a reward and I don't believe all that crap about testing us by giving this slave a head start. I think he has something else on his mind."

"Now look here, Levon. I don't think you have no call to be disrespecting Mr. Wheeler," Lo said as his hand slid slowly down toward the butt of the revolver protruding from his holster.

Wilson quickly reached into this overcoat, whipped out his Colt, pointed it at Lo and said, "Not so fast there, Lo. Let's not get hasty. The three of us here are all on the same side. Now, I've been feeling a little strange myself about this fishing expedition."

Lo, relaxing his hand, said, "I just don't think anyone's got no call to question Mr. Wheeler, that's all."

"Easy for you to say that, Lo. But Wilson and I have never seen this runaway. We're less than one day out and you consider pulling a gun on me. Now, maybe you don't have a problem with Josiah's methods, but I do. Now this."

Remembering the whispered conversation that Josiah and Lo had the previous evening, I asked, "So, Lo, exactly what did you and Josiah talk about before we left? It seems to me you two didn't want us to overhear."

Obviously flustered, Lo said haltingly, "Oh, nothing. Mr. Wheeler just told me to make sure we all stayed safe, but especially you because you don't carry a gun." Lo would not meet my gaze as he spoke, so I knew he wasn't telling a lick of truth.

I laughed incredulously "Oh, really, Lo? You said he told you to protect me, yet again you were going to pull your gun. You can't be so blind to see that Josiah isn't exactly warm to me. So excuse me, Lo, but from now on, I will still lead but Wilson is going to bring up the rear to keep an eye on you. You okay with that, Wilson?"

Wilson replied with a silly grin. "Of course, Cousin. This ways I can protect all of us from, ahem, an attack from the rear."

"Okay, why don't we all mount up, and, Lo, taking your advice, let's keep traveling. Maybe we can find your family up here to get some information, but least ways we got nothing to lose." Mounting up, we continued on for quite a few more uneventful hours before bedding down for the night.

The following day, we skirted the banks of the Potomac, continuing the monotony of chasing down runaways to peer into their faces. We came out of the woods that lay on the south bank of Blackburn's Ford and crossed the stream where our horse's hooves left holes in the mud that quickly filled back up. We were unsuccessful in finding Lo's family, who he claimed lived up here, and began to turn back.

It was at the junction of the Georgetown and Leesburg Pike in the town of Dranesville that we ran into a whole lot of trouble. At the time, I knew that at least Wilson and I hadn't figured we'd run into fighting with the Yankees because we thought they would be in winter quarters. Lo, on the other hand, was probably overjoyed that it bubbled up because he had been eager to shoot his weapon and "plug some Yankees with holes."

Suddenly, the rattle of musketry from behind us startled Sol's Mistress, and Wilson, Lo and I kicked at our horses to lead us away from a line of blue-coated troopers who just suddenly appeared. Just as soon as we began to gallop away, a smattering of minie balls bit at the dirt in front of us. What I assumed was a Confederate patrol in front of us, had caught us in a cross-fire between them and the Yankee troopers.

"Wilson, follow me," I yelled as we tried to ride out of the middle of the skirmish. Lo had foolishly taken out his pistol and was wildly shooting at the Yankees while simultaneously yelling over his shoulder at the mounted Confederates, "Don't shoot, fellas. We're on your side."

The mounted Confederates didn't pay Lo any mind, or most simply didn't hear him. Lo came to his senses, and realizing that his bargaining was useless, charged after us as we moved west on the Leesburg Pike.

I pressed my body close to Sol's Mistress for an hour or so until the sound of musketry had died away, leaving us reassured that we were out of danger for the moment, and so slowed our escape.

"What the hell was that?" gasped Wilson.

"Don't know, Cousin. I thought the fighting was over for at least the winter. Hell, the Ball's Bluff battle was way back in October. Guess I was wrong, you hurt?" I asked.

"No, no, I'm alright, but I got so scared I must have wet my pants. Lo, you all right?" Wilson asked. Lo, although still mounted, was slumped over the pommel of his saddle. Seeing the blood streaming down the saddle and his horse's flank, we had our answer.

"No, boys, I'm hurt real bad," Lo whimpered. We stopped under a stand of trees, and Wilson and I hurriedly dismounted and rushed over to help Lo off his horse.

"Jesus, boys, I can't believe I got shot. I had no idea it would hurt like this. First time I have even seen Yankees and I'm hurt." Lo moaned as he held his bleeding chest. I grabbed a saddle bag to prop his head up, then stood there, confused as to what else I should do.

Wilson took off his muffler to staunch Lo's wound, but it was no use. Lo probably knew his life was seeping away, as the bleeding would not stop. "Uh, Levon, I have to tell ya something because I am sure to go. Josiah didn't want you coming back. He thought you had turned yellow. That's what we had that chat about before leaving. But I think you had that figured out, right?" Lo said weakly.

"Yeah, Lo, I knew," I replied as I felt my mouth turn up in a slight smile.

"But, Levon…I didn't want to really do it. I was afraid Josiah would be disappointed in me though."

"Doesn't matter, Lo. You were only doing what I expect a good soldier would do. It's all right."

"Levon, are we really soldiers?" Lo brightened up slightly.

"Well, Lo, I guess you can say we are. We don't have any uniforms, and some, like me, don't have any guns but we are all fightin' now. Doesn't mean we want to, but we've been brung into it just the same."

Lo closed his eyes, and just like that, he was gone. Wilson sighed. He took his bedroll and laid it over Lo's body. "Okay, so what do we do now?" he asked. "We got to get his body back to his family."

"That would be proper," I said. "But I'm not going back. Josiah wants me dead and I don't think my chances of continuing breathing would be so greatly increased if I did," I said wistfully, rubbing my chin.

"I'm not leaving you by yourself, no sir. So I guess our minds are made up. But what do we do next? What do we tell our parents? How do we let them know?" Wilson asked wryly.

"Let's take Lo's body, tie him on his horse and lead it along till we decide what to do. Say, remember what those cadets back at the fair said, Wilson?"

"I remember that you talked with them a bit but I don't remember what was said. What are you talking about?"

"They asked me how well I knew Virginia, and I know it pretty well. Hell, we're practically at the border with Maryland now. They suggested I could be a scout."

"Hmm, now there is a plan. I can go along with that. It's like what you said to Lo. We are in this mess now, and today is just an indication. I can't see going back to work with Josiah, especially without you."

We carefully bundled Lo's body in his own bedroll, slung him over his horse's back and tied his body to the saddle. We mounted up and rode out to a muddy, uncertain future.

Riding along in uncertainty, I spied a train of wagons trundling along the Pike heading south. Being unsure of which side they were on despite the southward direction, Wilson and I decided to trail off into the trees alongside them to watch. We struggled through the thick woods, dodging low hanging limbs and getting scratched by the branches of others. We were able to stay pretty quiet, I thought, except when Lo's body bounced against the trunk of a tree we hadn't been able to avoid.

I thought I saw some of the horsemen wearing gray uniforms alongside the wagon train and alerted Wilson, who was trailing behind me, guiding Lo's horse by its reins. "What do you think, Wilson, they Confederates?"

"Could be. But how can we join them without being shot?" Wilson asked.

"It's not like they don't come across civilians just like us, and we are in Virginia." I said. "Why don't we ride up ahead of their train and approach them head on so they don't think we are spying on them?"

"Okay, let's see if we can't get some better headway here so we can put your suggestion in motion." Wilson smiled.

We urged our horses on a little faster, and not much later, my plans began playing out. We rode leisurely up toward the head of the train before the driver of the lead wagon hailed us. "Good afternoon there, strangers. Looks like you ran into trouble there if that's a body tied to that horse. It wouldn't have anything to do with that fight back there, would it? But this thing here does pose a bigger question. To whose allegiance do you show?"

He quickly brought his team to a halt, reached behind his seat, grabbed a musket and leveled it at us. "Care to answer that now, you two?"

"Whoa there, sir," Wilson said, pulling up alongside me. "No call for that, but we understand your alarm. We know how this must look, but let me explain."

"Please do," the driver said, keeping his musket trained on us.

I was thinking as we stood there that, up to this point, I had taken the lead, but Wilson was talking and doing a good job at it so I wasn't indignant with it at all.

"My cousin here and I, and yes, the unfortunate body back there, uh, his name was Lo, were trying to run down an escaped slave and got caught up in that fight of which I believe you spoke. We are slave catchers from down in Wythe County, so I think you can figure which side we would be on." Wilson continued.

"Your story seems likely but you are kind of far from Wythe County, if my directions and memory are correct. See, I'm not from Virginia. I'm from South Carolina. James Pagan, 6th Infantry of the Sixth Regiment, South Carolina Volunteers, I am. What are your names?"

Wilson answered, "Well, you met Lo back there. I'm Wilson, and my cousin here is Levon."

Pagan asked, "What's your plan now, boys? Gonna get your friend back to his family, are ya?"

"Sir, we are not really sure. We are not eager to go back down that way. A son of a bitch down there wants Levon dead. We thought we could offer ourselves as scouts and do some real good."

Just then, a rider came up and started yelling, "Pagan, damn you. Why are you stopping? The whole train is backed up." Spying us, he continued ranting. "And who are these men?"

Pagan replied, "They are slave catchers from down south, Lieutenant. Say they want to help out as scouts."

"Well, that's all fine and dandy, but right now, Pagan, let's keep moving out of trouble, and later on, I can take these two to the General. What about that third horse? My guess he holds a body. We will bury him later, now, let's move." The angry horseman shouted as he rode away.

Pagan snapped the reins. His mule team grunted and started again. "That's Lieutenant Pelham. He doesn't usually act like regular army 'less he wants to impress someone."

Riding alongside Pagan's wagon, I asked him, "Why are you up here in Dranesville? Wilson and I figured the fighting would have stopped during the winter, at least."

"The fighting was, for the most part. But we were on a foraging expedition in Loudon County while being protected by the fighting boys. I'm here because I'm in a commissary position. You know, supply food and such for the army," Pagan replied.

"We had decided our trip wasn't going to pan out and we were heading home when we got caught in the crossfire between us and the North," I said.

"Must have been our pickets and some Yankee patrol. Anyways, we're almost to our position at Centreville. We'll stop there, and I suppose the Lieutenant will take you to meet the general. See if he wants to take you up on your offer."

"Who is the general?" Wilson asked.

"Oh, top dawg would be General Jeb Stuart. Ever heard of him?"

Incredulous, I asked, "Would that be James Ewell Brown Stuart?"

He laughed. "The same. Those of us on more familiar terms just call him Jeb." We pulled up to a camp of tents while the wagon train rode on a ways and stopped. Pagan jumped down from his seat and walked back to us.

"You two can give your rides to Patch here. He will get 'em fed and tied to the line with the rest of the cavalry horses. We'll take your boy aside, get him buried and all, then we better get you fed. When's the last time you had something to eat?"

"Been awhile. A day or so, I figure," Wilson said.

"We've got some greens and mule that will fill your belly," Pagan said.

"I'm not eating that animal," I said disgustedly.

Pagan, noticing my disgust, laughed and said, "I didn't mean those ornery things. We call meat "mule" in my outfit. Come over here to my tent." He gestured. "I bet Lieutenant will be by shortly to take you to General Jeb. But first, we have to bury Lo."

Pagan helped Wilson and I untie and lift Lo's body off his saddle, then carry his body to the side of the camp. After digging a small pit and shaping a crude cross, we laid Lo's blanket covered body in and shoveled dirt over it. Strangely, I felt almost nothing when the last spade of dirt was tossed over Lo's body. I didn't know him that well, and although misguided, he had wanted to kill me. A lack of compassion perhaps, but I'd felt more sadness for a family pet's death.

Pagan looked at us. "It seems a pity to bury him away from home," he said. "It's happening though, and it's ever growing in number. Heck, bodies and the graves I've seen would fit an entire army before it's over. We don't have any chaplains about so I guess we can share a bit of the good book over his resting place.

"The Lord is my shepherd,
I shall not want.
He makes me lie down in green pastures;
He leads me beside the still waters.
He restores my soul,
He leads me in the paths of righteousness
for his names sake. Amen"

We hung our heads for a moment and kept them down 'til we got to Pagan's tent.

We followed Pagan in and ate, made small talk, and waited for our summons to the general, but it didn't come that night. As the sky darkened into night and it became apparent that we would not be seeing the general, Pagan reached into a nearby bag, grabbed a bottle of amber liquid and pulled out the cork.

"It doesn't look like the general will be seeing you two tonight so we might as well partake a little of this bottle. Before coming up here, I met a man named Daniels, from Tennessee, he was. Swore it was the best whiskey made." Taking a swig, he laughed and offered us the bottle. "I'm inclined to agree with him."

I took the bottle and let a small bit trickle into my mouth, and felt its burning trail all the way to my stomach. Wilson glanced at me, and after taking the bottle, took a drink.

Coughing, I lied. "Good stuff, that's right."

Pagan caught my lie, and with a chuckle, replied, "Sure, Levon. Don't have a penchant for the drink yet, eh? You two are young yet, but the general, he doesn't smoke or drink neither so maybe it's not about youth at all. That's okay."

Still coughing, I said to Wilson, "Cousin, let's go check our horses before turning in." I turned back the burlap flap of the tent and Wilson and I stepped out.

"The horses are down the line," yelled Pagan. "Just before the wagons."

Wilson and I walked down the line where the horses were tethered. It didn't take me long to find a slightly miffed Sol's Mistress, and Wilson found Mitch right next to her. As I moved to Sol's Mistress's muzzle, she shot me a baleful look as if to ask me why she was tied up with the others and not allowed to roam in her own pasture like back home.

"I'm sorry, girl, but it looks like we will be joining the cavalry. Sometimes you'll have to be tethered up, but not for long stretches," I said soothingly while stroking her muzzle. I grabbed a missed carrot that lay on the ground, fed it to her, then Wilson and I headed back to Pagan's tent.

We grabbed our bedrolls, and bedded down under a low hanging limb, and promptly fell asleep.

 SIX

Meeting the Knight
Early Evening, December 21st, 1861

Centreville, Virginia

The next day, we milled around the camp, being there weren't too many soldiers to talk to. Someone in passing had said that Stuart had set out again to possibly resume the fighting of the previous day. Later that evening, standing at the opening of Pagan's tent, we were approached by the angry lieutenant.

"You two want to be scouts, huh?" he said with a scowl.

"We were certainly thinking that would be the right thing to do," I said, struggling to keep the meekness of my voice low.

"We will let the general decide that. Follow me."

We followed the lieutenant to a big tent sitting on the edge of a circle of tents. A fiddler and banjo player played a jaunty melody in the center of the ring.

The lieutenant pulled back the tent flap and beckoned us in, saying, "General, the two boys who wanted to meet with you."

"Very good, Lieutenant Pelham. You can stay or go as you wish," he said.

"I'll take my leave, sir. I have some things to attend to," he said, then stepped out.

So, there we stood, in the audience of the Knight of the Golden Spurs himself, James Ewell Brown, Jeb Stuart. He sat behind a makeshift desk of discarded supply boxes with a plank laid across them. His gray uniform jacket was buttoned to the neck and a yellow sash was wound around his waist. His trousers were tucked inside knee high riding boots. His face was ruddy and he smiled underneath his full beard.

"Sit down, boys, sit down. Pelham told me that Pagan from South Carolina had encountered the two of you on the wagon ride back this way last night. According to the lieutenant, Pagan had said you two mentioned working as scouts. Is that correct?" he said, his eyes sparkling in amusement.

"Yes, sir, General. I think we could be really helpful. We both know Virginia very well, and like all Virginians, including you, excellent horsemen."

He laughed. "Well said, young man, and I thank you for the compliment. But I have some concerns. Number one is, what brings you up this way? Number two, you cannot possibly think that this war will remain in Virginia? Of course, not if you were involved with my pickets in Dranesville. Question number three is, how can I be assured you are not a spy for the enemy? The last question I have is that the both of you are quite young, although I have a young man on my staff, 17 year old Chiswell Dabney, so it is possible."

Wilson piped up, "Sir, with your permission I'd like

to answer your questions."

Stuart continued smiling while stroking his beard and said, "Go ahead."

After a slight cough to clear his throat, Wilson said, "Sir, we are slave catchers from Wythe County, which I know you are familiar with."

Stuart's eyes twinkled in agreement.

Wilson continued, "We've been pursuing a runaway who regrettably escaped. My cousin here," Wilson said, pointing at me, "cannot really go back down there. Our leader, as it were, has it out for his neck. We lost one of our party, if you don't know that, back at the skirmish at the pike, so we believe we should stay because we are here now. I disagree with you on one point. We have, for too long, thought we could stay out of the fight, be separated by distance. That is why my family fled the Missouri Territory and came to live with Levon and his family. I know the war won't be confined to Virginia, but I'm a good tracker, and Levon is the finest horseman. He did win the races at the Wythe County Fair."

Stuart said, "Did he now? Hmm."

"Yes, sir, I did," I said. "Beat one of your family's slaves too. We are Southerners, sir, through and through. We wouldn't be slave-catchers if we didn't believe in our way of life, and you answered the last question yourself. If your aide is only 17, well, we aren't much younger, 15 or so."

He laughed loudly, and leaning back on his stool said, "Okay, boys, okay, you convinced me. You may be of some use, and if you show some mettle, maybe a little spy work. The Yankees aren't too bright so you might go undetected. You won't wear any uniforms, not initially, at least. Scouts tend to change uniforms as the situation dictates. You mentioned another member of your party. Where is he?"

Wilson and I looked quickly at each other. "Lo, sir. His name was Lo." I said. "He got killed, sir. With Pagan's help, we buried him here."

"That's awful," Stuart groaned. "That poor boy lying so far from home and his family not knowing what has become of him, not to mention your families, but perhaps I have a solution. Some of my men have lost their mounts and will need replacements. As you stated, I'm well aware of Wythe County, having grown up at Laurel Hill Farm in nearby Patrick County. Perhaps we can uncover your friend's body, have it borne back home, along with messages to your families, and my men can gather more than enough able mounts." Before we could agree, he said, "Well, that's settled then. You young men go back and quarter with Pagan while I think of our future plans."

We stepped out of the general's tent and started back to Pagan's tent.

As we neared the tent, Pagan called out, "Come on in, boys, I got some information to share, but first tell me how your meetin' went."

"It was okay. General Stuart is considering us. I think we will be staying on," I said.

"That's great. I figured Jeb wouldn't have any problems with the likes of you. You boys are gonna get some education in fighting, I can tell you that. But here is what I wanted to tell you. In a couple of days, it will be Christmas, if you two had forgotten, but we have some problems we have to fix and right quick. Winter is upon us and we have to have cozier quarters than the flaps of this old tent. It's going to get real gloomy and cold.

If you're up to it, I say we lay down wooden planks on the floor and a lean-to over the top. That will make it warmer and dry. Damn, I forgot the horses. We'll get help, I'm sure, from all of the cavalry, but we have to make those pitiful stables more fit for the beasts. Can't let them suffer with all they do for us. I say let's work in the morning, even though it's near Christmas, and relax in the evening. Perhaps I can introduce you to some of Jeb's staff and you can get yourselves invited to one of the parties."

As the sounds of 'Sweet Evalina" emanated from Stuart's tent and drifted over the camp, Pagan uncorked the whiskey bottle and said, "Now boys, I figure you don't want to drink this if my judgment of your responses of last night are correct. But if you are so inclined."

After taking a pull off the bottle and offering us some, of which we declined, Pagan said gaily, "Merry Christmas, boys, and welcome to Camp Qui Vive."

After enduring a night of Pagan's drunken snoring, Wilson and I stepped out of the tent into a drizzling Christmas Eve morning. Most of the camp was still in a quiet slumber, but there were a few campfires sparking and sputtering, and a few men chattered around them.

Breathing in the smoke, I said to Wilson, "God, Cousin, is that bacon I smell? It's been so long since I smelled something so good."

"Yes, Cousin, I smell it too," Wilson said, taking in a deep breath. "Well, Pagan is a commissary, so I bet somewhere around we could find some of the same. Let's look."

Being careful to not wake him, we rummaged through his supplies, finding some salt pork and green coffee, and after building a small fire of our own, managed a satisfactory breakfast. We had just finished a sour cup of coffee when Pagan came barging out of the tent.

"You boys helped yourself, did ya?" he said, a bit testily, I thought. "No matter, you are with us, so forget it. Any more of that coffee left?"

"I'm sorry, Pagan, we were hungry. My cousin and I

shouldn't have taken the liberty," I said, handing him a tin cup of steaming coffee.

"It's okay, boys, as I said. I apologize, but too much of the Tennessee moonshine last night has left me a might cranky. But don't forget, we've got work to do. I know where there's some wood we can use."

We gathered some fallen timber to create some shelter over the tent and on the floor, and also added some strength to the stables for the horses. As we worked on shoring up the stables, Sol's Mistress angrily ignored me. It was dusk when we finished, and being tired, the three of us trudged back to our greatly improved home.

"Boys, we got all that done, and in only one day to boot. Since its Christmas Eve, I think we earned a little rest," Pagan said.

"I'm damn tired," I said, feeling the weariness in my bones. "You know we don't drink, but I wouldn't turn down some good chewing tobacco for celebration tonight."

Wilson, cackling, said, "Levon, what makes you think Pagan would have any plug? From what I've seen, chew would be as scarce as teeth on a hen."

Pagan, noting my implication, said, "Laugh all you want, you two. Even though I'm not a Virginian doesn't mean I don't have good tobacco. I saved some brown slug for special occasions. I just don't share that information with the rest of the outfit. But there isn't no more of a special occasion than Christmas, so take a chew."

So the three of us sat on the floor of the tent, Wilson and I chewing, and Pagan drinking, on that dreary evening.

As Pagan began to drift off to what I recognized to be his almost nightly drunken slumber, Wilson and I talked in hushed tones.

"Levon, you know we've stepped in it now. Who knows what this New Year is going to bring. It's dangerous, and like Pagan said, burying people is becoming more common. I'm scared to death, aren't you?"

"Sure I am, Wilson, and I know it sounds crazy, but isn't it safer to see what lies ahead on the road than looking over your shoulder worrying about what may be following you?" I replied.

"I disagree with you a bit there, Cousin," Wilson said, pausing to spit out some tobacco juice before continuing. "I'd rather ride away from a storm than straight into one. I learned that living in the Missouri Territory. That is, after all, what my family did. We moved out of the storm to the relative peace of your home."

"Okay, I concede that what you say is true since you lived it. What would you say now, though? We saw the slaves and their damn Hoodoo. We've seen how this whole business has turned people ugly, like Josiah. Lo gets killed just because we got caught in the middle of the Yankees and a Confederate patrol. I'm not even sure they were certain they were firing at the enemy, it happened so fast. Lo wasn't on either side, really. We cannot sit idly by. Circumstances have placed us in what you refer to as a storm. But the storm is widespread, and I think we are unable to ride out of it. We are a part of it. I don't intend for you and I to become sacrificial pawns in this game of chess." Realizing my analogy of the chess game, I said with a smile, "Besides, we ride along with the knight."

"Guess we'll just have to be strong, but careful. I'm still scared, Levon."

"Me too, Cousin. I am too. Let's get some sleep." We spread out the bedrolls, and after slinging blankets over our shoulders to ward off the cold, fell asleep.

I awakened early the next morning, and I mean fully awake since it had been a fitful night, and crawled out of my bedroll. Wilson and Pagan were still asleep as I found my way out of the tent flap that still served as the door, although the rest of our home was mostly now a hut, strengthened by our work of yesterday.

The drizzling of yesterday had turned into a slight snow that left snowflakes to landin' on my face before slowly melting away. I gathered what dry twigs and small branches I could muster and got a small fire started. I grabbed a kettle, filled it with water, and when it was hot, added some ground coffee beans to it.

Not much later, Wilson and Pagan staggered out and sat on the ground around the fire. They both clapped and rubbed their hands, keeping them close to the fire to warm them.

"Have some coffee; it may warm you up a bit. You two are shivering," I said with a smile, and handed them filled tin cups.

"Damn, it'd be nice to add some of Daniel's whiskey to this coffee. That surely would warm me up, but hell, its morning," Pagan grumbled.

I didn't reply but kept alternately sipping and staring at the cloudy liquid in my cup. Wilson was quiet as well, so we just sat there. Our gloomy solitude was broken by a whistling soldier who strode toward us on the worn path that cut through the center of our encampment.

"Aha, there you are Pagan. Pelham said you were hereabouts with your two young friends."

Standing up, Pagan yelled, "Do you have to be so loud, Chiswell? It's barely dawn for Christ's sake."

The young soldier laughed. "I've been up a couple of hours and so has the general, as well as most of the camp. Maybe you're getting softer, you old bombproof."

Pagan ignored the young soldier's barb and

introduced him. "Levon, Wilson, this here is Chiswell Dabney, one of Jeb's staff. Chiswell?"

"Glad to meet the both of you," Dabney said warmly as he shook our hands. "I bet the general sent me specifically because we are about the same age. He wants you to meet some of the others. Let's go."

As we walked toward the general's tent, Dabney asked, "What brought the two of you into the war? Obviously there are many as young as us, even drummer boys who couldn't be more than ten. I'm only 17, and you're younger, but…understand, I'm not judging you, I'm just curious."

"Well, mister, or do I say soldier, or…" I stammered.

"Chiswell is fine," he said.

"Well, Chiswell, I've lived in the southern Shenandoah my whole life, and my cousin here, Wilson, and his family came to live with us. They left the Missouri Territory. He and I were part of what loosely would be known as the Wythe County Home Guard, but we are plain and simply slave catchers."

"So you joined us to catch slaves?" he asked, confused.

"No, no, we got caught up in the action in Dranesville and one of our party was killed, and we kind of linked up with you here. Because slave catching is becoming somewhat dangerous for me, we both decided to see if we could join as scouts."

"Wait a minute, I'm confused. You think joining the Confederacy and the war that is being fought would be less dangerous than slave catching? You did say one of your party was killed, did you not?"

"That's true. One of our party was killed. But what waits back in Wytheville is this man who I know is hell-bent on seeing me harm. I'd rather know who the enemy is than looking over my shoulder, on my guard all the time, for a veiled threat," I replied.

"So you're not emboldened by the cause of southern rights, but more by a slim wish for self-preservation?" he said as we neared the tent.

"Make no mistake, Chiswell," Wilson piped up. "We are fully inspired by the southern states' need for independence. This man that Levon spoke of and slave catching was not something we felt would aid the cause at all. We felt we could do more."

"Okay, I guess that makes sense. Let's go in, the general will see you."

"General, here are the two boys you asked for. Will there be anything else?" Chiswell asked.

"No, thank you, Lieutenant. I wanted to commend you once again for your actions at Dranesville. You may go." Stuart said.

Chiswell, reddening with embarrassment, mumbled a thank you, saluted, and hurried out of the tent. Stuart once again was seated behind his makeshift desk while off to his side stood a burly, dour faced man.

"Good morning, young men. Levon and Wilson, isn't it?" Stuart asked.

"Yes," we replied in unison.

"I have considered your offer and I accept. Because you indicated the desire to serve as scouts, I would like you to go out with the most accomplished scout I have, Redmond Burke. Burke will be your teacher, and you must be earnest pupils. Listen to him and trust him. Lieutenant Burke, do you have anything to add?"

"No, Jeb. You boys get your mounts saddled up and we'll head to the Warrenton Junction where we currently operate. Let us take our leave," Burke said in his heavily accented English.

Wilson and I went to the stables to bring out Sol's Mistress and Mitch. I stopped in my tracks to admire a magnificent horse that was tethered alone. He had the newer McClellan saddle rather than the ordinary Jenifer saddle most of us owned. Embroidered in gold lettering on one side were the letters C.S.A.

Burke noticed me admiring both the horse and saddle, and said, "That's one of Jeb's horses, right there. Highfly is a spirited mount and well suited for the fancy saddle, he is. Jeb thinks that this particular saddle will be better suited for the horse should they become worn down. We do a lot of hard riding, as you can guess. We sometimes ask too much."

We went inside the makeshift stable and Wilson and I brought our horses out. Sol's Mistress began prancing and neighing, seemingly excited to have been sprung from the confines of her quarters. She seemed to know she would be taken out on a ride and was exhilarated. Exhilarated as a horse can be, I guess. Wilson's horse, Mitch, perked up too. We joined Burke already mounted and waiting for us.

Once we crossed Cub Run and Broad Run, I asked Burke why we were making what I thought was a circuitous route toward Warrenton.

"Good question, boyo. I have seen some skirmishing in the area north of the junction that I would like to avoid, being this is your first time out. I do appreciate that you know the area so well. Observation is a key skill of the scout. The mind and the eyes. We are the eyes of the Confederate army, infantry, and cavalry alike," Burke said in his heavy Irish brogue.

Continuing, he said, "To be captured by the enemy is almost certain death. Doing that, they will have blinded Stuart, Johnston, and all of our leaders to their intentions. That is the eyes to which I have spoken. The mind of the scout is of equal importance. You must, as accurately as you can, figure out the presence of the enemy, as we have already done at Warrenton. You must also gauge their strength in numbers of men and the arms they carry. Note their condition. Are they worn and dispirited, or fit and eager to fight? If you can figure out by sight that they are eager to fight, that may give an indication as to their intentions."

Occasionally, we heard distant weapons discharge but I felt safe where we were. If it is possible for an animal to transmit and infuse its owner with its feelings, then that was what was happening between Sol's Mistress and me. I know, I know. You would say that such things are not possible between man and beast, but I felt it. I felt invigorated by my girl's eagerness to be ridden again. It was like our days back home when I felt so attuned to her and her to me. My daydreaming was broken up by Burke's hurried whisper.

"Into the trees, be quick. Quiet now, let me look."

The three of us nudged our horses into a thicket of gnarled, bullet scarred pines and hunkered down in the shadows of their boughs wet with dew.

"Listen, boys. Did you hear any sound? What do you make of it?"

I heard nothing but the birds chirping in the trees and our horse's slight breaths, and told Burke so.

"Then you are not really listening!" he hissed. "You must hear what others cannot. It can mean the saving of lives, those who serve the Confederacy. Listen harder."

I glanced at Wilson who simply shrugged his shoulders. We bent our shoulders forward so our ears might grasp what had previously been unheard by us. It came to me as if a trumpet had blown and its music had cascaded out. I heard the almost imperceptible sound of the creak of a wheel and the jangle of traces. The scuffling of boots and the gentle beat of horse hooves on the soft ground. Burke watched me and saw my expression widen in realization.

"Now, boyo, what do you really hear?" he said with a slight smile.

Wilson spoke first. "Wagons. I thought I heard wagons and men marching along the road. Am I right?"

"Aha, you are right, Wilson. And you, Levon, did you hear the same?"

I replied that I did before Wilson broke in. "But how do we know if they are the enemy, us, or just ordinary citizens?"

"We use our eyes. If we move just to the edge of these trees, I'll pull out this eyepiece and have a look."

Burke pulled a mariner's spyglass from a pouch on his saddle and peered through it into the darkness provided by the trees.

"As I thought. I knew it wouldn't be us. We are back in Centreville. But I wasn't completely sure it wasn't an ordinary family either," he said, continuing to look through the spyglass.

"The hint of blue. It's not an enemy patrol though. Too large, and they wouldn't have a train of wagons. We will follow them and see where they may lead. I should have noticed them sooner but they kicked up no dust due to the wet ground."

For hours we rode parallel to the wagon train, watching them, but keeping out of their sight. When they finally stopped short of Bull Run and seemed to make camp, Burke said, "Let's ride further up the road and make camp for the night. We can watch them, but no fires. We can't give ourselves away. I think these poor mounts need the rest, too."

That evening, we unsaddled our horses, took everything off them, and covered the equipment with a blanket to ward off the snow. We curried, watered, and fed the horses, then tethered them to a tree to afford them with as much shelter as could be provided. Sol's Mistress didn't seem to mind the inclement weather too much, preferring it to the confines of the stable.

The light snowfall continued to fall but didn't blot out a star-filled night. Because we couldn't light a fire we would share a cold, miserable night bundled in every available bit of clothing or bedding we had. The fires in the valley beckoned to us with their promises of warmth, while around them sat people who would surely like to see us dead.

"Lieutenant Burke, we have heard many reasons as to why people have joined the Confederacy. Why did you join?" I asked.

"Son, when I was a younger man, I was faced with the same aggression as we presently face. I, and others of a shared belief, were encamped at a farmhouse in Tipporary, Ireland, fighting for our very independence. Betrayed, we were, and those who did not run, were captured. I ran. My sons had been born and I brought my family here to America. It was 1848, and the thought that I ran has gnawed at me ever since.

I could no longer face my image in the mirror or the thought that my sons would see me as weak, unwilling to make a stand. My sons serve with Johnston, and I find myself here, with Stuart. It is curious to me that many of my compatriots, the Brothers of Erin, would fight for the Union though. The Irish Rebellion will continue, but in this instance, the Rebels will gain victory and this will not be dragged on, for I will not run nor be defeated."

I did not speak as Burke raised the spyglass to peer down at the enemy campfires. I don't recall how much time elapsed till the winking of the enemy fires dimmed. Shivering, I finally fell asleep in a sitting position on the cold ground, on the hill that looked over the enemy.

SEVEN

Breaking Winter Quarters
March, 1862

The next morning, I was shaken awake by the beefy hand and vigorous voice of Redmond Burke. "Wake up, boy, we must be getting back to camp."

"Wha…where am I?" I said as I tried to rouse myself and shake off the ice crystals that blanketed me.

"You look like a snowman, son. I knew you and Wilson weren't froze to death because I checked for your breaths by the rising and falling of your chests. I've been up for several hours. We have to be moving out to give Jeb what we have found out. I don't think the Yankees below are going to move out. Although they are not a large bunch, my guess is they are just waiting on some friends. McClellan seems to me to prefer to gather enormous forces always, but tends to move too slowly.

That man, I think, is overly cautious and that gives us a great advantage. I'm concerned with this buildup though. He may make a push toward Richmond. Let's move."

We saddled up, and riding the horses at a trot, headed back toward our winter quarters. Not more than a mile from our destination, as we slogged through the snow, we heard laughing and the jangling of traces just over a rise. Coming to the crest, we peered into the slight depression to see a couple gaily sleighing through the snow.

The man was clad in a Confederate uniform, and the striking brunette next to him was all bundled up. They seemed to have not a care in the world. I thought to myself, *What idiot would be out on a sleigh ride with a war going on?*

"Well, doesn't that beat all?" Burke said. "That's General Jeb at the reins. I swear to my God that man treats this war as if it were a play put on for his amusement."

Laughing heartily, he continued, "I can't fault his methods. He has his fun and still holds himself to the full competency of a great soldier."

Stuart stopped the sleigh upon our approach and called out, "Lieutenant Burke and his two charges. How are you this fine morning?"

"Fine, General. We are all fine. I don't think we have any information that would drastically change your strategy, but I will file a report and tell you of my findings, or rather, impressions," Burke replied.

"That will be splendid, but we will get to that later. Gentlemen, I want to introduce you to my companion today. This is Miss Laura Ratcliffe," Stuart said, making an exaggerated sweeping gesture.

"Pleased to meet you, gentlemen," the comely young woman said.

"Ma'am," I said, tipping my hat.

"Miss Ratcliffe lives in nearby Frying Pan with her mother and her sisters. She has very graciously accepted my invitation to a sleigh ride today, and we had a chance to go horseback riding, as well. Well, gentlemen, we will talk later. I would say we will meet at my tent in two hours, and Burke, I would also like to know how my two newest scouts fared," he said with twinkling eyes.

"Very good, General," Burke said, then we continued into camp.

We tethered Sol's Mistress and Mitch in the ramshackle stables, and after brushing them down, went to our home at Pagan's tent. "Hello, Levon, Wilson. How did it go?" Pagan bellowed.

I took my hat off, and wiping my brow, I answered, "Serious work, Mr. Pagan. I think we learned a lot, at least, I think I learned a lot. How about you, Cousin?"

"Yes, I think we did. It's kind of scary though," Wilson replied glibly.

"It is serious work we all do. Both sides. Is it scary? It surely is, and we all get scared. Wouldn't be natural if we didn't. I understand from the talk around camp that you have an excellent teacher. Redmond Burke is an excellent scout and I know he has Jeb's trust. He also has Jeb's ear. You could do far worse for a teacher. But, boys, you look hungry. Wilson looks like he's gonna shrink away. Boy, you were puny when you got here. What say I get you boys some food?"

Exhausted, Wilson said weakly, "Yes, I'm hungry, but for the love of all things, make it hot."

"You boys sit down out here. I got some mule," he laughed at his joke, remembering that I had taken it literally the first time. "I'll heat up some hominy; give you some bread and hot coffee. That should take care of you boys, don't ya think?" he continued.

"Oh, please, Pagan," Wilson said before plopping

down on the wet ground.

I was too tired to answer. I sat down next to Wilson and tried to warm myself by the fire.

The meal, I think, reinvigorated me, and Wilson too. After being able to wrangle two plugs of chew from Pagan, Wilson and I contentedly sat drinking the last of our coffee and spitting out streams of tobacco juice until Burke walked up.

"Boyos, the General wants to see you now. Let us not keep him waiting."

We got up, shook off the cold, and with Burke, trudged down to Stuart's tent. Stuart was seated on a stool stripped of his jacket but still clad in his gray trousers and knee high boots.

"Burke has not yet told me of the information you have deduced, or your educational experiences. I told him I wanted to wait for you. I also wanted to introduce you to the newest member of my staff. The gentleman to my left is Lieutenant John Singleton Mosby. He is an able cavalry man, and like the two of you claim, a fine rider. But enough of the introductions. Lieutenant Burke, what have you learned of our enemy?"

"Jeb—I mean, General," Burke stammered and then stopped, embarrassed, I think, by his lack of military protocol.

Stuart chuckled and said, "It's okay, Lieutenant. We are most familiar with each other, so your choice of calling me by name is fine. Please continue."

"We did spot a small squad of Yankees moving this way. They stopped before crossing Bull Run. I didn't notice any large numbers of fighters, but it seemed to me to be more of a supply train. I think McClellan will intend to mass before making any push. When we met you and your companion, I said I didn't think the information would be new to you."

When Burke made the comment regarding Stuart's companion and the sleigh ride I tried to hide a sneer and hoped Stuart hadn't noticed.

"What about your two pupils here? Forgive me for using military jargon, but did they pass muster?"

"Indeed, they will be, but as of yet, are still very green. I've tried to teach them to listen and explained all the traits I believe a good scout should possess. I believe they have passed muster for being their first time out. I would recommend they stay with me a little longer."

Stuart looked at Wilson and me, and what he said next made my throat tighten. Looking directly at me with his eyes not holding his usual mirth, he said, "I notice you seem to disapprove of my going sleighing with young Miss Ratcliffe. Is that so?"

"Uh, no, General, I made no such judgment," I lied.

"Verbally, you did not, but my belief is that your eyes told a different story. A judgment born of disdain, as it were. But let me be clear. Gaiety and amusement relieves tension. I have found it to be a valuable tonic that I encourage in my men, as well. Does the diversion detract from your capabilities as a warrior? I think not. When situations cry out for calm and strong resolve, it is awakened. This wakefulness is not bound by the stupor of slumber. You are instantly alert and in command of your faculties because you have relieved yourself of tension.

I see all of us as knights, those of us in the Confederacy. Upon reading, 'Idylls of the King', the narrative of King Arthur's life, my connection to it came upon me. As King Arthur sought to embrace ideal manhood and create the perfect kingdom, I believe I have been similarly called. Yes, King Arthur and his Round Table of Knights lived hundreds of years ago, that is true. But I believe in my heart that we are the knights of our time and I will act accordingly, even if it is only me. One other thing, respect and trust me as I will you, and we will build what King Arthur failed to accomplish, that perfect kingdom.

For the time being, I agree with Mr. Burke. You stay close to him and continue to learn from him. I received word that Johnston is to abandon our present quarters before the mass that McClellan is accumulating. But, as always, McClellan is slow to act. We will move out tomorrow and act as the rear guard for Johnston's forces. Relax for the rest of the day because, young men, further tests await you. Be ready in the morning. That is all."

His words would prove to be prophetic.

I left Stuart's tent in a state of horror, realizing that I had angered him. I felt that I must prove myself to him to change his feelings. I would have to show him through my actions, my loyalty, and allegiance to him, and through him, my allegiance to the whole cause. I glanced at Wilson who met my gaze only briefly before he turned away. The rest of the day was spent in silence as we helped Pagan pack up the wagons and our belongings.

Early on the morning of March 7th, 1862, we withdrew from the Manassas area to the Fredericksburg area below the Rappahannock. We were not in any scouting position now so we rode along with the wagon train and the bulk of Stuart's cavalry, which I felt a part of, however tenuous, acting as a rear guard for Johnston's larger army. Our usually surefooted horses slipped and slid on the snow covered roads of frozen mud. We rode to the point of evacuation of Johnston's army along the Alexandria line, when Burke and the recently arrived...what was his name again? I tried to think...oh yeah, Mosby, rode up.

Burke appeared more surly than usual and barked out orders. "We are going to lay the torch to the warehouses here so the advancing enemy cannot use what lies here and you will help. Now, boys, this is not scouting work, but you are going to join in and participate in it, understand?"

"Yes, sir," Wilson and I replied in unison.

"Good. See that fire that's been built over there?" he shouted, gesturing at a hastily built bonfire that had been built on probably the only dry patch of ground for miles around. "Here are two planks of wood to use as torches. Light them up from the fire and get to work."

Mosby looked at us with a studied gaze but said nothing.

I guided Sol's Mistress over to the roaring fire and lit the plank while she flinched not a bit, and Wilson did the same. I rode up to the first warehouse and applied the torch. The wet outside walls of the building sputtered before coming to life, being fed by the dry food, weapons, equipment, and soldier's baggage we left untouched inside.

So it went, for hours, as warehouse after warehouse went up, and a cloud of bluish smoke hung over the area. I heard some grumbling from a few of the others about how we could certainly benefit from what we were burning, but I didn't care. My place, I felt, was not to question orders but follow them to the letter, even if I wasn't considered a part of the army yet.

We rode away from the flaming ruins and kept on the move. Some of the soldiers spoke of retreating from McClellan, but since I was not familiar with the word, just kept riding along in silence.

The next few weeks were filled with what I could only describe as routine. Wilson and I tagged along with Redmond Burke on almost daily rides. Although there wasn't much scouting being done, as far as I could tell. I'm sure our education continued as Burke tossed out nuggets as we rode along the picket line that stretched as far west as the foothills of the Blue Ridge Mountains.

Around the first few days of April, the routine changed. The four of us—Burke, Mosby, Wilson, and I, were approached by a gangly figure on a road that straddled the Potomac. He strolled along the road toward us, bouncing with each step. He was dressed in plain work clothes, and as we reined up in front of him, he didn't appear to be overly excited despite the news he was about to deliver.

"I know you gents must be Confederates. Am I right?" he said lazily.

"What if we said we were?" Burke asked.

"Could be important news for you. If you're Yanks, maybe not."

"How would you know if I was lying to you or not? What if I was a Yank who told you I was a Reb?"

"I wouldn't know, necessarily. If you are a Yank, then let me be. If not, can you prove it?" the gangly fellow said.

"What if I showed you this?" Burke asked, pulling aside his heavy overcoat to show a piece of his gray uniform.

"That don't mean nothing. You know scouts often wear the uniforms of the other side."

"Enough of this," Mosby shouted, pulling his revolver out and pointing it at the man.

"If you're Yank and I give you this information you will kill me," he whined.

"I'll kill you if you don't. We are with Jeb Stuart. Now tell us what news you have!" Mosby growled, cocking the hammer. "Besides, how do we know you aren't a spy for them giving us false information?"

"Fair enough. I guess we are just going to have to trust each other and believe what we say to be true as well. Besides, sir, you are the one with the advantage," the gangly man said, pointing at Mosby's pistol.

"So, what news do you have, pray tell us?" Mosby said sarcastically.

"I have a place near the Potomac. I saw the Yanks loading up on transports to be put out on the river. Lots of them. I think they must be building up to attack Richmond, so I approached your lines to give you what information I have."

Mosby let the hammer down slowly, and easing the revolver down as well, said, "Thank you, sir, that is important information. You have provided a great service to the Confederacy."

"I'm not telling you that for the Confederacy's great cause. But I sure don't want troops marching through my land. It upsets my cows."

"Well, thank you just the same," Burke interjected.

As we started back, Burke said, "I don't think Jeb is taking this latest advance seriously enough. His methods work, but we are certainly on the run. Even though we approach Richmond, we seem to move languidly. McClellan has now massed his troops and I do not know if he plans to come from the land or by water. He could attack from the James or York rivers and be within easy striking distance. I think we better get back to the general with the news."

When we got back to camp, neither Wilson nor I were included in the conversation I assumed was conducted between Stuart, Burke, and Mosby, nor did I expect to be. The next day, we simply continued the slow retreat toward Richmond. When the soldiers first spoke of retreat, I hadn't known what the word meant, but now I felt that it was the same as defeat and I damn well knew what that meant. We had lost and the Yankees had won.

Feeling disconsolate, I was confused by the warm welcome we received from the citizens of Richmond when we paraded through town on April 18th. I was dumbfounded to see cheering crowds throwing flowers in front of us. I thought celebrations were reserved for conquering heroes, not an army in defeat. I looked at Wilson astride me and he was smiling, basking in the adulation.

Stuart's young aide, Chiswell, was suddenly beside me, inquiring, "Why so glum—Wilson, isn't it?"

"No, Levon, Wilson's my cousin," I replied.

"Then, why so glum, Levon? The people of Richmond love us."

"How can they be this way when we are in defeat?" I fired back.

"Defeat? Are you kidding me? This war is far from over. They're cheering our gallant defense of their homes. We have yet to lose to the Billys." Chiswell laughed.

"We may not be in defeat, but then retreat. I sometimes jumble the two meanings," I shouted over the din.

"I understand that because of your lack of military training, it may lead you to believe we are retreating, and therefore, in defeat. We are only repositioning ourselves to a more advantageous ground on which to fight. If our horses remain fit and do not suffer too many more breakdowns, we will be all right, okay?" He spurred his mount and rode away without waiting for an answer.

We arrived in Yorktown and met with the army of Joseph E. Johnston dug into works, I found out later, constructed a year before by a General Magruder. The talk in camp was that we had delayed McClellan's advance, but I was skeptical. They seemed to be constantly nipping at our heels.

We were only there a short time before command had decided to evacuate Yorktown, which we did on the evening of May 3rd. Retreat or defeat had become so blurred in my mind that despite Chiswell's explanation, it had become almost impossible for me to distinguish the two.

We happened to be close to Stuart when an excited courier returned and told him that the enemy had closed the road at Blow's Mill, the road from which we had just come.

Stuart called out for Burke, but when there was no answer he set his gaze on us.

"Wilson and Levon, this is it. You will not have your teacher, only his teachings to rely on. I hope you have learned your lessons well. Ride down there, find out what the devil is going on and report back to me. God bless you, boys, and I trust you will prove yourselves well."

Wilson and I wheeled our respective horses around and headed out at a gallop. It wasn't much of a gallop because the ground was like a swamp, but we had a good gait. The road was ringed on either side with dense underbrush, so I figured if we got into those woods, we might escape detection.

Up ahead, the road seemed deserted, so the two of us took the opportunity to ease the horses into the woods and set back from the road. I loosely tied Sol's Mistress to a pine as Wilson did Mitch.

We watched the road intently for what must have been fifteen minutes or so, when suddenly, two blue clad troopers broke through the underbrush to my left with their Colts pointed directly at my face.

"Don't move, boy. Will you look here, Bill? I think we have a little Johnny Reb. What are you doing spying on us? Are you a scout with the traitors?" the one not named Bill said.

"No, sir, I'm not," I replied.

"That's a lie. Why else would you be out here hiding

in the brush? Unless you got a little lady back there," he said as he looked past me.

We are dead when he sees Wilson, I thought. But when I looked back, I didn't see Wilson either. He'd been right next to me but now had disappeared.

"Check him for a gun, Bill. I wouldn't want this scrawny son of a bitch to shoot me."

Bill searched me. Pulling out my jackknife, he laughed loudly "Can you believe it? All he's got is this knife."

"Give it to me then, I need a souvenir for this kill," he said with a cold sneer.

"All you got is this boy?" he said fingering it slowly. "It's strange to find one of the enemy armed with just a knife. Maybe you're just stupid. But I don't believe you are not a scout, and I do believe you know what both sides do to a scout."

I felt the trickle of urine drip down my leg, and seeing that, they both burst out in fits of laughter again.

"He's so scared he wet himself. Yes, you have it figured out right. We are going to execute you. Say hello to your mother when you see her in hell."

Just as I figured, he was going to pull the trigger. The sharp report of a pistol boomed over my right shoulder. A red hole appeared on the Yank's forehead, and with mouth wide open, and his eyes doing the same, he toppled backward. Bill frantically looked for the shooter but he was shot dead by Wilson too.

Wilson screamed, "Let's go, Levon, run." We untied our horses, guided them to the road, and took off. I looked quickly over my shoulder and saw, sure enough, a thin blue line of cavalry coming fast, but still some distance away.

We raced toward our men, paying no mind to the muddy road and hanging tightly to our horses. Upon reaching Stuart, I yelled, "General, they are certainly coming."

"What was it, just a scouting party or a whole body of men?" Stuart asked.

"I'm sorry, General, I don't know," I wheezed. "We almost got killed by a couple of them, but Wilson got 'em."

"Good job, you two. Excellent. Colonel Goode take some of the 3rd Virginia down there and take care of the problem, you hear?"

"Very good, General," Colonel Goode said, snapping off a salute and charging away.

"Stay with me all the way to Williamsburg. Maybe we will get a chance to talk there."

We reached Williamsburg just after dark. I struggled to catch my breath all the way into the next morning, rendering sleep impossible. The next morning, the battle of Williamsburg began. The deplorable condition of the ground made it impossible for the cavalry. We retired to the rear of Fort Magruder to wait out the results under a drenching rain and enemy cannon fire.

A happy faced Burke sought us out late in the day. "You made me proud boys, you surely did. Made Stuart proud too, he told me. So, Wilson, you killed a couple, did ya? What about you, Levon?"

"No, Captain, I don't carry a gun," I said sheepishly.

"You don't carry a gun, son? That just doesn't make a lick of sense," Burke said.

"I'm afraid to, Burke. I don't like guns."

He patted me on the shoulder. "It would only be through fear or ignorance for a man not to carry a gun," he said. "Just as the blacksmith has his hammer, and the farmer his plow, the gun is a tool. A soldier must always have his tool. I have an extra Navy colt I'm going to give you."

He handed me the revolver. I turned it over and over in my hand. It would take some time for any sense of comfort to come over me.

EIGHT

The Great Chickahominy Raid
June 12th — 15th, 1862

Chickahominy River, Virginia

With the fighting stopped in late May, and the cavalry limited in what we could do, I tried to get used to handling a gun. Handling a musket wasn't completely foreign to me though. I had done some hunting when I was younger, but I did practice with the Colt and a Sharps Cavalry carbine that Burke had also given me. The carbine had a nice sling that hung from my saddle. Wilson had a carbine by then too, but I don't remember how he came to have it. I wasn't offered a saber, and if I had been, I would have refused it. I wouldn't have known how to use the damn thing anyway.

All my shooting practice was done on horseback, naturally. I figured all the fighting I'd be doing on horseback anyways. Wilson reminded me, and yes, even chided me about always practicing shooting on horseback.

"Remember, Levon, I killed those two Yanks while standing on the ground."

"Yes, Cousin, I remember quite well," I said wearily. "But I don't think I'll be fixing to get in that predicament again. Now that I got my friend here," feeling the warm grip of the Colt in my hand.

"Tool," Wilson said. "Burke said it was a tool."

"Tool, okay, tool. I get it!" I said testily.

Now, remember, my horse, Sol's Mistress, had been skittish around gunfire, but I noticed a change in her almost instantly. It was as if she had accepted my evolution and stood stock still or ran fluidly as I asked, never flinching, not even once.

Burke rode up one day while Wilson and I were practicing in a field. "How's the shooting going there for you boys?"

"Oh, its fine, Lieutenant," I said, trying to sound cheerful.

"Are you getting used to the feel and heft of the two weapons? I will tell you that you will get more use out of the pistol in the close fighting we do here in the cavalry. Of course, there will be times when logic points directly at the Sharps."

"What happens next, Lieutenant? I'm starting to get anxious," Wilson said.

"Well, McClellan has moved within, I would think, 10 miles from Richmond, so it could get hot. There has been fighting in Fair Oaks, and General Johnston has been wounded. But, Wilson, you sound just like Jeb. He's been fidgeting like a cow who knows he's been cornered and is about to get himself branded. Very uncharacteristic of him. He knows we are not able to maneuver our cavalry in these heavy woods but I know he isn't happy just acting as an aide to Longstreet. I don't believe we will be idle too much longer though," he said, fishing into his pocket and pulling out a cigar, lighting it with one easy strike of a match.

"Boys, I think my teaching of you is done. I have taught you all that I know." Blowing out a small trail of smoke, he continued, "Don't get me wrong, you will continue to learn. Sometimes these lessons are learned by your actions, so carry on until we meet again."

He rode away and I was left with sadness, although it didn't feel like it was a final farewell, and it was not. Johnston got some backbone and with none of our assistance. He had forced the Yankees away from Richmond. I immediately regretted the fleeting feeling I had of the lack of courage on Johnston's part. He had been badly wounded and had placed himself in harm's way more times than I probably ever would. I would never again question another man's courage.

Wilson and I lived out in the open in simple bedrolls, and occasionally, we put together enough scraps to construct a lean-to. We hadn't seen Pagan since the parade through Richmond. Of course, he was in a supply train, and now I felt that we were in the Confederate cavalry. Wilson and I were simply strolling through camp on a warm June evening when someone called out, "Stuart's looking for you. You best get over there."

I waved at the voice in acknowledgment and went to Stuart's tent straight away. As we approached the clearing where Stuart's tent lay, I heard the familiar strain of, "Jine the Cavalry," Stuart's favorite song. Sam Sweeney, who I'd come to know as Stuart's favorite banjo player, and a fiddler, played the tune. We announced ourselves and Stuart asked us in. We stepped inside and found Stuart his usual jovial self, and if I do say so myself, elated.

"Thank you for coming, gentlemen. The purpose of my asking for this meeting was to outline a mission I consider exceedingly important. If you don't already know, the Yankee forces under their General McClellan, were forced back from their attempted stranglehold of Richmond. Regrettably, General Johnston was wounded, but General Robert E. Lee, of who I am most familiar, has taken charge. We have been badly hampered by the weather, and therefore, under-utilized. I have sent a communication to Lee of my ideas regarding campaign strategy and to suggest an attack on the enemy's right, but he has not responded. Without yet receiving a response, I wanted to outline a mission that may convince him. I've entrusted this gathering of vital information to you five."

Gesturing with his arm, Stuart continued, "Levon and Wilson, I believe you have already acquainted yourself with Mr. Mosby here through previous service, agreed?"

Mosby gave a slight smile and nod.

Without pausing for an answer, Stuart said, "Mosby here is not altogether comfortable with traditional soldiering so I believe he would be a good fit with the two of you who have a lack of military training. I have no questions regarding your courage, however, nor do I have any questions regarding Mosby's either. Now, Mosby has brought along with him Mr. Beattie and Mr. Frankland. Although I'm not personally familiar with them, he has vouched for their trustworthiness."

"What I desire of you is to perform a reconnaissance along McClellan's right flank to see if it is as unguarded as I believe it to be. You are then to return with your observations. Be off with you," he said with a dismissive wave of his hand.

The five of us exited the tent. Mosby, with another slight smile on his face, said, "Let's mount up, boys, and see if we can find the enemy."

We moved out at a slow gallop, straddling the Richmond, Fredericksburg, and Potomac Railroad with the intention of finding a large body of Yankees. We made a few quick dashes into the covering woods to escape being seen by some small scouting parties before finally coming upon the enemy's right flank, largely unprotected as Stuart had thought. After observing them for a while, we rode quickly back to Stuart to deliver the news.

Upon receiving our information Stuart laughed heartily and fairly shouted, "It is as I thought. I must speak with Lee immediately." He quickly pulled his boots up, grabbed his hat, and instructed an aide, whose name and face I wasn't familiar with, to saddle up his horse. When Highfly was led to him, Stuart quickly mounted up and tore out of camp, leaving me scratching my head.

Just after midnight, on June12[th], Wilson and I were roused by the young aide, Chiswell, who told us excitedly that Stuart had ordered the command to be ready to ride in ten minutes. Still groggy, Wilson and I got Sol's Mistress and Mitch saddled up, grabbed some equipment, including our guns, of course, and waited in the muggy Virginian night for Stuart. Looking around, there seemed to be over a thousand horsemen who waited with us. This was no scouting party, but a much bigger affair, to be sure. I recognized detachments of the 1st Virginia Cavalry, 4th Virginia Cavalry, 9th Virginia Cavalry, the Jeff Davis Legion, and several artillery pieces.

Seated upon a sweating Sol's Mistress, I tried to figure out what Stuart's plans were, but nobody knew. Wilson sat upon Mitch, rubbing the sleep from his eyes. I knew he didn't know any more than anyone else about what could be up. I thought maybe we were going to meet up with the almost mythical Stonewall Jackson and his army.

When someone inquired of Stuart, how long he would be gone, he said plainly, "It may be for years, and it may be forever."

And so it was that we rode out, not knowing where we were going, but trusting in General Jeb Stuart's instinct would have to be enough. I had learned, in just my short time with Stuart, that he had his men's complete trust and loyalty. In that instant, I realized he had mine as well.

The air clung to all of us, drenching us in a combination of dew and sweat. We rode steadily northward up the Brooke Turnpike, traveling the same path Mosby and the rest of us had done earlier that evening.

Near a place called Yellow Tavern, we left the turnpike and went this way and that before crossing the Richmond, Fredericksburg, and Potomac Railroad and headed east. That night, we camped at Winston's Farm, which was close to Taylorsville, having covered 22 miles.

As soon as we stopped and begun to relax, Wilson and I were summoned to Stuart, yet again. We came upon Stuart, still mounted.

"I'm desirous to know what lies ahead," he said. "Before turning in tonight, Mosby, I want you, Levon, and Wilson to ride out ahead and tell me how the going looks for tomorrow morning. Mr. Lee and I will not be staying in camp tonight, but visiting a friend at the Lee home at Hickory Hill. If I'm not here when you return, wait for me and further instructions. That is all." He wheeled his mount around and rode away with Rooney Lee. We watched until the darkness enveloped them.

"Damn, we just got the horses unsaddled and now we have to go back out," Wilson grumbled.

Mosby, who was usually reserved, lashed out. "Shut up, Wilson. Your commanding general has given you orders. You will obey."

Wilson snarled back. "He is not my commanding general. I'm not even in the cavalry." Apparently, Wilson hadn't embraced Stuart as wholeheartedly as I had, yet.

Mosby, growing angry spat back "Then what are you doing here, boy? Are you here just for your amusement? You are in the cavalry, boy, at the very least attached to it. No, you don't have a uniform or title, but you have been here. We are not playing parlor games, we are at war. Didn't you kill two Yanks saving your cousin? That's what I heard."

"Yes, I did, but that was to save Levon's life," Wilson sputtered back.

"That is what war is all about. We kill the enemy to save our families, our friends. Congratulations, boy, you are in the thick of it now, whether you like it or not. Saddle up!"

"C'mon, Wilson, let's go get the horses," I said, gently grabbing the now sniveling Wilson's shoulder and guiding him to the horse's picket lines.

We said no more, but went and got Sol's Mistress and Mitch saddled up again. Even with all the riding, Sol's Mistress didn't seem all that annoyed to be ridden again. *Damn,* I thought, *the girl likes to be ridden.*

We rode along the road to Old Church, slowly and cautiously, but encountering none of the enemy, we turned around to report back to Stuart. When we returned to camp, the three of us were surprised to find Stuart waiting for us.

I spoke first, "General, the road to Old Church seems clear."

"We encountered no one in the hours we've been out," Mosby added. Wilson was mute, pouting, I thought.

"Well done, once again, young men. Get some rest, you have done more than a day's work. We will move out in a few hours, and I might send for you then," Stuart said.

We unsaddled the horses, brushed them down, laid blankets over their backs, and walked away from the horse's picket line searching for a place to lay our bedrolls and maybe get some coffee.

"I'm whipped sorely, Levon," Wilson said quietly.

"But you will still do the duty even if you don't feel like you're a part of all this?"

"Yes, I will, I guess. But, Levon, do you feel like you are in the Confederate cavalry?"

"Maybe not all the way in, if it means having a uniform, rank, or even pay. But we are doing a job. We are helping out. I do respect General Stuart, and he seems to do good deeds like the knight he is," I said with a grin. "I haven't had to kill anybody yet, but I think the time is drawing near. Maybe when I have to, I'll feel like a real soldier, a real part of the Confederate cavalry. But, Wilson, you have already done that."

"I know, but it was to save you. I didn't really want to, but I didn't have time to think about it. I saw that Yank fixing to shoot you so I shot him first," Wilson said blankly.

"It was like Mosby said. We will fight to protect our family and our friends. Now, let's see if we can find some friends who will lend us some coffee," I said.

We did find those friends who did indeed lend us a cup or two, along with a promise to wake us when we began to advance. Obviously, we looked like we were tired and prone to doze off, hence their promise. I dozed off almost immediately.

"We are on the move. Get up soldiers," a gruff voice roused us.

Wilson and I gathered up our bedrolls, ran to the picket line, saddled up our horses and trotted toward the lead column. We chatted with a few troopers we were friendly with. They told us that the advance was moving toward Hanover Courthouse and Old Church. When it was relayed to Stuart that the enemy was spotted in Hanover Town, they admitted they were not sure what Stuart's next step would be. One trooper familiar with the area said he thought he knew what Stuart was up to. "We must be skirting the flank of McClellan's forces, heading for his rear end along the banks of the Pamunkey."

"To strike a blow?" I asked.

"To strike a blow. A mighty big blow judging by the size of this group," he said matter-of-factually.

Wilson and I rode hard toward the front and reunited with Stuart just as Fitz Lee's regiment did the same. I don't know where Lee had been. I was still groggy, desperately trying to clear my head by shaking it.

We trailed Stuart who led us by Taliaferro's Mill and Enon Church, to Haw's Shop where a few of Stuart's lead troopers captured some unprepared enemy pickets and charged on toward Old Church. I rode Sol's Mistress hard, splashing through Totopotomoy Creek, hot on Highfly's heels.

The cold splashes of water to my face, and the breeze as we raced along, did what the shaking of my head had failed to accomplish. I was now fully awake.

A brief fight ensued at the edge of the creek in a deep ravine whose banks were fringed with laurel and pine. Wilson and I were not involved in that, or a larger fight that occurred soon after.

After those two fights, our army regrouped and Stuart talked in an animated manner with a few of his regimental commanders, most notably Rooney Lee of the 9th Virginia. After their discussion, Stuart decided, I guess, to completely circle McClellan's army. At the time, I thought it was complete lunacy and utterly risky, but this was Stuart, and I trusted Stuart.

Wilson still had not completely bought into Stuart's competency, or rather, his instincts, and was screaming in my ear as we plundered an unescorted wagon train, "We are in Virginia, sure, but we are completely surrounded. He is going to get us all killed."

I looked at him as I ate some captured rations from one wagon. "Not to worry, Cousin. Although it may appear rather bleak to you and I, look at Stuart." Both of us shot a glance at Stuart, who was not far away. "Does he appear worried or confused? Of course not. He has complete confidence in his abilities. Look at it. Embrace it. Perhaps that will be enough. C'mon, do not fret, let us continue on."

We galloped into Tunstall's Station, a depot on the York River Railroad, just behind an echelon of our men led by someone named Robins. As his small group was busy rounding up wide-eyed Union soldiers, I jumped down from Sol's Mistress, grabbed a bayonet from a confiscated rifle, and began shinnying up a telegraph pole to cut the wires.

Don't ask me how I knew that to prevent an alarm, I should cut the telegraph wires. I had not seen it done, nor had Redmond Burke taught me. Perhaps it was some unseen spirit who has moved me to do it. Maybe it was God. As I sawed through the wire, Wilson and others were felling trees to block the tracks from approaching trains.

After I finished cutting the wire and started to come down, the steam of an approaching locomotive stopped my descent. The train was running at top speed, and I was sure that it wasn't planning on letting those logs stop it. I dug my heels into the telegraph pole, dropped the bayonet, pulled my Colt and just started shooting. Gunfire erupted from the train and my fellow troopers on the ground. I wasn't fired upon, perhaps because the shooters in the train were too occupied by their attackers on the ground to notice someone up in the air. The train barreled through the blockade, pitching the fallen timber in its wake. Now I shot blindly and got off four shots, although I don't know if I hit anybody.

I slid down the rest of the way and helped Wilson tear up more track and placed some logs over them. We applied the torch to the bridge over Black Creek and plundered another wagon train before burning it as well.

Although nightfall was fast approaching, Stuart led us about five more miles into Talleysville. We had swung a sword of destruction on the enemy and captured 165 of the unfortunates as well. Although we were not out of danger yet, Stuart stopped to let us rest. Wilson and I watched our horses graze as we helped ourselves to some delicacies pilfered from a sutler's store we had broken into. I stuffed some canned meat into my trousers while Wilson stuffed some candy into his. We both bit into figs, looked at each other, and burst out laughing.

"Oh, my God, this has been one hell of a day! I can't remember when I've been so scared and yet triumphant at the same time. It's about more than a man can take," Wilson said.

"Oh, so you're a man now, are you?" I said with a grin, and we both burst out in laughter again.

Back in the saddle at midnight, Stuart led us toward the Chickahominy, and then what I hoped would be Richmond. Although it was a full moon, it didn't provide much light as we struggled on to Sycamore Springs. Sycamore Springs sat on the bank of a now swollen and raging river. What had usually provided a practical ford, was today offering anything but that.

Stuart stroked his beard pensively, locked in conversation with not only his brother-in-law, John Esten Cooke, but Rooney Lee as well. They were discussing what to do when I overheard Cooke ask the others on their thoughts. Stuart calmly replied, "Well, Lieutenant, I think we are caught." Stuart dismounted and strode along the bank, examining the terrain and the churning water.

Redmond Burke, accompanied by Mosby, rode up next to me and said, "You two follow me. I have an idea."

We rode a mile downstream to the charred remains of Forge Bridge where the water ran far shallower, and the bridge's abutments remained. When we reined up, Burke announced, "By God, boys, we can fix a damn fit bridge from the remains. Levon, ride back to Stuart and give him the news while Mosby, Wilson, and I get started."

I rode back and gave a delighted Stuart the news, and soon, he, I, and the others were busy building the bridge. I tell you, he might have been a general but he rolled up his shirtsleeves and pitched in like a private.

Our entire column crossed the Chickahominy just after 1:00 pm, I figure, then the bridge was set ablaze. It was not a moment too soon as our enemy pursuers had reached the far bank but could only watch in frustration as we disappeared into the woods.

Wilson and I were fortunate in being selected to guide our party the rest of the way into Richmond. We led Stuart up the banks of the James River by way of the Charles City Courthouse, inside the capital's defenses to Richmond and freedom.

Scant days later, I recalled all that we had done. Stuart's belief that McClellan's right was unprotected was proven. We had harassed and annoyed our enemy to no end, destroying supply lines and communication lines, and forcing the Union to abandon their foray to

Richmond. We had gained vital information, captured 165 men and over 260 horses and mules, and had not lost a man, I thought at the time. Even more astonishing to me was that we had traveled over 150 miles while spending 65 hours in the saddle.

We had the adoration of the entire South and were lauded by the Richmond Dispatch. Stuart modestly received the accolades and added a title of Beau Sabreur, but I bet he reveled in it in private. We had given confidence to the South that we could not be defeated. Some called it "The Ride around McClellan", or the "Pamunkey Expedition", but I can tell you, my friends, that I will always remember it for what it was, "The Great Chickahominy Raid."

NINE

Chasing McClellan Away
Late June, 1862

Stonewall and his army had finally arrived from the Shenandoah, or at least, I finally became aware of it. I learned that Lee planned to launch a major offensive north of the Chickahominy, and with Stuart, we were going to finally accomplish what I thought we had planned to do initially before it became the raid. This time our mission was to guard the flanks and rear of Jackson's advance. Funny, we did many of the same things as on the previous raid but were not near as effective.

Stuart had added to his already resplendent uniform an ostrich plume stuck in his hat. The first time I saw him with it I almost burst out laughing. Within days, we headed toward Mechanicsville. Before we saddled our horses, Wilson made an admission that, to be sure, wasn't totally unexpected by me. He had been coughing for days, and just the night before, his nose had bled. He was weary, as we all were, but maybe he labored with it a little more.

"Levon, I don't know how much longer I can do this," he said wearily.

I didn't interrupt him, but let him continue as we saddled up.

"I know at the outset of serving here I agreed with it. There didn't seem like there was anything else we could really do. I wasn't going to face Josiah and I didn't want to part from you. You and I are more like brothers than cousins anyway. I guess you feel like this last raid was just one big adventure, but we could have been killed. Me, I miss my family, and you never say so either way but I can't understand it if you don't. I don't want to die. Maybe I'll ride back home alone to our home, or rather your home."

I stood there, silently waiting for him to continue, but when he didn't, I spoke up, "Listen, Wilson, we are all scared, just like Pagan said so long ago. None of us wishes to die or even court death. But how long will it be until our home in the lower Shenandoah will be drug in? To fight here to me is the point. Preserving paradise down there, in my opinion, is to keep the defense and fighting up here. C'mon, look, maybe we can write a letter and get it to our families. Please just stick with me a little longer."

Wilson reluctantly agreed, at least I think he agreed, because he did mount up and we rode north of the Chickahominy toward Mechanicsville and Beaver Dam Creek. One day in the saddle and nothing happened.

On June 27th, as we entered the territory around Gaines Mill, the action ignited as kindling ignites to the flame of a match. We charged a small band of Yankee skirmishers, and leaving my Sharps inside its sling, pulled the Colt for the close work Burke had told me to expect. Both sides had men drop as bullets found their intended targets. I was shooting as I charged forth, and that moment will be forever burned into my memory as I killed another human being. The Yankee sitting tall in the saddle raised his carbine and our eyes locked. I pulled the trigger of my Colt just before he shot. My shot ripped into his blue jacket, and I swear I saw threads of blue tear away from his jacket. Thankfully, his shot was too high and whistled away. His body jerked, then he fell from his horse, one boot caught in the stirrup. His horse stumbled and lurched to the right dragging his body away.

The enemy turned and thundered away in the general direction of White House. We pursued them for a time before Stuart halted us. We headed toward the York and Pamunkey. At Dispatch Station, the work we had become adept at doing during the Chickahominy Raid, commenced. We tore up tracks, captured prisoners, and I shinnied up a pole and cut the telegraph wires.

Stuart eyed me as I cut the wire and yelled, "Levon, I'm going to start calling you, 'Wirecutter,' for you have the talent for it."

I didn't tell him how a revelation had spurred me to do it the first time, I just slid down the pole. I noticed something distinctly different with Wilson. When we had been slave catching, then scouting, and now cavalry, Wilson had been by my side, but now I had to almost go looking for him. He hung back in the column, his head down. I don't even know if he had shot his pistol, or even been active in the pursuit. If he participated at the destruction at Dispatch Station, I don't know, but in his defense, I had been busy with the telegraph wires.

I slowed Sol's Mistress to give Wilson time to come alongside me, but we didn't talk. I tried to engage him in small talk to get a conversation started, but he remained quietly slumped in his saddle.

About dawn on June 29th, we halted about four miles from White House Landing near the former estate of Rooney Lee. The sky was darkened by smoke that hung in the air for miles it seemed. I was on a scouting mission with noted scout, Frank Stringfellow, Mosby, and a few others, but not Wilson.

Approaching the James River, Mosby quickly silenced us. We slid out of our saddles, handing the reins to one of our party, and edged closer to look at the Union gunboat anchored ashore.

Stringfellow whispered, "Would you look at that damn thing? I recognize it from the siege at Yorktown. It's called the "Marblehead." I wish we had a cannon to blast that floating piece of crap right out of the water."

Mosby snickered, and patting Stringfellow on the shoulder said, "Simmer down there, Frank. Pelham's not around to take that boat there but we don't need a cannon to take those boys," He pointed down to a group of Union sailors on shore.

"Let's grab our rifles and break up their little beach outing."

I crept back to Sol's Mistress and grabbed the Sharps out of its sling. I crept back up to a dune dotted with grass. I brought up my rifle and took aim. The others did the same and we began shooting. The startled sailors hunkered down on the bank as several skiffs departed from the gunboat heading for shore. *Damn, they got reinforcements,* I thought. I kept shooting and felt rather safe behind the dune, even though I could hear their shots thud into the dirt. Not long after, we got our reinforcements to match them. Stuart apparently sent a party of about 70 men to aid us.

I thought I saw a glimpse of Wilson with them, but I

wasn't sure. Finally, a field piece of Pelham's drove the sailors back to the gunboat and it moved away from shore. After the gun battle, all we could do was watch the remnants of Rooney Lee's beautiful estate smolder. I was told that Lee was disconsolate. There was some consolation for the rest of our army, however, as the retreating enemy left a well-stocked commissary of which we took full advantage. Rations and whiskey was plentiful, but after a rumor circulated that the whiskey was poisoned, we ate, but just poured the drink into the dirt.

We rested for several days and I reconnected with Wilson the very first night. At least he said a few words, but it was like pulling teeth.

"Did you join the attack on the Union gunboat anchored near the bank today?" I asked.

"I was there," he said.

"How did you feel about it? Are you still feeling the same?" I asked, studying his face for an answer.

"It'd take more than one instance to sway my mind. It wasn't no great victory and I didn't feel any safer. It sure didn't cure my homesickness."

"I know, I know. But give it some time. Remember what I said about fighting here to preserve our home?" I urged.

He fell silent around the campfire we built for ourselves that night as I wrestled with my own guilt. I had killed a man today, and tried to kill more. The struggle I had wrestled with had come to pass and the scale had tipped heavily in the continued use of a weapon.

It was a bit easier to come to grips with it after that Yank had pointed a gun at my face, and many more would follow his lead. Plus, Burke's words echoed in my head, "It's just a tool." We ate a little as we talked that night, and collecting our bedrolls, stretched out by the fire and slept.

July 1st started hot and muggy, and after Robert E. Lee's courier gave Stuart a message to link up with Jackson, we were on the trail again. It took us most of a day to locate Jackson and it frustrated Stuart to no end since we missed, what I am told, was a horrific battle at Malvern Hill. When Stuart was informed that McClellan's rear guard had not yet reached the James River in their retreat, we pursued them. We captured stragglers from the battle at Malvern Hill, and a shore party from the ironclad ship, Monitor, in our pursuit.

In the predawn darkness of what I believe was July 3rd, and after a hard night of riding, we came upon the rear guard of McClellan's forces. They had stupidly camped in a valley below a ridge at Evelington Heights. After we chased a Union party from the heights, I shook my head, unable to figure out why the Yankees sometimes would take their sweet time in making their way.

While Burke had questioned our languid retreat, the term I still used to describe the movement toward Yorktown and beyond, the Yankees always seemed to travel lazily both in their attacks and retreats. Their column lay scattered below the ridge in a disjointed jumble.

I dismounted, as did the troopers, to offer support, and once again, Wilson was right there with me. We had called an unspoken truce with each other in the hopes of repairing our close relationship. Wilson was still very quiet. Before, he had seemed content to let me lead the way and had followed along. I was older, but only by a year, and I never thought we had anything more than an equal level of maturity. Hell, he was the first to defend himself with the gun.

Stuart had commanded Pelham to bombard their camp with a single howitzer. I assume Stuart commanded Pelham to do it, because slightly after 9:00 am, the cannon sent a barrage of fire raining down on the enemy camp. We watched as the cannon caused havoc, breaking up their shelters, destroying supply wagons, and sending soldiers scattering. It went on for a few hours until the artillerists had to abandon their work because they ran out of ammunition.

With the capture of quite a number of frantic Yanks, we abandoned the ridge and moved away. I looked back and watched the Yankees swarm over the heights and occupy the position we had just left.

We hadn't even arrived at Stuart's new headquarters at Atlee's Station on the Virginia Central Railroad before Stuart was coming under broad criticism for his perceived reckless behavior. Some in Stuart's own command, as well as many other supposed strategists, said Stuart should have waited for the Confederate infantry to arrive. A large amount of McClellan's army would have been forced to surrender, they said.

By unleashing Pelham's gun, Stuart had alerted the enemy to their precarious position and the moment had been lost, according to the critics. Now, I'm just a scout, but I was there on that ridge and saw the damage the howitzer inflicted. How could it not be considered a success?

The arrival at Atlee's Station was a joyous relief. Everyone and everything was worn from the hard campaign and constant riding of almost a month. I think even Sol's Mistress was worn out. I wished I could get my hands on one of the newer McClellan saddles. I've heard it offered the horses relief from the torturous Jenifer saddle I placed on Sol's Mistress.

 TEN

An Unexpected Trip to the Enemy's Capital
Late July, 1862

The next few days were consumed by reviews, refitting, and rest. Stuart, at this time, relocated his headquarters to Hanover Court House 7 miles north of Atlee's Station. Although Wilson and I weren't in Stuart's inner circle, and maybe never would be, we always bedded down nearby where Stuart could call on us for important duties.

During the day, we never were called to drill because we were only scouts, but simply lollygagged around and picked up information from the talks in camp. At night, we were serenaded by Sam Sweeney's banjo accompanied by Mulatto Bob on the bones. It was during one of those evenings that we were approached by Mosby.

"Hello, boys. I had to step away from Stuart because he doesn't smoke or drink."

He slung himself down on the ground and said, "I had to enjoy a cheroot."

"Would you care for a smoke?" he said, offering us some cigars.

I took one, but Wilson declined because he was still feeling poorly, what with nosebleeds and the shits.

"I heard a commotion. What's going on over there?" I asked Mosby trying to sound nonchalant.

He laughed. "Well, it looks like the North got tired of their General McClellan's failures and put a General Pope in charge, and that McClellan will work in conjunction with him, apparently. Combined forces too. Seems like we'll be fighting the Union Army of Virginia for now. I almost forgot to tell you what the commotion was about. Jeb's been promoted up to major general and in command of two brigades, but that in itself is not bad. He wants Fitz Lee as commander of the First Brigade."

"So what's the problem?" I asked, taking a puff and starting to feel my body relax.

"It's the selection of Wade Hampton in command of the Second Brigade," Mosby replied.

"Who is he? I haven't ever heard of him."

"Well, first, he isn't Jeb's choice. It's President Jeff Davis's choice," Mosby said. "He's some wealthy planter from South Carolina who has some battlefield experience. Some say he's responsible for the flight of a portion of his men at Manassas and Seven Pines. Plus, he ain't a soldier. He's not from West Point, or our glorious VMI, as other leaders of ours are. To top it off, he's old, nearly 44, and I'm sure his conservative manner will surely clash with ah, let's say Jeb's more cavalier style. I've seen it already," Mosby chuckled.

"But I have something I think would be more to your

liking and I wanted to run the idea past you," Mosby continued. "I'm weary of all this politicking that goes on. I've been talking to Jeb about participating as more of a loose outfit of irregulars."

"What would you do?" I asked, coming alert.

"As a loose outfit we could harass the enemy from different spots rather than face to face assaults. We could do essentially what we did on the Chickahominy Raid. After surprise attacks, we would just blend in with the good folks of Fauquier and Loudoun counties, predominantly. I think we could be of great benefit to the cause of this undertaking."

"We?" I asked stunned.

"Yes, us. Wilson, you, I, and others," he said quickly.

I asked warily "Why us, Wilson and I?"

He laughed "You two haven't been formally enlisted yet, you've been with Jeb for some time. You're young, daring, good horsemen, and don't forget, I've witnessed your work. I think you could grab a little glory and not be stuck in a rather drab situation. Not that what we do isn't important, because it is. But this would be on a much grander scale and not confined to a strict military life. I know I often chafe under its confines."

"Maybe we prefer its confines. I think it might be safer," Wilson said with a cough.

"Suit yourself, but I talked to Jeb and he has given the go ahead on the idea. The three of us would try to get around the back of Pope's army and see what information we can get. Pope's rear is supposed to be in the vicinity of Manassas and the Fairfax Court House area. Jeb wants us to meet up with old Stonewall. I got a letter of introduction from Stuart right here in my pocket," Mosby said patting his jacket.

"Wilson, I won't deny it's dangerous, but we'd be doing a great service," Mosby added.

I said, "I'm in. Wilson?"

After a brief bit of disagreement, Wilson reluctantly agreed. "Okay, we'll ride out tomorrow," Mosby said as he stubbed out the end of his cigar.

Early the next morning, after a quick breakfast, the three of us were mounted up and ready to ride out. I hadn't seen Stuart, but I didn't really feel like I had to because Mosby said he had received the okay from him, so we rode off.

Heading north, we hoped to catch up to Stonewall and the rear of Pope's army almost simultaneously. We rode down the roads three abreast, and I think maybe a bit too carelessly. Since the raid, and even before, like at Dranesville, the Yankees and us seemed to bump into one another in the unlikeliest of places. I guess Mosby knew what he was doing because we rode quietly, with the silence only occasionally broken by Wilson's moan or cough.

So two thoughts gnawed at me. One, shouldn't we be a little more cautious and ride on less traveled roads? Two, would Wilson even make it? I questioned Mosby on our seeming lack of caution.

"John, er, Mosby, how do you know we're not going to meet up with an enemy patrol riding like this?"

"I don't, but I feel inclined to go the shortest route we can. It's not like we're stranded on some island. Jeb is heading west, has been commanded to head west to seal off the enemy threats around Fredericksburg. If we get in a sticky situation we will run back to Stuart, or Mother Hen," he said disgustedly.

We looked over at Wilson. He looked a little wan, and had for some time, when Mosby asked him, "Wilson, you all right?"

"I've got an awful stomach ache and I've been coughing, but let's just keep on," Wilson answered unsteadily.

As we neared Beaver Dam Station, which sat on the Virginia Central line, Mosby suggested we board our horses and catch a train. We reined in our horses in the yard at the front of the depot and tied them to a hitching post.

"Why don't we load them on the train? We are going to need them,"

Mosby agreed, and he and Wilson strode over to look for a suitable way to load the horses on the train. I went into the dilapidated weather-beaten depot office to search for periodicals or newspapers in which to bide my time while on our ride. I finished making some purchases and headed out the door into a hot, dusty wind when a patrol rode in.

My heart skipped a mite when I realized it was a Yankee patrol. I slid under the planks at the front of the depot and watched. Surprised, Mosby just threw his arms up in surrender as several riders encircled him. Wilson started to run, but only made it a few feet before stumbling and falling into the dust.

Wilson hollered, "Oh damn, it I think I broke my leg." He clutched at his ankle and writhed on the ground before two Yankees dismounted and jerked him to his feet.

With pitiful eyes, he looked for me but didn't see me in the shadows of the plank porch of the depot. Fortunately, neither did the Yanks, I didn't think. Then I saw the pant legs of three troopers approach my hiding place, and thought, *Oh hell, they've seen me.* But they stopped short at the hitching post and untied the horses. Sol's Mistress neighed her objections as the troopers led her, Mitch, and Mosby's horses away as well.

I watched as they bound Mosby and Wilson, placed them on their horses, and with one final look around, rode off with them. I buried my face in the dirt and cried.

I laid there for I don't know how long before I began to think of what I should do. I couldn't attempt to rescue them for I was simply outnumbered and it would be madness. I had to get a horse and get back to Stuart. He would certainly know what to do.

I crawled out from my hiding place, dusting myself off as my stomach began to churn. Think, think! I prodded myself. There were no other horses tied to the hitching post so I went around the back of the station where I thought I had seen horses boarded in a ramshackle stable of sorts. In a pen, there sat a few horses, though none who could match Sol's Mistress in endurance and quality from what I could see. Oh God, I had lost her too. I must stay strong. In a tack room I found some saddles. I looked around and didn't notice anyone so I stole into the room and grabbed a bridle and saddle.

I peered out of the door, and still seeing no one, approached a bay and quickly had him saddled. I opened the gate, guiding the bay out, jumped on him and tore off in search of Stuart.

I took the less traveled roads to avoid any other Yankee patrols, while a thousand thoughts whipped around in my head like they were caught in a whirlwind.

For the first moment in my entire life, I was alone. I had pestered Wilson to continue on and now he was in the hands of our enemy along with Mosby. I hoped that the Yanks would not find the letter of introduction Mosby had from Stuart to Stonewall, but felt sure they would. I had lost my mount, Sol's Mistress, who I had raised since she was a foal. How would I get anyone back?

I continued to race along, as did my thoughts. I had heard troopers in the camps speak their beliefs about what war does to a man, how it changes them. Now I felt the effects. I had killed a man, and as morally wrong and awful as it had been, I had been driven to accept it. Killing was part of war, something I had known, and continued to know, so little about.

I had eaten from the sutler's stores we had broken into and looted, never thinking of payment. It had never crossed my mind being so caught up in that moment. To boot, I was now atop a stolen horse. I had become a thief, a common criminal. I scarcely remembered the ride as I charged into camp.

Sentries yelled and Chiswell Dabney joined them, "Levon, what the heck are you doing? You come charging into camp like that?"

I dismounted and gasped, "I got to see the general right away."

Chiswell grabbed my shoulder to steady me. "Levon, what's going on? What's wrong?"

"I have to see Stuart, now."

"Okay, I'll take you."

Stuart stood as soon as Chiswell drew back the tent flap and I stepped in. "Levon, what are you still doing here? Didn't you leave with Mosby?" he asked with alarm.

"I did, General. Mosby and Wilson have been captured," I blurted out.

"How and where?"

"We were waiting to board a train at Beaver Dam Station. We were surprised by a Yankee patrol."

Stuart exclaimed, "You're as white as a ghost. Are you injured? How did you escape? Chiswell, go get Dr. Eliason."

"It's not necessary to get the doctor, I'm not injured. I'd just come out of the station office when the Yankee patrol rode in. I got under the front porch of the station and hid. Mosby and my cousin were in the yard inspecting the train and were surrounded pretty quickly. Wilson tried to run, but he injured his leg. They bound them both and rode off with them. I couldn't do anything, there were probably 20 or so. I decided to get back as quickly as I could. What will we do?"

"Sit down, Levon, let me think. Sometimes it is better to run than fight, especially against the overwhelming forces we all face, that you faced. Lieutenant Dabney, get this man a drink. He looks like he needs one. Pardon me, Levon, but as you know, I don't drink."

"General, how are we going to get them out?" I asked shakily.

"I don't know if we can, at least, not easily. I know that out of the loyalty to your cousin you must at least try to get them out. Lieutenant Dabney, see if Stringfellow is about. He may be of some help with this," Stuart said, remaining perfectly calm as always.

Snapping off a salute, Chiswell said, "Very good, General, I will look for him." He stepped out of the tent, leaving Jeb and I alone.

"I know, Levon, that getting Wilson out of prison would be of upmost importance to you, but you must be patient. He is young and therefore may be exchanged fairly early I think. But Mosby is much different. I do not wish to sound indelicate, but getting Mosby out is of greater importance to all of us."

"But, sir, he is my cousin," I pleaded. "He, I think, wanted out. He said as much to me. Besides, he's sick."

"I see," Stuart said, stroking his beard pensively. "If the enemy were to find my letter on Mosby's person, they may realize he is very valuable to us and perhaps bargain with us for his release. If that is so, the stakes may be quite high. I have no experience in prisoner swaps, but I do know one thing. Do you recall during our first meeting that I thought you might prove to be most effective as a spy? Due to your youthfulness, you may go into enemy territory and not arouse much, if any, suspicion. That can work to our advantage. I will let you go because of that, and the fact that they have your cousin as well."

Chiswell announced Franklin Stringfellow as he pulled back the tent flap and Stringfellow entered.

Stringfellow, in a private's uniform came to a snappy salute. "General, you have asked for me?"

"Relax and have a seat, private," Stuart said casually. "We have a slight problem where I believe your expertise may be best suited to fixing, as it were."

Stringfellow inquired, "Yes, General?"

"I believe you have worked with young Levon here before, correct?" Before Stringfellow could answer that it was true, Stuart continued, "Good. Mosby and Levon's cousin, Wilson, who I also believe you worked with, have been captured. I believe they will have been taken to the Old Capitol Prison is Washington."

"Undoubtedly," Stringfellow replied.

"I want to send Levon here to check on them, and without arousing suspicion, press for their release. By the way, how is Major Norris?"

It wasn't clear to me till much later why Stuart had asked the question. I was angry with Stuart for inquiring about the well-being of someone they both obviously knew when Mosby and Wilson were in mortal danger, as far as I knew.

Stringfellow smiled and said, "Quite well, General. I have spoken to him rather recently." I found out that Major Norris, of who they spoke, coordinated the "Secret Line," a group of Confederate spies that worked between Richmond and Washington-Baltimore. Stuart's question was in fact to find out how active and recent Stringfellow's spy activities were.

Stringfellow continued, "We don't need Major Norris so much as we need General Howell. Getting Levon to Washington won't be the problem. Since General Howell represents the Confederacy in prisoner exchanges and releases, it is he who we need to contact. Suspicion may be a problem though."

"Do you have any ideas?" Stuart asked.

Stringfellow puffed up his chest and swelled with pride that Stuart had asked him for his thoughts. "How about this? We get Levon some nicer clothes, dressed perhaps as a dandy, and get him to the prison to check on the welfare of Mosby and Wilson. He will have to come across as a solid Union man who is just concerned for his misguided rebel relative's health. If I can get an audience with Howell, we could accomplish at least a visit."

Stuart clapped his hands in glee. "Very, very good. But how do we put him in contact with General Howell?"

"You know I have contacts." Stringfellow then turned to me and said, "Levon, I know you can cross the Potomac and get to Washington. When you get there you must proceed to Fred S. Cozzen's, a mercantile store. It's at the corner of Pennsylvania Ave and 14th Street. There is a young girl employed there who works for us. To make sure you have not placed yourself in danger, you will remark, "Dixie is sure down today." She will have to reply, "All the way to hell," then you will know you can feel quite safe with each other. Sil is rather clever, so you may not need Howell at all. At least you can formulate a plan to get to the prison if you choose not to see Howell. Any questions, Levon?"

"No, Private. When can I leave, General?" I asked.

Stuart replied, "Give the private here some time to setup the communications. That should take no more than a couple of days. That is correct, is it not, Private?"

"That's right, General. Levon will have to get some

better clothes, of course," Stringfellow said as he glanced at me once again.

"You have told Levon this, but you need to know, Levon, that this is extremely dangerous. I know Wilson is your cousin and so it is natural to have some emotion, but people like us, spies, must keep our emotions in check. To show any undue emotion and you could be joining Mosby and Wilson in a cell. They don't execute spies like they do scouts, not yet at least. But Washington, unlike Richmond, is a sewer. The war is not popular there, and why should it be if you're losing?"

Stringfellow rubbed his whiskered chin and continued, "Yes, we do have people there that can assist you, but you are largely on your own, understand?"

"I do."

"Good, then I will take my leave and begin preparations."

After Stringfellow left, Stuart and I were again alone and he studied me with his gaze. "Levon, are you ready for this? Of course, I have already given you my consent so how you respond is somewhat insignificant."

"General, may I be completely honest with you?" I asked.

"Of course, Levon."

"I really don't know much about spying, but then, I didn't really know as much about being a scout as I thought I did. I understood the danger, or at least, I thought I did. I guess the thought of being a scout had me believing that I wouldn't have to actually shoot anybody. I thought it would be only mildly dangerous, but could be pretty exciting too. Pretty stupid, huh?"

"Levon, we have all been called on to do things we didn't imagine we would ever have to even confront. Of course, for me, it is to be expected. I have chosen the life of a soldier and am aware that my choice is fraught with danger. But you are different. This life has been thrust upon you. In many ways, I respect you. It is not what you chose, but you have accepted the challenge to protect your home, your family, our very way of life. You are scared, and I know that. What else may I say?"

"Nothing, sir. I will perform these duties just as any normal soldier would do, but I have one question that puzzles me. Why do you think Stringfellow wants me to dress as a dandy, I think that was the term he used? What difference would what I was wearing have to do with it?"

"Point taken. But look at yourself. Your clothes are torn and bloodied. You have been involved in the fighting clearly. If you are to visit Mosby and Wilson and not attract attention, perhaps you should be in finer clothes. People in Washington may ask you why are you not with your unit fighting for the Union. Are you a deserter? Or they may ask you once you get to the prison what your affiliation is to the Confederacy? I think the best instance is for you to go in disguise, as it were. As Stringfellow said, you are a solid Union man showing concern for your misguided relative, that is all. It's really very, very good. But, Levon, get some rest and we will talk again in a day or so."

I rose and snapped to a salute. "Thank you, General."

He smiled at my attempt at military protocol as I stepped out of the tent.

For the next day, or maybe two, all I could think of was getting Wilson free. I admit, Mosby wasn't really all that important to me, but he was to others, and they had said so. The days till I left, I was in a daze. I could always talk and share time with Wilson, but he was gone. Sure, I could talk to others in camp, but I didn't feel much like it. I looked for Redmond Burke, Wilson's and my teacher, but he was out on a mission, and even Stuart's aide, Chiswell, was busy. I still bedded down close to Stuart's tent, though. I walked down to the stable to look at the bay I had rode in on, but it just reminded me that I had lost Sol's Mistress too. I knew the chances of me ever getting her back were about zero.

Early one morning, which I figure must been around the 25th of July, Stringfellow shook me from my daze. I was sitting by a small fire having a small cup of coffee when he walked up. "Got you some clothes to wear when you're in Washington. Mind if I join you?"

"Not at all. Care for a cup of coffee?" I said, my mood starting to brighten.

"Don't mind if I do. We can leave today, everything is set."

"You going with me, Franklin? It's alright if I'm calling you Franklin, isn't it?"

He laughed. "Well, hell yeah, I've been calling you by your first name. I don't even know your last name. I'm sure it must have been mentioned, but I've just plumb forgot."

"Lewis, Levon Lewis," I said with a smile.

"In answer to your question, Levon," Franklin said, pausing to sip from a tin cup. "I'm only going part ways toward the Potomac, then I got to take care of some other business. After we finish our cups, we can saddle up and get out of here. Any more questions been stirred up?"

"When I get to Washington, I know I'm supposed to go to Fred S. Cozzen's store, you gave me the address. I'm supposed to meet a girl and give her a code phrase but I don't even know her name."

"Oh, her name is Sil Burrows. Now, Mr. Cozzen, the owner, is a staunch Northerner, so having Sil working there is quite a feat. She is purely on our side though. You may face some problem getting across the Potomac, but if I was you, I'd pay some ferry to get you across. Once you meet with Sil, she will be able to guide you the rest of the way. That girl is very resourceful," he said, shaking his head and chuckling.

"Let's go then," I said after dousing the fire.

"Let's," Franklin agreed.

I bundled up my belongings and we set off to the stables. I found the bay and started getting him saddled up when I noticed Franklin looking at me with a puzzled look.

"I thought you rode that beautiful roan. My God, she's a superb horse. I could tell just by looking at her," he said.

"I lost her, Franklin," I said, my throat tightening. "She was, I guess you could say, captured, along with Mosby, Wilson, and their mounts, as well."

"At least you know she'll be better fed than what we can currently supply in feed, but I know that's a small consolation. They don't know what a prize they got," he said with sympathy.

"No, they don't, and they can't know how her loss affects me. To me, she is more than just a horse."

"Perhaps there will be others. Other horses equal to her in quality, but maybe never replaced in your heart. Let me say though, that you may find that these horses will perform just as admirably. Even this bay you're riding," he said as he gently slapped my bay on the rump.

"C'mon, let's go," Franklin said as he pulled himself up into the saddle. I mounted the bay and we started toward the Potomac.

Just south of the river crossing into Alexandria County, Stringfellow urged me into the trees. "Get in here, quick."

We guided our horses into the woods as I was asking Franklin what the ruckus was about. "Let's dismount and I'll show you," he said quickly. We tied the horses to a tree and made our way to the edge of a clearing.

He pointed his finger toward the sky and said, "Look there, do you see it?"

I looked northward, up into the sky. What I saw in the distance caused me to gasp. A round canvas ball with several ropes attached, and a small basket beneath it holding several figures. It was an enemy observation balloon! I had heard others mention it but I had never seen one. It was a glorious sight, even though it was the Yankee's balloon.

Franklin then explained to me what I already knew. "Observation balloon. I don't expect them to see us, but I wanted to make you aware of its presence as you get closer to the river. I'm going to take my leave of you here. Now, I know you haven't any weapons, so if you encounter enemy patrols you better hope you can outrun them. Sil will be able to provide you a pistol when you see her. Good luck, Levon."

After giving me a hug, Franklin guided his horse out of the stand of trees and trotted off. I inhaled deeply to steady my nerves and guided the bay out of the trees, carefully keeping to the side of the road.

I kept glancing up at the balloon as I got closer to the river. I realized I was close when the vegetation got decidedly more green and leafy, and the rushing water of the river became my compass. I led the bay along the river's edge looking for a calm, shallow place to cross. I was ever mindful of the other bank, not wanting to meet anybody just yet. I found a smaller river feeding the Potomac, but it still seemed to run too fast and deep. Too deep for my horse and I to cross.

Just then, I heard a splash in the water. I crouched low on the horse's back and squinted into the lush grass. I thought I saw a small homemade raft constructed with rough logs lashed together moving slowly along the bank. I couldn't make out who piloted it, so I jumped down and crept toward the bank for a better look.

I crawled through the silt, wet from the river's flow, and parted the grass. No more than ten feet from me a set of eyes stared back at me. The eyes were almond shaped and yellow like that of a feral cat. They didn't register any surprise like I know my eyes did, so we just locked onto each other for a minute or more.

I didn't know what to do until a voice accompanying the eyes spoke, "Well, stranger, you need some help?"

I swallowed hard, and giving a quick thanks to the Lord that it wasn't a growl, replied, "I need passage across the river."

"I can help with that, stranger. But first, I must see you fully. Be aware that I have this belly buster aimed at you, so it'd be right smart of you to not be holding a weapon. Stand up and be comin' toward me." Following the comment, a shotgun barrel poked through the weeds. I didn't have a gun, and Franklin's hope that I could outrun whoever was holding that gun, was impossible. I just did what the voice commanded me to do and stood up.

I walked toward the figure holding the shotgun, and parting the weeds, stepped through. The owner of the gun and voice was a waif of a woman dressed in rags, her hair hanging dank and dirty. Her face was sallow and pockmarked with acne.

"Well there, boy, you wanting passage are ya? Which side you on and why aren't you carrying no gun?" she said lazily.

I carefully searched for the right words. I didn't want to anger her, yet I was curious about her as well. I had questions of my own. Who was she and why was she out here, being a woman and all?

"Well, boy?" she asked again.

Thinking quickly, I said, "I'm not on either side.

That's why I'm not carrying a gun."

"So you are not on either side but you are seeking passage to the other side of the Potomac. Why?"

Thinking of the lady I was to meet in Washington, I replied, "To visit my sister. She has been ill."

"But you live in Virginia or further south?"

"I just moved down to Virginia several months ago. I now want to go back."

"Quite young to move down there. What were you doing?"

Stalling her while I searched for an answer I began peppering her with questions. "Who are you and what are you doing here? You are a woman, after all."

"Nice of you to notice, boy," she said sarcastically while going into an exaggerated curtsy.

"But it don't take no man to pull this trigger," she said, cocking the hammer back. "But since you asked, and I feel pretty safe with this here piece, I'll tell you who I am. Name's Pearl. I make a living ferrying people back and forth across the river."

"But you are alone. Why are you not with your family?" I continued to press forth as a distraction. I was still uncomfortable with continuing my fable.

"I'm an orphan. My father and mother got taken by the typhoid. We lived close to the river, so I'm trying to continue living here. I'm not on either side of the issue neither. Couldn't care less about the Union staying together and I don't give a damn about the South and them trying to prop up their way of life. They own slaves or not, I don't care."

"There was a business opportunity for my family down in Virginia, that's all," I lied.

Pearl said, "Oh sure, bizness opportunity. You lie pretty good."

"You gonna ferry me across or not?" I said with

resignation.

"Sure enough. How you plan to pay me?"

"I got some coins here" I said extending my hand with the coins.

`She guffawed. "Coins, you say? Boy, how can I use coins? Do you think I'm gonna go traipsing into town? How about that horse you got hid behind you?"

"I'll need him to ride," I protested.

"You ain't gonna put him on this raft. There ain't enough room, and he'd be too heavy to support. What do you say, boy?"

"How am I going to get to Washington?"

"You are about as stupid a person as I come across. You can walk, and it don't look like your legs is broke. It ain't that far, neither. We got a deal?"

"I guess. Let me get my things. What do you want me to do with him?" I said, pointing at the bay.

She muttered something under her breath and said, "Just leave him tied up there. Climb aboard. I'm gonna lay the gun down so I can pole us across. Don't get any bright ideas, not that I think you can conjure it up, but I'm pretty quick. I can drop this pole, pick up the gun, and put a hole through you."

I grabbed my bundled up clothes, climbed aboard, and watched her surprisingly muscled arms strain the fabric of her shirt as she grabbed a trimmed branch and started us across. I watched as the pole dipped in the brown swirling water and felt us inch forward. I allowed myself to feel a little confidence. I had gotten across the Potomac.

When the raft bumped on the other bank, Pearl planted her leg on the shore to steady us. "Here we is. You tromp about a mile thataways and you'll run into the road the boys in blue used to get back to Washington after the Rebs whipped their asses at Bull Run. Nuther two miles and you're there. Good luck, secesh," she said, breaking into a grin of rotting teeth.

I gathered my things and glared at her, but said nothing. I trudged through the underbrush searching for the main road Pearl had mentioned. Thickets and plants running along the ground kept holding me back until I felt like I was the captured prisoner trying to escape, rather than getting Wilson and Mosby released from their imprisonment. I worried how I would negotiate the road which was sure to be crowded with Yankees moving back and forth.

Before I arrived in the city, I would have to change into the clothes Franklin had given me. Stuart had used the word disguise, and how could I do that? Stepping off the road may attract attention to my strange behavior but I didn't want to be gaily walking down the middle of the road, either. Hell, I could run into, or be run over by, a Yankee cavalry patrol. I prayed under my breath that I would not run into a soul. I'd certainly been surprised by Pearl the River Rat's questioning, and she had seen right through my story.

If I wasn't more convincing going forward, I would surely be put in a cell right along with Mosby and Wilson. The distance to the road seemed to be a right good estimate of Pearl's mile. Because of the moisture of the ground caused by recent rain showers, my trousers were soaked to the knee, my shoes waterlogged, making a squishing sound with each step.

The road was muddy as well, and puddles of water formed in the worn wheel ruts of the ground. The puddles danced as mosquitoes landed and took off on their assaults of man and beast. I hoped that through my scout work, my hearing had become more acute so I could hear approaching hoof beats as they hit the puddles and I could move out of sight.

I continued my walk, and looking up, noticed I was directly under the Yankee observation balloon. *At least I've made some headway,* I thought cheerily. I kept to the side of the road, and I figure almost to the limits of the city, when a symphony of clanking canteens, squeaky leather and the muffled voices of men caused me to scamper into hiding.

I hid behind the trunk of a large pine, and peering around, watched a Yankee infantry troop march by. With their clean and pressed blue uniforms and smart march, I knew they hadn't seen combat yet. I chuckled softly as I wondered how long it would take before their rigid marching would slow, their uniforms became torn, and their boyish pink-cheeked faces took on the haggard look I had seen on battle-hardened veterans. They were in for a big surprise, much as I had been, and yet, I hadn't done much scrapping at all.

I waited until they marched out of sight, then continued my walk. Reaching the city limits of Washington, I again scampered into the woods, untying the twine that held the fancy clothes. I slung my tattered clothes off and dressed in the finer things. I found a top hat that hadn't even been crumpled up, placed it on my head, and wadding up my regular clothes, tied them up. I stepped out and tried to avoid the puddles. I came into the city and noticed that it appeared as Stringfellow had said, a sewer.

The streets were muddy, and human feces mingled with the trash and the rats. The streets filled with people from every walk of life. Yankees soldiers stumbled by in groups of two and three, and occasionally flashed me angry stares. Women brave enough to venture into the streets, hurried by, keeping their eyes downcast. From boardinghouse stairs, painted ladies of ill-repute called to me with promises of pleasures unimagined. With my face hot and reddened in embarrassment, I hurried on.

After walking for what seemed to be only a few blocks, I was greeted by the sight of what I figured was the White House. It seemed likely it was from people's description, for I had never seen it. So, that is where the Yankee President, Lincoln, lives. Did he know he was hated, or was he just scared, because he had a lot of guards.

Ringing the outside were thousands of tents and campfires filled with Yankees. I'd never seen so many in one place. I knew they weren't really guards, nobody is that important, but I allowed myself the silly thought. It calmed me down a bit. I lingered a little longer than I knew I should, then went looking for the corner of Pennsylvania Avenue and 14th Street, where the Fred S. Cozzen's store was located.

I wasn't more than a few steps from the store when a man bumped into me and spat out, "Watch where you be going, boy." Before I could get out an apology, I was surrounded by a group of street toughs. Brutal looking, I knew nothing good could come from our meeting.

"Dressed mighty fine with this war going on," one of the group said.

Another of the group stepped forward until he was no more than an inch from my face. "Why you not fighting? War too good for you?" he said, his breath smelling of sour whiskey.

"I, I didn't…." I stammered.

"You didn't want to fight in a war of common folk, that it? You pay someone to take your place?"

Before I could answer I felt a sharp pain from a kick to the shin that sent me sprawling.

One of the group shouted, "Let's show him he's no better than us. We will convince him to fight, we will." I tried to shield myself from their flailing fists and kicks as they descended upon me. I felt myself getting lightheaded and I could hardly even feel their beating anymore when a shrill voice gave them pause.

"Stop it. Stop it, this instant!"

"But, Miss Burrows..." one of the group started to say.

"Don't you but me, you drunkard. Get your hands off him."

"We just thought..." another stuttered.

"That's the problem, you don't think. You think because he's nicely dressed he is a coward like you," she said, her voice rising even more shrilly.

"Uh, c'mon, Miss Burrows. You know I've been fighting. Still would be if it weren't for this wound in my leg."

"You've been nursing that wound," she said sarcastically, "for over a year now."

"What's this boy to you?"

"He's my brother. He's dressed nicely because he's been studying abroad. He just got back and he's more eager to fight for Lincoln than you obviously are," she said pointedly.

"I didn't know you had a brother."

She answered back, "There is a lot you don't know about me, Mr. Filler, and you never will. Come on, brother, let me help you up. You idiots skedaddle."

I staggered to my feet, dizzy from the beating, while the girl steadied me. She guided me into the store and called out, "Mr. Cozzen, is it okay if I take the rest of the day off? I have some personal things I need to take care of."

A bespectacled man looked up, and seeing me, said with alarm, "My word, is everything okay, Miss Burrows? That man you're propping up looks hurt. Are you in trouble?"

"No, but my brother got beaten up and I want to take care of him."

Mr. Cozzen remarked, "I didn't know you had a brother, Miss Burrows. You never mentioned it."

Her answer this time held nothing in the tone she had when she answered Filler. "There are things I haven't shared with you yet, Mr. Cozzen. I'm very sorry. Is it okay?"

After a quick survey of the store, he said, "Go ahead, Miss Burrows, it doesn't look like it will be getting too busy today. Miss Storey is due to arrive in an hour or so anyway, so go ahead. Take care of yourself young man."

"Yes, sure," I said drunkenly.

The girl, Miss Burrows everyone was calling her, hurried me down the street, up some stairs, and into her room at a boardinghouse.

"Sit down on the bed. Let me get something to take care of that gash on your head," she said gently.

My vision began to clear as she went to a cabinet, and I got a good look at her. She was petite, really, with brown hair that, although parted in the middle, was swept back into a ponytail. She wore a long sleeved blouse, a dress that went to the floor, and a white apron around her waist. Then it dawned on me. I had been near the store and everyone called her Miss Burrows. Was she my contact, Sil Burrows?

"Sil?" I asked.

She looked at me with amusement in her eyes and said, "I think you were supposed to say "Dixie is sure down today."

"Then you are her?"

"All the way to hell," she laughed as she used our code. "Be quiet now, and let me take care of that gash."

She applied what I assume was tincture with a cloth bandage to my head. It stung, and jerking back, I howled.

"Oh, you men are such babies. Hold still," she scolded.

I looked at her face as she focused on the wound. *She didn't look too old, and she is very pretty,* I thought. With a little upturned nose and small mouth, her face resembled the face of a china doll my sisters owned back home.

Noticing my stare, she said with a smile, "What are you looking at, Mr. Lewis?"

"Oh, nothing. Lately, it seems I've been helped out by a few women. But none as nice as you."

"That all?"

"None were as pretty as you," I said, emboldened.

"Thank you, kind sir. So, we have a charmer here, huh?"

"I didn't mean to upset you, though. You are very pretty."

"I'm not upset. I don't often get that kind of compliment from a man, that's all. I'm not used to it."

"I can't believe that," I said.

"It's true. There are not a lot of suitable men here. It's the Union, after all. But enough about my love life, let's talk about you. I know you need to find out about Mosby and your cousin, but little else."

"I didn't want to get involved in this war business. I was happy down in the lower Shenandoah with my family. I hoped the war wouldn't go down that far."

"Before you go on, would you care for a drink?" she said.

I declined her offer and continued. "Anyways, the slaves started acting strange, so a group of us formed a Home Guard of sorts, but all we really did was catch runaway slaves."

"It could be quite profitable, I imagine," she said, swirling a black liquid in the small glass she held in her hand. "Go on."

"One man had it in for me. I didn't like the way he treated those we caught, and said so. We disagreed. Then Wilson and I, along with another, were running down one around Dranesville this past winter and got caught in a skirmish. Lo got killed."

"Who got killed?" she said, listening raptly.

"Lo, he was the other guy with my cousin and me. He admitted before he died that he was ordered to take care of me, and not in a nice way neither."

Putting her hand to her face, she said, "Oh my, that's awful."

"Wilson and I decided then and there that I certainly couldn't go back. Wilson wasn't going back without me so we stayed. We figured we might serve a little better by being scouts. The ride around McClellan and all, I admit, was exciting, but Wilson wasn't really seeing it that way, and now this. For me, Stuart is hard to resist, he has a gallant side that draws you in."

"You're not the only one who has been drawn to him," she said smugly.

"What do you mean?"

"Well, in my duties, I correspond with Laura Ratcliffe, who lives in Frying Pan. She is also strong for the cause. Anyway, she has been drawn in by Stuart, just like you. Even more intimately, you might say."

Wasn't that the name of the woman Stuart had been sleigh riding with at winter quarters?

My eyes started to feel tired and I rubbed at them.

"You should have that drink now. You look like you could use one. Your journey has been hard and you look tired."

"Maybe your suggestion is a good one. Maybe a little." I took a drink and my eyes felt heavy.

"Here, let's take your boots off. You can lie back in

my bed."

I did as she said. As I began to drift off, I wondered, when she was talking about my journey, was she referring to my trip here to Washington, or the journey that had put me in the war?

I awoke to raindrops tapping on the window, and Sil's gentle humming. The curtains in her room were not drawn and the sunlight filtered throughout the room. I suddenly realized I was naked beneath the blankets. Had she undressed me as I slept?

Sil smiled when she noticed I was awake.

"Hello, sleepy head. How are you feeling?"

Embarrassed, I pulled the covers to my chin. "I'm feeling better, but…"

"But what? You can't tell me you're worried because I stripped you naked? Your clothes were wet!"

"I know, but…"

"But nothing. No woman ever seen you naked before except your mama? Boy, you are young."

"How long have I been sleeping?" I said, yawning.

"Long enough for me to find out some information. I went down to the Old Capitol Prison."

"Did you see Mosby or my cousin?" I asked, forgetting that she had never met Wilson.

"Mosby's gone. He's been released or pardoned, whatever they want to call it. He's been sent down to Fort Monroe, and from there, he will be exchanged, I guess. Tomorrow, you and I will go down there to see about your cousin."

"Tomorrow?" I protested. "Why not right now?"

"Oh, sure, it's raining like all get out. Some more rest is in order for you, for sure. I'm not going back out there and catch no cold, and I won't let you neither. I don't have to work till later tomorrow so we can go in the morning."

"Well, where can I stay? I've got to look for a room." I scratched at my head. "I hadn't thought it out much, only about just getting here."

"Silly, you will stay here. I'll get some bedding and you can sleep on the floor. I'm sure not going to sleep in the same bed with you."

"Wouldn't be appropriate," I added.

"Appropriate ain't the half of it. Now, I'm going to turn my head, and you get out of that there bed and throw some clothes on."

I crawled out, and searching for my clothes, began tossing them on. I looked up into a large hanging mirror. I'm sure I caught her looking at me, but just as quickly, looking away.

The rest of the afternoon floated away as Sil and I made small talk. We changed into our night clothes with a great deal of shyness, and bedded down. She blew out the oil lamp and murmured, "Good night, Levon."

"Good night, Sil," I replied.

I awoke the next morning with a cramp in my back and aches over the rest. Sleeping on the wood floor coupled with the beating, had left me feeling quite poorly, as you can imagine. I sat up and saw Sil lying propped up in her bed, smiling at me as she ran a brush through her hair.

"You sleep well? You may be young, but you snore louder than any grown man I have ever met."

"I do not," I replied.

"Tell my sleepy eyes that. I didn't catch hardly a wink. Can't let that stop us though, got to get going."

We dressed hurriedly just as shyly as the night before, then went out into the street. "How we going to get inside, Sil?" I asked.

"Oh, this one guard is pretty sweet on me. I done told him that I'm providing the word of the Lord and some comfort to the prisoners. I told him I'm trying to show the prisoners the error of their ways. They have been falling for it ever since. That's why I'm toting the Bibles," she said as she opened the satchel she had been carrying. Nestled inside were four or five bound copies of the Good Book.

As we approached the brick building, we were hailed by a Yankee officer, "Good morning, Miss Burrows. You're a little early today, aren't you?"

"Good morning, Captain Walker. I have to work later today so I've come early," Sil said, batting her eyelashes.

"Who do you have there with you?" he asked, not a bit suspiciously.

"Oh, Levon, is my brother. He is just back from studying abroad. Since he has only heard about the war, I decided to show him how humanely we treat our foe. The Lord tells us to forgive, you know."

"That he does, Miss Burrows. I only wish the Rebs holding our boys down there in Andersonville received His word. It is hell," Captain Walker said.

Sil replied, "I wouldn't know about that. Shall we go in?"

"Sure, Miss Burrows. I'm sorry, I forgot my manners, and nice to meet you, Levon," Captain Walker said, extending his hand. I shook it and we stepped into the stale hallways.

As we walked through the corridors between the cells, all that I saw was wretchedness. From behind the bars, mute figures dressed in tattered Confederate uniforms, or in some cases, remnants of them, simply stared at us. Others walked in circles mumbling in incoherent speech.

I gagged at the sight and the smell. Sil glared a warning at me to remain composed as to not raise suspicion. I just held my hand to my mouth and over my nostrils. We turned the corner with Captain Walker leading, when I ran into a shuffling prisoner. Captain Walker sneered, "Oh that there is Little Will. Came in with a broken leg and a case of malaria. He wouldn't harm no one so we keep him on as a trustee. He isn't locked up much and he keeps our boots shined and brings us our meals. I can't believe he's a Reb sometimes, because he does whatever we tell him. But he did come in with a couple of others. Boy, they all looked frail like him."

I was hot with anger at the Yankee's attitude until "Little Will" looked at me with his lifeless eyes, red-rimmed with the fever. His hair was tousled, and dried vomit and spit stuck to his cheeks. I had to stifle a scream when I realized the creature before me was my cousin, Wilson.

Sil seemed to sense my discovery and sought to distract the Yankee captain. She clutched his arm and steered him away. "Dear Captain, I need to talk to you privately for a moment," she said.

"Wilson, is that you? We've come to get you out," I whispered.

"Wha...out of where?" he slurred.

"Out of here, to freedom."

"But I am free," he mumbled.

"You most certainly are not," I said trying hard to shove down my rising anger. "You are in prison and are held by the enemy."

He gave me a look that even I found myself unable to describe. In two weeks, he had literally crumbled; his mind and his heart, too.

He coughed and swayed from side to side as we stood there. "You are sick and we need to get you out of here. Have you forgotten your family?" I said with insistence.

In his delirium, which I surely thought it to be, he said, "We have been away from our family for so long now I have trouble remembering them. All the fighting, I cannot do it."

I had to control myself from reaching out and shaking him. "Let me get you out of this place and I promise I will take you home."

"I'm safe here. I don't have to fight no one, and they take care of me. I have reveled in your sins but will do so no longer."

"Oh jeez, Wilson, don't be stupid."

He ended our conversation by saying simply, "I cannot go. I'm waiting for someone."

I was about to answer his madness when Sil rushed up to me and whispered angrily in my ear, "Stop this now. You want us all to get thrown in here? You're starting to create a scene. We must go."

As she hustled me toward the front of the prison, I protested, "But we may lose him."

She replied, "Perhaps he is already lost. But we can do him no good imprisoned with him." With a hurried goodbye to the bewildered Yankee captain, she shoved me out the front door.

We stalked back to her room. After stomping up the stairs, she opened the latch to her room, slamming the door closed behind us with a bang.

"Are you insane? What are you trying to do? Did no one tell you do not betray yourself by showing emotion? You could have got us killed," she said, infuriated. "We all know he is your cousin. I don't believe you are ready for this game." She poured a drink and tossed it down.

"It's not a game to me," I said weakly in defense.

She sighed in exasperation. "I didn't mean it was a game. It was a poor choice of words and I apologize." Pulling me close to her, she pleaded, "Go back to Stuart.

Go back to the world where you have a sense of yourself. I will continue to try to win your cousin's release."

"What will I tell his family?" I sobbed.

"You must mix some truth and some lies. Tell them he is brave, because he is. Tell them he is imprisoned, because he is. But lie to them by telling them he is healthy, because he is not. There is so little to gain by hurting them with the truth. I must go to work now, but I bid you leave. You should go back to Stuart. His camp can ease your burden, leave now," she said with sympathy.

I hurriedly packed up my belongings and we walked down the stairs to the street. Sil gave me directions to a stable. Pulling me close, she said, "Do you have money to purchase a horse? It cannot be Confederate money, but you know that."

"I have some gold coins," I said.

"In these times of suspicion and doubt there is one thing that trumps them both, greed. I'm sure the stable owner will gladly accept the payment. Good luck, Levon, and Levon?" she said.

"Yes, Sil?"

"Dixie will not go down," she said with a wry smile.

"I know, and Sil, thank you for helping me to at least see Wilson."

"It is okay. Now go," she said. As she turned hurriedly away, I swear I thought I saw a tear in the corner of her eye.

I walked to the stables, and without any questions, I was able to purchase a horse after shoving a few coins into the owner's hand. *Greed, indeed,* I thought. *Just as Sil had said.* I rode down toward Fort Monroe, which Sil had mentioned as the destination of Mosby. I rode close to the fort which lies near to the entrance of Chesapeake Bay and Hampton Roads. I watched from the banks of the James River where it appeared the enemy was building up, judging by the amount of ships they ran through Hampton Roads.

I knew I couldn't get close enough to Mosby, and didn't really care to get close to Yankee imprisonment. I'd had quite enough of that for a while, thank you. I crossed the James River without much difficulty. I got lost in the bustle and no one gave me even scant notice. Near the Rappahannock, just by happenstance, I ran into Stuart. More correctly, I ran into Stuart's advance column.

ELEVEN

Tit For Tat
August, 1862

One cavalry man I wasn't familiar with, leveled his carbine, shouting, "Halt. Who might you be?"

Great, I thought, *now I'll have to fight my own.* "You can put the gun down. I'm one of General Stuart's scouts. Let me be," I said grumpily.

"Well, where do you think you're going? I don't believe you're a scout. You're too finely dressed."

"I've been in Washington trying to get John Mosby released. I'm sure you have heard of him?"

"Yep, and so has half of this country." The carbine-toter continued. "Why don't I just ride along with you and take you to the General?"

"Suits me fine," I said with a shrug.

We trotted down the line together. I was glad our

conversation had fizzled out.

As he rounded a bend, Stuart spied me immediately. "Levon, you are back. Where are Mosby and Wilson?"

"See. He does know me, just like I said," I remarked with childlike smugness.

"Yeah, okay, I'll be leaving you here then," the carbine-toter grumbled before riding off.

"There have been some problems I would like to inform you of," I said.

"Very well. Let us pullout of the column here and rest our horses. General Lee, assume command and keep pushing. I want to have a talk with young Levon here," Stuart barked.

"Very good, General," Fitz Lee, himself a general, replied with a salute.

We both dismounted by the side of the road. Stuart eyed me. "Your tone was somewhat ominous. What has happened to our companions?" he asked.

Shaking my head to relieve some of Stuart's obvious concern, I said, "It's not all bad, General. When I met with Sil, the girl Stringfellow directed me to; she was able to find out that Mosby had already been released. I'm somewhat surprised he is not here. But, then again, I just stumbled upon you myself."

"Go on," Stuart said eagerly. "Your cousin was with him then?"

Biting my lip I blurted out, "It's bad, General."

"How so?" Stuart asked.

"Well, he is sick and I don't think he wants to come back."

"You can't be serious? Did you talk to him?"

"I did, General. He says he feels free even though he is caged up. Those damn Yankees treat him no better than a damn dog. He accused me of being a sinner, and I guess he meant all of us in the Confederacy. He also said the strangest thing. He told me he had to stay because he was waiting for someone."

"You don't say. Imprisonment does strange things to a man. But he is but a boy as you are," Stuart said, stroking his beard reflectively.

"Well, General, he is sick. Of that I'm certain."

"Certainly, but you cannot pause to grieve for him, for he is not entirely lost. Perhaps our friends in Washington can win his release. For now, you stay close to Chiswell. Being young as you and your cousin are, he may aid you in some way. If Mosby ever gets back, you may ride with him. Your familiarity with the both of them, I think, will be beneficial to you. Oh, there is Chiswell now. Lieutenant Dabney, I need a word with you."

He and Chiswell huddled in conversation. The gold stitching of C.S.A. on Stuart's saddle sparkled in front of my eyes. Several times during their hushed conversation, Chiswell would steal a glance at me and nod his head up and down. After some time, Chiswell rode over.

"Levon, we need to get you some new weapons. As the general has no doubt told you, we will ride together. I have an extra rifle I will loan you. Do not fret too much about Wilson. I'm sure good things will come to pass. Let's go get that rifle."

We rode toward the back of the column to the train of wagons. Reining up at the first one, Chiswell jumped off his horse into the bed of the wagon, tossed me the reins and pulled back the canvas.

"Here you go. It's an Enfield, I think. I also have a revolver here somewhere," Chiswell said, continuing to rummage around the wagon. "Ah, here it is. I didn't get a holster for it so you will have to tuck it into your belt."

He handed me the Enfield rifle and the pistol before jumping down off the wagon and took back the reins of his horse.

"I almost forgot. Here's a sling for the rifle too."

I attached the sling to the saddle and slid the Enfield in, then jammed the Colt into my too tight belt. I noticed Chiswell looking at me with a bemused smile on his face.

"What?" I asked.

"I noticed you still got on those fancy duds. Getting used to the feel of them, are ya?" he said mockingly.

I chuckled a bit and replied, "I've been a little busy. Haven't had time to change yet."

"It's just that I noticed you had a little trouble getting that pistol into your belt. Thought those pants may be just a bit snug," he jeered.

"No, no, no. I got my regular clothes bundled up here," I said, pointing to my belongings tied to the back of the saddle. "Might need me a bedroll though."

"Oh, don't worry about that." he said. "We'll come upon one before we stop for the night. Let's catch back up to the front." He spurred his horse forward and I quickly followed.

We soon made contact with the Yankees and pushed them on the line of the Ny River. I had quickly forgotten Wilson for the moment and fell in with the 9th Virginia, whooping and hollering. The Yankees were in full retreat away from the Virginia Central Railroad, which is exactly what Stuart had intended them to do. They were heading back toward Fredericksburg.

I rode down one Yankee as he was running, and sent him to the ground by clubbing him in the back of the head with the stock of my rifle. Another just stopped in his tracks, threw down his gun, and raised his arms up in surrender. I sat there on my horse with my prisoner as other members of the cavalry charged on, rounding up prisoners and supply wagons.

"Don't shoot me, little Johnny Reb," my prisoner

wailed.

With a mixture of anger and sadness, I said gruffly, "Don't give me cause to. Now move on down this road here and you can introduce me to your friends."

With the gunfire stopped, the prisoner slowly stumbled down the road of his defeat while I occasionally prodded him along with the rifle. The scene we soon came upon, I could only describe as jubilant chaos. The eighty or so prisoners stood to the side under guard while the 9th gorged themselves on the spoils of the captured wagons.

Someone tossed me a hunk of beef and I dove into it, tearing off large chunks with my teeth and swallowing. I couldn't remember the last time I had eaten, and being so hungry, I didn't wait to dismount, but just devoured it sitting in the saddle. I did dismount shortly thereafter to lead my horse to water, and feed him some captured grain.

Anything we didn't consume we gave to the grateful citizens. We made our way back to Stuart's headquarters at Hanover Court House with 85 prisoners and 11 captured wagons. I mused that we had probably halted any further attacks on the Virginia Central Railroad. As small schoolchildren finally learn their lessons under a stern headmaster, our pupils, the enemy, had learned theirs.

For the next several days, Stuart would leave the camp. Where he traveled, I did not know, and he told no one. What I did notice was that Fitz Lee's brigade was drilling incessantly. Something was amiss.

During the lull, as it were, I had come to grips with the issues that had plagued me since seeing Wilson imprisoned. I would never again show the enemy any mercy. The way they treated Wilson in that God awful prison had angered me, and I wanted to strike back in retaliation of his treatment until he was released.

Second, I would have to write a letter to our respective families explaining the situation and ask for their understanding and forgiveness in not writing sooner. The latter, to me, seemed the most daunting. To seek understanding for Wilson's imprisonment would be almost as bitter of a pill to swallow for them as it was for me, since I was the cause.

One evening, which I estimate was perhaps the 10th or 11th of August, I sat down by the campfire with Chiswell, and with his assistance, crafted the letter.

Dear Family,

I beg your forgiveness for my lack of communications thus far. The times having been trying, as you may have guessed when Lo's body was returned. You may have asked yourself why Wilson and I did not respond as men and tell you of our plans face to face as mature men surely would. When we left to go after the last runaway, we were kept from returning because of the impression I had that Josiah Wheeler wished harm to befall me. I learned as much from Lo's dying breath. Wilson and I were reluctant to part for he is as close to me as Caleb is my brother, and Alexandria and Quinn are my sisters. After discussion, we felt we may be better able to help the cause, however vague the meaning, as scouts. We have been with Stuart through many of his exploits, including the Chickahominy Raid, which you no doubt have read about.

Wilson and I have been inseparable as he has shown himself to be very brave, even more so than me. However, he has recently been captured and I have had a chance to visit him. It brings me great sadness to tell you of this news. I hope that you will, along with me, pray for his release and soon. Above all, I want you to know that the choices I have made were the best choices I felt I could make at the time. I cannot come home in all conscience until Wilson is with me. I beg for your understanding.

Your obedient son,
Levon

On the last of Stuart's mysterious trips in August, he returned with a companion. To my delight, it was John Mosby! I didn't approach them right away when they rode in because their grim expressions warned me away.

I wanted to talk with Mosby, welcome him back, but I had to wait a few hours because of a meeting taking place inside Stuart's tent. As I said before, I am not a member of Stuart's staff, and therefore not included in such talks, nor do I expect to be. Sometimes I felt that I enjoyed some favors that other scouts did not, but I never saw any need to question it.

After those few hours of me not doing much of anything, Mosby exited the tent and quickly approached me. The grim expression he had ridden in with was replaced by a slight grin when he saw me.

"Levon, so good to see you. Jeb said you were here," he said as he grabbed me in a warm, but unexpected, embrace.

"I'm glad to see you too, John," I said, forgetting past formalities. He didn't seem to notice, which I was happy about. I was struck by the quick thought that at the least I was in the inner circle of Stuart's command.

His expression turned stern at once when he said, "Stuart told me of your trip to Washington to secure my release. Fortunately, I had already been released." His voice faltering, he continued, "I also was told you met with your cousin. He is not well. You would agree?"

"I would agree. Sil, who is part of the spy ring, told

me of your release. But she had never met Wilson, so the next day, we went to the prison and found him. I don't know what to do. He doesn't seem right in the head."

"Probably the fever. He has been saying some strange things. He kept saying he was waiting for someone, or maybe something, I'm not sure," John said, rubbing his lip. "I hope it's not the reaper, but perhaps it is our Lord offering him his deliverance. Beyond that, I don't know."

"He told you the same thing as he told me?" I said, shocked.

"Told you the same thing what?"

"That he was waiting for someone," I replied, shaking my head.

"Hmm, that is strange. Do not dwell on it right now. It makes me uncomfortable, and so I cannot imagine how you must feel. But on a slightly more joyful note, I have been instructed to take you into my charge. I know you have been with young Chiswell, but he is presently away. I do believe you will be accompanying some of us to see General Robert E. Lee. Jeb is none too happy with one of his officers, Beverly Robertson. Says he's incompetent."

"Never heard of him," I said tersely.

"No matter. We are set to board a train bound for Lee's headquarters later on in the day. It will be a long trip so I suggest you get some rest, but also get ready," he said before walking away.

Before leaving to board the train, I watched Stuart in an animated conversation with Fitz Lee, so my previous thoughts proved correct. Something was definitely up. I wasn't frightened by it. I had participated in some very dangerous activities before, but I couldn't prevent some uneasiness from creeping in, which I guess was due to Wilson's capture.

In the early evening of August 16th, I boarded the

train, along with Stuart, the big Prussian, Heros von Borcke, Lieutenant St. Pierre Gibson, and of course, Mosby. We set out westbound toward Gordonsville on the Virginia Central line.

The steady clicking of the train wheels on the rails lulled me to sleep. I was roused for a brief time as the train switched onto the Orange and Alexandria Railroad for the final destination to Lee's headquarters.

When the train finally ground to a stop, I disembarked. The sun had begun to fall, leaving the sky in the orange hue of dusk. I was still tired and dusty as if only a few hours had passed. I ran headlong into confusion. It had been dusk when we left.

Mosby yawned and remarked, "Finally got here. Damn, that was one long ride." He noticed the confused expression spread across my face. "What's wrong, Levon?" he asked. Before I could pose the question he realized what it was and answered, "It took a day."

I was hoping to catch a glimpse of the great General Robert E. Lee, but he ducked out of sight with Stuart and a few others. I had never seen him, but had heard that his manner of carriage was rather stately and grand.

We all sagged in our saddles as we rode away from the Orange Court House to meet Fitz Lee's command. By keeping my mouth closed and ears open, I was able to find out what the plan was. Fitz Lee was to stop at the Rapidan and strike Union General Pope's army before they could escape north of the Rappahannock. Further, Lee was to destroy a railroad bridge near the depot, effectively trapping the Yanks between the two rivers and forcing them to fight both Stonewall and Longstreet without reinforcements. Now, I'm no military genius, but I chuckled at the plan. Pretty damn smart, I'd say.

When we got to the village of New Verdiersville, we met not with the 2nd Brigade, but Chiswell and another of Stuart's staff, Norman Fitzhugh. Stuart seemed unconcerned however, and decided that we should stay on the Orange Plank Road because he knew that it would be the route taken by the 2nd Brigade.

When they did not arrive that night, or the next morning, Stuart decided that we would spend the night on the porch of an old house along the plank road.

Stuart stretched out using his cloak as his bedding, his plumed hat his pillow. I sat back against a railing, while the others lay scattered around the porch or out into the yard.

When dawn broke early the next day, I mean, it really broke. Shots rang out and I flew awake to see Stuart out in the yard starting to run. As I broke into a run toward a forest of trees, I saw who I thought were Mosby and Gibson charging toward us with a passel of Yank cavalry hot on their heels. Von Borcke lunged onto his horse, not a small feat for a man of his girth, while Chiswell, a few steps ahead of me, was heading toward the same stand of trees. The Yankees didn't pursue us, letting us watch from the trees. Major Fitzhugh, he wasn't so lucky. To be sure, he was lucky he wasn't shot, but he was captured. He had in his possession the orders of General Robert E. Lee's offensive, but the Yankees became visibly more elated as several of them admired Stuart's famed plumed hat, crimson-lined cape, yellow sash, and gauntlets. As they rode away, Stuart muttered, "I intend to make the Yankees pay for the price of that hat." I was sure of that.

Von Borcke appeared guiding some horses as we exited our hiding place. After mounting up, von Borcke taunted Chiswell when he noticed that Chiswell had lost his gauntlets, saber, rifle, and pistol. "Comfortable?" he said.

Chiswell reddened in embarrassment and stared at

me wistfully, knowing I had lost the weapons he had given me, as well. "I'm going to miss that Enfield," he said with a slight smile. Dispirited, we rode to camp.

Stuart stewed over the loss of his hat and opportunity as we bivouacked near Mitchell's Ford on the Rapidan. He laid most of the blame on Fitz Lee's tardiness.

Stuart, following what I supposed was Lee's orders, and his own intuition, led us across the Rapidan and upriver toward Waterloo Bridge and Hart's Mill. The sole objective, I'm sure, because it was so apparent to me, was to harass Pope's rear by damaging his main supply line of the Orange and Alexandria rails. We entered Union-held Warrenton without a shot being fired as the Yankees just fled. The townspeople gave us a glorious welcome.

As Stuart soaked in the adulation, he managed to retain enough composure to shout out for Stringfellow and I to scout the route the rest of the way to Catlett's Station. For the first time since I had known Stuart, I thought I caught a hint of anxiety.

Once again, I was sufficiently armed. There never seemed to be a lack of guns, only food and warmth. The weapons were not Southern made but captured from the Yankees.

Stringfellow and I stayed to the side of the road, keeping our eyes and ears open. As we rode along, quietly ominous black clouds overhead threatened us with their deluge. Stringfellow, because of his experience, noted points of strategy and which areas were guarded when we reported back to Stuart. I'm ashamed to admit it, but felt that I had just been along for the ride having nothing to add to Stringfellow's report.

We left Warrenton and followed a rain-punished trail to Auburn, arriving just after dark. Stuart stopped the column briefly and instructed Stringfellow, a Captain Blackford, whom I knew very little of because he kept appearing and disappearing, and curiously, me, to scout out the station.

Riding along, we came to a bridge that carried the Orange and Alexandria rail over Cedar Run. Franklin remarked, "I bet Jeb would like to see that bridge go down. That would certainly create some problems for Mr. Pope."

We inched closer to the station. I looked on, noticing sleepy pickets guarding what looked like an enormous amount of supplies and wagons crowded together. To see so much of what we did not have made me drool.

In a hushed voice, Blackford said, "We could sure use those supplies. Let's get back to Jeb. There's no time to lose." We turned our mounts and headed back.

Just before getting all the way back to Stuart, we encountered a small band of our pickets surrounding an excited colored man.

Reining up, Blackford angrily shouted, "What in the devil is going on here?"

One of the pickets drawled, "Begging your pardons, sir, but this darkie here is saying some peculiar thangs."

"Go on," Blackford said earnestly.

"Says he knows the acquaintance of our Gen'l from some days back. Say's Yank Gen'l Pope's personal belongings are at the depot."

"You don't say?" Blackford said.

"No, I donts, he does," the somewhat dull-witted picket said. "If that don't beat all, he says he is free."

The colored, his eyes bright and wide in the darkness said, "What I say is true. I can show you boys where Pope's baggage is. I've been there."

"Well, good man, let me take you to Stuart and get to the bottom of all this. Hop up behind me." Astonished, I watched Blackford's gray glove reaching down to grasp the black man's arm and help him up.

"I'm not sure I remember you, but my men say you have some information about the station up ahead," Stuart said when we arrived back with the colored in tow.

"I does indeed, Gen'l. Pope has his headquarter baggage stashed at the station along with all the rest of their goods. I can lead you there."

Stuart leaned back in his saddle. "Then, by all means man, lead on. Leave the artillery, the roads are much too soggy to carry their weight."

As we neared the station, Stuart made his assignments. I was going along with the 9th Virginia again, commanded by Rooney Lee. We were to attack the supply base north of the railroad, while Rosser's 5th Virginia would hit from the south, and another detail would destroy the bridge which Stringfellow had suggested during our earlier foray.

The bugler blew the charge which I only faintly heard through the din of rain, wind, and thunder, then charged in with the 9th. Yelling and screaming, we startled the sleepy Yankees, and with guns blazing and sabers flailing, took down several of them. I didn't have a saber, and frankly, had no use for one, so I used my pistol to shoot down one of the Yanks in the throat as he stepped out of his tent. Others meekly surrendered, realizing that we had them surrounded. I heard the faint whistling of a bullet as it sped past me and toppled one of my fellow riders.

Seeing several flashes of musket fire coming from some nearby warehouses, I grabbed my rifle and swung down from my horse. I raced to the side of a building and jammed my pistol into my belt. Loading the rifle with hands slippery from the rain, I peered around the corner. From, I'd say, nearly fifty feet away, a Yankee crouched behind a wagon wheel, and unaware of me, continued loading and shooting. Without any warning, I steadied my eye and shot him dead. I leaned back against the wet planks of the building and exhaled. This particular bunch of Yanks were pesky, and did kill a few of us before being chased into the woods.

The ensuing scene reminded me of parts of the Chickahominy Raid. Along with the 5th, I helped myself to the bounty of more weapons, ammunition, horse equipment, clothing, tents, and edibles that made me drool even more than when I had imagined them. I took a discarded bayonet and stabbed open a can of peaches savoring each slice as I stuck them into my mouth with the end of the bayonet. Several troopers and I just smiled and laughed at our good fortune.

Stuart appeared carrying a sparkling brand spanking new Yankee dress uniform and exclaimed, "Would you look at what Pope has left me as a gift?"

"Well, General," I said, feigning an air of haughtiness, "Perhaps he may be willing to trade you back your things for his gift."

Stuart laughed boisterously. "Splendid idea, Levon. I will have to inquire with him about that very thing when I see him."

I grinned and slid another chunk of peach into my mouth. Down south of camp, there was an uproar of shooting that startled me and momentarily stopped our enjoyment. I heard later that Rosser's attack was unsuccessful due to the fact of the large amount of captured prisoners. Apparently the prisoners had come to believe they were to be executed and attacked our men. Thankfully, they were persuaded that this was not the case and quieted down. The bridge didn't get burnt neither, the wood being too wet to light.

The biggest buzz through camp was the capture of a collection of General Pope's official letters detailing his army's fitness and fear for the security of his supply lines.

Supply lines that we had just looted. Stuart unashamedly gloated over the capture of the papers, Pope's uniform, a half million dollars in greenbacks, twenty thousand dollars in gold, more than 300 prisoners and almost twice that much in horses and mules.

The next day, as we marched away from the smoldering ruins, I smiled to myself and thought, *Yes, surely Stuart's bill has been paid in full.*

 TWELVE

Second Manassas and the End of Pope
August 25th — September 2nd, 1862

Manassas Junction

I did not hear the report of the musket until after the flight of the ball had passed before my heavily lidded eyes. Even as tired as I was, the shots caused me to rouse myself.

A pesky bunch of Yankee skirmishers along the river's bank near Waterloo Bridge were not going to show me any charity and let me sleep. Wearily, I slid my musket from its sheath and haphazardly pulled off one or two shots. Thankfully, I heard Stuart order Colonel Rosser and the 5th Virginia to respond while the rest of us made it back to Warrenton Springs.

Upon arriving back at camp, I hurriedly dismounted, brushed and fed my horse, and went looking for a place to sleep. Sleep proved to be elusive though, because by

2:00 am the next morning, Stuart had us back in the saddle.

Along with some of Stonewall's army, we waded the Rappahannock near Henson's Mill and turned north toward the hamlets of Orleans and Salem. God, I was weary and a bit lonely too. Sure I was within the security of the Confederate cavalry, but I allowed myself some time to miss Wilson. Hell, it wasn't really allowing myself to miss him, for it was unavoidable. Mosby and Dabney were no longer accompanying me, or rather, me accompanying them, so there was no one to really talk to. Maybe I should have felt some pride that Stuart didn't feel like I needed a shepherd anymore, or more likely, he had more important things to worry about. So I continued to soldier on. A soldier without a uniform, a soldier without a rank.

We did finally catch up with the mythical Stonewall at the head of his column just short of Bristoe Station. Stuart and Jackson had a short conversation as I slouched in my saddle nearby. I thought Stuart appeared slightly irritated as their conversation ended.

Stuart approached me and barked, "Levon, go find Longstreet and advise him of our position. Jackson and Longstreet are to move in conjunction so that we may finally put an end to Pope."

It wasn't until later that I found out the source of Stuart's apparent irritation. Jackson had ordered the cavalry to guard his flanks and that rankled Stuart because there wasn't much cause for action. That just didn't fit with Stuart's style. Pageantry and glorious feats were what Stuart craved and sought out, I had come to believe. I had no quarrel with that. I was a lowly pawn in this never-ending chess match, and Stuart was, well, the knight. While I was away, Stuart had sought to break the monotony. On the 26th of August, Fitz Lee had seized a forage train near Haymarket, and later on that same day, Stuart attacked Bristoe Station, capturing it, and once again, tore up some tracks.

I, of course, was not included in that capture but had some action on my own while I ferried messages to Longstreet. But first, I had to find him. Before I left, Stuart he mentioned to me that Longstreet may be near Gainesville. He told me that General Robert E. Lee's master plan was to link Jackson and Longstreet together to face Pope, and keep Pope in the dark.

I decided that the quickest way to get to Gainesville area was to use Thoroughfare Gap which cut through the Bull Run Mountains. I was making good headway for several miles until I ran into trouble.

"Halt, you there, stop!" I heard a voice holler from in back of me. I turned and saw a Yankee cavalry patrol charging up fast. How did they get behind me? I hadn't encountered them along the ride, thus far.

I kicked my horse's flanks and wished like hell that I was mounted on the lost Sol's Mistress because I knew how she would respond. I guess I would find out the mettle of the bay gelding I was currently riding.

The Yankees realized almost immediately that I didn't intend to obey their command and started shooting. I wasn't gonna slow myself down by pulling my pistol and shooting back at them so I just kept myself lowered to the horse's back. I knew I couldn't outrun them on the road because, with a quick look back, their horses looked much larger. I figured my only chance was to get off the road and into the mountain terrain, where the differences in the size of our horses might work to my advantage. I jerked on the reins and veered into the dense woods.

I kept myself flat on the geldings back so I wouldn't be unceremoniously dumped by a tree bough while the horse stumbled and slipped on the rocky ground. Please, dear God, let us keep climbing and not be sent tumbling down this mountain. It was tough going, really rough riding, but as I had thought previously, that the bigger horses would not be able to follow proved correct as the gunfire and curses grew faint and then disappeared altogether.

My heart was thumping madly as the horse and I, bleeding from cuts and slick with sweat, came to a crest and stopped for a moment. The road was concealed by trees and I simply sighed. Escaped danger, yet again. Whew, welcome to the life of a courier.

After dismounting and willing my heart to stop pounding, I took the reins, and on foot, we walked along a small trail that was clear of trees. After about a mile or so, I jumped on the horse's back, certain that he was cooled down enough. I continued guiding the horse along the trail and slowly began to descend the mountain.

I was frightened by the thought I would encounter more Yankees before reaching Longstreet. I got back onto Thoroughfare Gap, and luckily, didn't come across any more enemy patrols before finding Longstreet and delivering the message.

"As you see, young man, I am here. I believe that I will engage the enemy no later than August 28th. Tell General Jackson that Lee's plan, I believe, should come to its successful conclusion shortly. And one more thing, young man. Except for some cuts and bleeding, you seem to not have any serious wounds. Am I to believe you didn't encounter the enemy at all, or is that why you have those cuts?" Longstreet asked incredulously.

His questions and the manner in which he asked brought a slight smile to my lips.

"Oh no, General. I met up with an enemy patrol, but made my escape by taking my horse into the rocky terrain off the road. They couldn't follow me and these scrapes came from the trees," I said, rubbing a particularly angry cut on my arm.

"I see. It is not that we have not encountered the enemy, but being such a large force we have easily routed them. But you are one man, and young at that," Longstreet replied.

I responded with a shrug of my shoulders.

"You may go back to Jackson and deliver the news. Bid him that we catch Pope unaware."

"Oh, I'm not from Jackson's command, sir. I ride with Stuart."

"You don't say. That explains your bravery and gallantry, or maybe even foolhardiness. Some of General Stuart must have rubbed off on you. Go and report the information, but try to remain safe."

"Yes, General," I said after trying my best at a salute. I was able to make my way back to Stuart and Jackson just short of Manassas Junction late on the evening on the 26th of August.

Stuart hailed me as I approached. "Levon, you have found General Longstreet? What news do you bring?"

"Yes, General, I found Longstreet's whole army just prior to them entering Thoroughfare Gap. He bids me to tell you that he believes he should be on the field on the 28th, and hopes that Pope will remain unaware of his approach."

Stuart looked at me, bemused. "Very good, then. I will let General Jackson know. General Jackson has ordered me to take Manassas Junction and I left that to the charge of General Trimble. You will have to tell me later of the exploits that led to your current appearance. Accompany me to the Junction to see how the attack is going."

We rode closer to the Junction until Stuart halted the column. In hushed tones he conferred with his command leaders. What happened next is a point of contention. My understanding was that Stuart felt the approaches, and yes, even Manassas Junction, were too heavily guarded for cavalry alone, and wished to wait for daylight and infantry. An adamant General Trimble said that he was ordered by Jackson, and Jackson alone, to attack and did as much prior to dawn. Now, I don't wear a timepiece, but I know what is daylight and what is nightfall, and we entered the Junction in clear daylight. Now, Manassas Junction was not defeated when we rode in, so I would call in to question when the attack was made. True, I am only a scout, and as others always are quick to point out, young, but I was there.

The plunder that we took advantage of was even bigger than that at Catlett Station, if it can be imagined. Food and clothing was stacked high in the yard. To the side of the ransacking of the stores, I saw sullen Yankee prisoners glare at us. Did we need the food and clothing so badly that we would tear into the supplies like a pack of wild dogs? Always, I would answer yes. Like before, there never seemed to be a shortage of weapons to kill one another, but a lack of anything else. What we lacked could sustain life and I felt a bit melancholy as I watched my fellow ravenous soldiers.

Coupled with the supplies, were eight new cannons, over 300 prisoners, and a good deal of coloreds, to boot. Stuart rode through the Junction with a look of smug satisfaction on his face, and allowed us to take part in the eating, drinking, and resting for most of the 28th before again hitting the saddle.

I'm happy to say that I managed to sleep more than a few hours despite the noise of the looting, being more sleepy than hungry. Early in the evening, I was awakened by the soft nudge of a boot. I awoke staring into the face of the smiling Chiswell.

"Missed me, did you, sleeping beauty?" He laughed.

"Oh hell, Chiswell, leave me alone," I replied groggily.

"Oh, no time to sleep, Levon. There's plenty of fighting left to do today. The trap set for Pope has not yet been sprung. Longstreet has not even shown himself to Mr. Pope yet. Plus, we gotta burn this damn Junction now that we've emptied it of everything of value. I bet Pope ain't too far behind us, and I know you don't want to be caught napping, nor burnt neither."

"Yes, yes, of course, you're right," I said, staggering to my feet.

"I was even nice enough to bring you your horse all saddled and ready to ride."

I mounted up, and along with Chiswell, headed toward Stuart and Jackson as the smoke from the ruins of Manassas Junction chased after us. The infantry veered north toward Groveton on the Warrenton Turnpike as the cavalry, the part presently with Stuart, headed toward Haymarket.

Alongside me, Chiswell piped up, "Levon, what have you been up to? It has been some time since I have seen you. The last time must have been, let's see," he said, lifting a finger to his face in thought. "When we almost got captured along the Plank Road, that right?"

"Ah, it was indeed," I said. "Do you remember when we were in the woods hearing Stuart vow revenge for the loss of his hat, among other things?"

"Yes, I do remember that. Of course, Major von Borcke was reminding me of my loss, so I must admit, I was somewhat preoccupied," he said ruefully.

"Well, Stuart did pay him back, and in spades," I said triumphantly. "We captured Catlett's Station with quite a few supplies, although much less than what we just got. We also got one of the general's dress uniforms and some of his official papers. Least, that's what they say."

"So I heard. So, go on."

"General Stuart then had me ride out to locate Longstreet and deliver some messages. Then I rode back to the Junction."

"So, very busy you are. Are you thinking of enlisting, then?" Chiswell asked.

I was stunned by the question. Really, it had not entered my mind fully. I had given some thought about having the uniform, and the pride and air that it would convey.

"Surely you must know that it is time. You have ridden with us, fought with us, scouted, and done some courier service, so it would seem, the time is surely right," he said with a glint in his eye.

"Perhaps what you say is so," I said, pausing to suck in some air. "But the soldiers like you, Chiswell, are different from me, I think. I'm not really into the military things. My brother is, of course, that's why he is at VMI, or was, but I don't feel that pull. I'm not afraid to fight, although originally, I was scared. I don't mind doing things for Stuart or helping the southern cause. But I don't want to drill and all that," I said with a grin.

"Oh, so you don't want to do all that we must participate in like drilling, giving and reacting to orders and commands?" Chiswell said, baiting me.

I chuckled when I realized what I was really saying. "Okay, so maybe I'm a tad lazy. I just like riding and traveling all over the valley. Maybe I don't like all the discipline that goes along with all the soldiering, although I would never not obey orders, or others, like my folks, for instance. I kind of joined up here, but I've never been called on to do sumthin' I didn't want to do. I feel free to do some things I enjoy and don't do things I don't. Really, it's as simple as that."

Chiswell just shrugged and uttered, "Hmmph," in response.

Sometime later, there was a commotion at the head of the column. Apparently, some troopers had captured some Yank dispatches indicating that their cavalry had been ordered to Haymarket. I eased my horse into a slow trot as we proceeded with caution. In the early afternoon, Stuart sent for me as I was aways back from him.

"Levon I want you to ride ahead and see what lies in our path. It is important that I locate General's Lee and Longstreet. I wouldn't want the trap to be sprung before it snares the prey. Do you understand?"

I replied, "Yes, General, I do." I gently kicked the gelding's flanks with my boots to urge him on. I was happier with this horse and his abilities when we had, shall I say, scaled the mountain to escape our pursuers, when I had acted as a courier. I kept to the sides of the road while riding ahead. I heard the clamor of marching feet, the creak of leather against men and animals, and the banging of supplies that caused me to pull up short. I saw the road ahead was well guarded, and knowing that Fitz Lee's command had not returned, felt that we were out-manned, I turned and rode back to Stuart.

"General, the road ahead is well manned by Yanks. I'm not fer sure, but I'm bettin' there's more of them than of us," I said to Stuart upon my return.

"I trust your insight, Levon. Better to err on the side of caution. We will not seek the generals out right now but head back toward General Jackson."

We did meet up with Jackson late in the evening of August 28th. Too late to join with Jackson's fight near Groveton left Stuart disgusted. *At least we can sleep,* I thought. I was still very weary, and the troopers around me grumbled their agreement to my silent wish.

Stuart awoke us early on August 29th to begin his

second attempt to reach Lee and Longstreet. I was still tired as all get out, but managed to get a quick fire put together from some dried twigs and heated some water for a quick cup of coffee. When the orders to move out came, I shook off the cold, wrapping my new overcoat that I had helped myself to at Manassas Junction tight around me, and with a last drink tossed the remaining liquid on the fire to douse it. We quickly began to retrace our path toward the Bull Run Mountains.

An hour out, our column was fired on by Yankees who were hidden in the pines that lined the road from Groveton to Sudley Springs. A slight storm of bullets blew in, toppling a young trooper near me from his horse. I quickly grabbed my rifle and blindly fired into the trees, unable to draw a bead. We rushed down the road, eager to alert the companies, of what I believe was the 17th Virginia, of possible attack as they were guarding Jackson's wagons overloaded with the plunder of Manassas Junction.

Riding further, we fell into the right side of Longstreet's column headed toward Manassas. The Confederate infantry veered north toward the sounds of battle, while we continued on toward Manassas. Stuart sent me on another scouting mission where I shared a pleasant reunion with Franklin Stringfellow.

Riding up next to him, I yelled out, "Franklin, good to see you again."

He had not seen me ride up so he jumped in his saddle at the sound of my voice. Surprised, he grinned at me and yelled back, "Ahah! Great to see you, Levon. Ready to stir up some trouble today?"

"I don't know if I want to stir up more trouble, but maybe we can find some and let General Stuart stir the pot."

Laughing loudly, Franklin said, "Yes, Jeb is pretty

good at stirring up things, and finishing them up too. Let's keep moving." It weren't too long till the both of us spied some of the Union's Army of the Potomac coming from Bristoe Station. We made a mad dash back to Stuart with the news.

Stuart, fearing the worse, concocted a plan to delay the Yank approach. He instructed quite a number of us to dismount and chop down branches from the surrounding trees. We quickly remounted, and following Stuart's shouted instructions, rode up and down the road dragging the branches through the dirt. We stirred up clouds of dust, and that was just what Stuart wanted. The stirred up dust led the Yankees to believe that a heavy column was headed their way. Tricked, the enemy slowed, and then withdrew all together. Stuart's cleverness showed through yet again.

On the morning of August 30th, we were reunited with Fitz Lee's men, and rode alongside Longstreet's flank. I could only watch in wonder at what played out that day.

Early in the afternoon, the trap was finally sprung. Longstreet, undetected, perhaps fatally, by the Yankees, fell upon them screaming the Rebel yell. The attack was devastating and complete. Now, devastation may be a big word for me, but I sure knew what it meant and it is what I saw.

The savagery was almost impossible for me to describe. Now, sure, I had committed violent acts, and to be sure, would probably continue to, but this was something else. What I saw done was what real soldiers do and that is why I had answered Chiswell the way I did. I could not do what the soldiers were currently doing. That day, I was free to watch, but Stuart was constantly busy directing multiple attacks with great speed. Riding along the back of the lines, keeping my distance from the fighting, I watched the boys in blue stream across Stone Bridge and other fords from Centreville, Fairfax Court House, and beyond.

Meeting with Stuart, I immediately noticed his frustration at being unable to prevent the enemy's flight. The reason to me was almost laughable. The reason he could not cutoff the retreat was because the roads toward the enemy's capital of Washington was clogged with the soldiers of both armies making progress impossible. He let our infantry continue and set camp for the night.

Stuart seemed to be incapable of rest, and before daylight on what I believe was the 31st, we were back in the saddle and set to work capturing the inevitable stragglers. Not one or two, mind you, but small bunches of stragglers. Stuart was driven, I believe, at least for the moment, by lust. He wanted a large battle against a large number of Yankees and was actively seeking it. We had a brief but bloody fight near Chantilly where Stuart led Jackson's men, as well. A somewhat stout defense and a driving rainstorm finally stopped Stuart's ambitions for a time.

I spent the miserably rainy night hunched under a poncho I had also gotten at Manassas, shivering and listening to the raindrops splash on its surface. I know, as had been pointed out, I was young, but thought stupidly, surely now the war would soon be over.

On September 2nd, Stuart led an attack on an outpost of Flint Hill at full strength. The artillery of Stuart pounded the outpost relentlessly, causing them to join their comrades in retreat. The war was not over, but at least the Yankees were driven from Virginia.

THIRTEEN

Maryland, My Maryland

I sorely needed the rest, and did so for a whole two days. I felt triumphant, although I hadn't played a part in the fighting. Simply carrying messages back and forth between the generals would have to be enough. We had driven the Yankees out of Virginia, and the remnants of their flight littered the area around Fairfax Court House. Walking through camp, I looked at the dropped haversacks, weapons, and clothing that covered the ground.

In the distance, I watched litter carriers and soldiers with shovels do what should always be done: tend to the wounded and bury the dead. It didn't always happen that way, and many a field was littered with the dead. I was curious, watching Yankees and Confederates alike as they worked side by side. Why weren't we fighting or capturing the Yankees out there? I learned in the sad aftermath of the battles fought, a sense of soul and respect for the dead marked the time. We had fought, we had made our point, and the loss was felt by both sides equally. Differences were to be set aside. We are not savages but human beings. I noticed a scrap of paper fluttering on the ground and stooped down to pick up what turned out to be a photograph.

Staring back at me, rather forlorn it seemed, was a young girl, maybe five or six years old. Her light hair loosely hung on her forehead, and pigtails clung to the sides. Her patterned dress was simple, and she stood straight as could be. Who had lost her? Was he a Yankee or one of us? Was he alive or dead? Her father had carried that picture with him into battle as a reminder that she was part of him. What would her memory of him be? I thought of my sister, Quinn, who was probably about the same age. Was she okay? My sister, Alexandria, my parents, Wilson's parents, were they okay? My brother, Caleb, surely he was fighting somewhere up here, although I had not seen him.

Mosby got word to me that Wilson was still imprisoned, but alive. Sil, the Confederate spy, watched out for him as best she could. I mourned them and the loss of my horse, Sol's Mistress, as well. Although the gelding I named Climber, for his ability, soothed her loss some. For some reason, I don't rightly know why, I tucked the picture into my breast pocket and wiped away the single tear that began to trickle down my face.

Before mounting up later in the day, my head was awash in a mixture of triumph and melancholy. We began the march toward the Potomac, and Stuart spread us out so that our actions resembled the breaking of waves against some coastline, crashing on the shore and ebbing away as we clashed with any foolhardy Yankees that remained. From Dranesville to Lewinsville, Falls Church to Georgetown, we surged forward. We were going to carry the war to Maryland. Finally, the North would feel the war close to their bosom as we had been forced to do in Virginia for too long.

General Lee instructed Stuart to bring up the rear guard, which we did on the road to Leesburg. Bands began playing, "Maryland, my Maryland" as we began crossing the Potomac. I knew my horse was small and would probably drown if I was aboard him as we crossed the surging Potomac, so I jumped down as we plunged into the river. I grabbed the pommel of my saddle and swam next to him. Climber snorted as we splashed across, struggling with the current, and I was sure I would freeze to death in the waters of the Potomac, cold with melted ice and the turning of the seasons toward winter.

We struggled up the opposite bank and I shook with the wet and cold. I stripped off the overcoat and rode in my undershirt, which, although wet, did not carry as large an amount of the Potomac as my coat did.

My fellow cavalrymen's spirits lifted, and dang if my spirits didn't also. The air seemed fresher, the plants greener, and the crops along the road promised a bounty that I'm sorry to say, no longer existed in Virginia.

Nearing the Poolesville area, city folks shouted in joy at our arrival. I knew that Maryland was a state that had people who showed a clear liking to one side or another. We sure had plenty of boys from Maryland in the Confederate army. A trooper riding next to me remarked in disgust, "They's probably happier with the suspension of the Yank draft than us showing up, I bet."

Stuart pitched headquarters at Urbana on the evening of September 5th, content to let the main army continue toward Frederick. He kept me and other scouts busy scouting McClellan daily.

Early morning on what must have been September 8th, Chiswell hailed me as I ambled through camp.

"Levon, I was looking for ya. Come on, you're gonna come with me and Major von Borcke. We have work to do."

"What kind of work?" I said, puzzled.

Laughing, he said, "Don't worry, it isn't really that kind of work. It'll be fun, come on."

We quickly mounted up, myself, Chiswell, and the big Prussian von Borcke who had some large satchels strapped in back of him. We rode just a short way before pulling up in front of a two-story building. It was nicely put together but empty, 'cause there wasn't no one around, as far as I could see.

As I cocked my head in confusion, Chiswell began to explain. "Jeb has decided to host a ball tonight. Maybe it's just in celebration of our being in Maryland. We have this abandoned academy here, and Jeb thought it would be grand to hold it here. A lot of the town folks from Urbana have been invited. It'll be fun."

As we dismounted, Chiswell continued, "We have some decorating to do. It's supposed to be just Jeb's staff, but I'm sure I can get you in."

Von Borcke grabbed the satchels off his saddle, and with Chiswell opening the large oak doors, we strode in. I took in the staircase that ran around a spacious room of polished oak. It smelled somewhat musty, I figured because it had been closed off, but the stairs appeared to gleam yellow with the application of linseed oil.

Von Borcke said in his thick accent, "Vas get these regimental flags up. Hang dem from the stair railings." He began pulling the flags out from the satchels and handing them to Chiswell and me. I bounded up the stairs carrying not a regimental flag at all, but the first National Flag of the Confederacy, and slowly draped it down over the railing. So it hung with its three stripes of red, white, and red, while in the upper left hand corner seven white stars stood against a blue relief. It was truly grand, taking my breath away. I knew it wasn't really true, but allowed myself to feel that it was the first time the Confederate flag had flown in the state of Maryland.

It was while I was hanging a regimental flag, I believe it was one from Cobb's Georgia Legion, that a few townspeople from the surrounding area arrived, bringing in tables, chairs, and bouquets of roses. Von Borcke welcomed them and they chatted like they were old friends. Curiously, I wondered if they had known each other before, but probably not. He had surely met them earlier to organize the ball. That must have been what it was. I suddenly felt like I was being watched. And then our eyes met.

She stood just paces from von Borcke and the adults, and stared up at me with slate gray eyes. She must have been about the same age as me, but slight. Her hair hung in light brown ringlets and she was plainly dressed. But her eyes, her eyes bored into me, and I shifted uncomfortably. Continuing my gaze, I drew myself up and threw out my chest trying to impress upon her that I was a proud and strong soldier.

Chiswell, standing next to me, noticing the stare, cackled, "Oh my, what do we have here? Seems like to me that there may be some attraction going on between you and that young Maryland belle, heh, Levon?"

Shouldering him away, embarrassed, I said, "Shut up, Chiswell. I don't even know her; she's just staring at me."

She saw Chiswell and I talking, and no doubt knew we were talking about her, which we were. She dropped her gaze and walked out of sight, hiding behind the adults. We finished hanging the flags and I stalked out. I avoided her and the others, mounted up, and rode back to camp.

As I sat, fairly stewing in camp, Chiswell walked up. "C'mon, Levon, don't be angry. I was just having a little amusement with you."

"That girl. I don't even know her, never met her even. You sat there poking fun at me, and her stare was kind of, I dunno, spooky, I guess," I said, still angry.

"Why you so angry? I just think she might like you a bit, that's all," Chiswell said.

"Perhaps you're right. I'm not used to female attention, if that's what it was," I said.

"Look, we are going to have fun tonight. We're going to spruce you up and see how things go, okay?"

Beginning to cool down, I answered absently, "Okay."

"Good, first we got to clean you up, and I think I can fit you into one of my spare uniforms. Come on, let's go over to my tent where you can get out of those clothes. You're beginning to smell like the Potomac, and about as filthy." We sauntered down to his tent, with Chiswell chatting gaily the whole way.

"Okay, first just strip your shirt off," Chiswell said as he lifted a bucket out of the fire.

"Dip this here cloth in the lye water and scrub your chest and arms. Ah, hell, get your face too. Now sit down on this stool and you can shave."

He examined my face and said cheerily, "You don't got much to shave, but let's do it anyway. I got a mirror and straight razor. Leave your face wet while I look for my spare uniform."

While Chiswell rummaged through a trunk in the corner of the tent, I picked up the razor and a small part of a mirror and got the first look at myself since my time in Sil's room in Washington.

I looked drawn, or maybe weary would be a better

term. I saw the small cuts I got when I escaped the Yankees during my service getting messages to Longstreet, and my hair was a little long, the benefit of not having a proper haircut for some time. Did I look older? I smiled at the thought. I've only been with Stuart a little over a year, so I couldn't possibly have aged too much, and I was right. The experiences, though, seemed like more than a year.

After I finished shaving of the few whiskers I had, I washed the razor in the bucket, and with my hands wet, ran them through my hair, slicking it back.

Chiswell approached with his arms full and told me to take my pants off, leaving me nearly naked excepting my thermals. "Put on these trousers."

I quietly did as I was told and put on the sky blue trousers, the pants of a cadet. Solemnly, he handed me a red undershirt and a tunic of gray cloth. "Now this."

Putting the undershirt and tunic on, I admired the yellow piping on the sleeves. I noticed the tunic extended halfway between the hip and knee. I slowly exhaled.

"Keep the boots you got and step back so I can admire you," Chiswell said, maintaining a solemn tone.

Chiswell, stating the obvious, remarked, "Now you surely look like a private in the regular army, excepting the yellow facing of an officer. It will have to do."

I felt different, oddly kind of shaky. "You sure General Stuart won't mind, me not being enlisted and all?"

"He won't mind, I already checked. He says he regards you as Confederate cavalry already, and no uniform doesn't matter one whit. Now, leave me so I can dress, and we will go presently."

I stepped out of the tent and waited for Chiswell. Somebody offered me a cheroot as they walked by, and I accepted it along with a light. I still felt real strange though. First a uniform, what's next, an enlistment and rank? I really stepped in it now, and pausing, took a long puff from the cigar.

Chiswell stepped out just as I began to calm my uneasy stomach, and mounting up, we rode to the ball. After tethering the horses next to the others outside the academy, we walked in, but not before Chiswell whispered, "Let's see what that Maryland girl thinks of you now."

When I stepped into the hall, my eyes immediately fell on the gleaming sabers stacked against the wall. The townspeople had come all decked out in their Sunday best. The men in nice suits, and the women in elegant gowns, chatted amicably with Stuart's staff. I looked over the crowd, searching for the girl with the slate gray eyes. I don't know if she scared or excited me. Maybe she did both. I didn't see her immediately, and that probably was due to the fact that Stuart was holding court, always the center of attention. He was completely surrounded by a group of fawning women, and enjoying himself as always. His gray uniform was impeccable with gold trim and a yellow sash wound around his waist. I noticed that even though dancing was expected, he had his gold spurs on.

Chiswell motioned me toward the punch bowl just as Stuart hushed the crowd and spoke up.

"Welcome to all the citizens of Maryland who have accepted our invitation tonight. We, the Cavalry of the Confederate States of America, are honored to be your hosts tonight. It is my hope, as well as my staff's, that we may extend the same hospitality that the Cockey family has shown us, and tonight's ball is in part a celebration of that.

Tonight's musical accompaniment is provided by the 18th Mississippi, commanded by Brigadier General

William Barksdale, who I see is also in attendance. Thank you for coming, General," Stuart said with a nod of acknowledgment before continuing. "So, let this night cast a light in the darkness of this tragedy we all feel so fully. Gentlemen strike up the music."

The band, already assembled, struck up a waltz, and men and women began partnering up. I felt self-conscious and out of place, so after getting a cup of punch, stood to the side still searching for the girl. I stood there nearly an hour, shuffling my feet, until a trooper burst in and rushed up to Stuart.

After a short conversation with the trooper gesturing wildly, Stuart yelled out, "If our guests would excuse us, men to the horses. We need to enter a fight to aid Hampton. Pelham, bring along your command."

While Stuart's staff rushed to their sabers, I quickly went to mount up, thankful that my rifle was still in its scabbard on my saddle.

We quickly rode toward the fighting as Pelham's horse artillery trundled behind. Stuart attacked with his saber aloft. I dismounted and ran behind a small rise to join the infantry already there. Pelham's cannons unlimbered, roared to life as I looked for a target. I didn't witness the saber charge because it was up ahead and obscured by the woods, so I concentrated on the job at hand.

The Yankees were not in ranks, but running pell-mell over the outpost. I pulled the trigger but the shot missed. I quickly reloaded and took what aim I could. That shot also missed, but others alongside me proved to be more accurate, and the Yankees began to break off their attack.

Stuart and the other mounted men trotted back, sabers, streaked with blood, held aloft. Not a word was spoken and we rode back to the ball.

Stuart, unconcerned and unruffled, strode back into

the hall. "Please accept my apologies for our brief departure. Please, let us continue with the festivities."

Uncomfortable again, I grabbed another cup of punch and took a seat leaning against a wall. Suddenly, the crowded dance floor parted and a beaming Chiswell approached with none other than the gray eyed girl on his arm. Her face pink, was framed by light brown ringlets and she had replaced the simple dress with an elegant orange gown with a tight bodice. As they got closer, her eyes held that unnerving stare and I started to sweat.

I stood up and brushed at my tunic while Chiswell began his introduction. "Private Lewis," he said with a wink. "It is my pleasure to introduce you to Miss Lilly Greene."

"Pleased to meet you, Private Lewis," she said, curtsying and offering me her hand.

It felt like my whole body was sweating, creating rivers of their own, as I took her hand.

"Uh, I'm, uh, pleased to make your acquaintance," I said, grasping her delicate hand. I was surprised at its softness and warmth.

Chiswell, recognizing that I was holding her hand for an uncomfortably long time reached for her arm, and pulling it away, said, "Yes. Well, Miss Greene here is the daughter of Urbana's town constable. Isn't that correct, Miss Greene?"

Her eyes seemed to search my very insides as she said softly, "That is correct, Lt. Dabney. Urbana is a quiet town, so my father's job is somewhat safe, although he works very hard. Of course, this war stirs people, and it has become less peaceful, so I hope that it will end soon, Chiswell. Oh, my gosh, I called you Chiswell. Is that okay? It's so improper." She giggled and raised her hand to cover her mouth.

"Well, of course it is. I called you Lilly." Chiswell

laughed. I stood there dumbstruck, not knowing what to do, much less say.

"Private Lewis's first name is Levon. For God's sake man, can't you speak?"

His question was like throwing a rope to a drowning man, as I was drowning in the beauty of her eyes. "I, I, uh…" I stammered. I felt helpless to speak, and so just slumped my shoulders in defeat.

"Levon, are you okay?" Chiswell said with concern.

"Yes, Levon, are you ill?" Lilly asked.

I struggled to regain myself. I had never been touched like this. I couldn't gather my thoughts and felt lightheaded. I didn't even know what I was feeling, to be particularly honest with you.

"Perhaps I need to sit down," I said.

"Do you need a cold compress? Perhaps some water?" Lilly asked as she began to back away.

Anxious for her to stay I summoned every bit of chivalry I could and said, "No, I'll be alright. Please stay."

"Okay, I will sit here with you," she said.

Chiswell, seeing what was going on better than I, said, "Oh, I think he'll be alright. Would the two of you mind if I went back to the dancing and our other guests?"

"I don't mind. Levon?" Lilly said as she placed her hand in my lap.

"Okay, Chiswell. It's okay with me."

"I'll take my leave then," Chiswell said with a bow and walked away.

"Are you sure you are okay?" Lilly asked.

"I'm sure. Maybe we could just talk," I replied.

"That would be grand. You seem so much younger than most of the soldier's I've met." Looking around the hall, she continued, "Certainly you and I are the youngest here tonight."

"Well, I was just living with my family down in the

lower Shenandoah, and just sort of became involved in what's going on."

"Oh, please tell me. How did it happen that you became a part of the Confederate cavalry?" she said breathlessly.

"Lilly, or, uh, Miss Greene. War seems so indelicate to speak of. You are a woman, after all."

"Nonsense. I'm a woman, certainly, but this war involves us all. We are powerless to ignore it. Please tell me how you came to be here. All of it! And, Levon, please call me Lilly."

I raised my head to look at her, and the eyes which had first scared me, and then stunned me, looked warm and inviting.

"I began doing slave catching. Bringing the runaways back to their owners. I guess it was foolish, but at the time, I thought I could do a small part toward preserving the Southern way of life, but not have to carry a gun. I was with my cousin and another man in Dranesville chasing down a slave and we got caught up in crossfire. The other man was killed."

"Oh, that's awful," Lilly murmured.

"It was, and at that moment, I knew I couldn't go back. The man that was killed admitted to me that he was along to make sure I didn't come back. The leader of our group, of what he called "Home Guards," were in disagreement and so Wilson, that's my cousin's name, and I decided to see if we could meet up with General Stuart and do some scouting. Of course, we did not know whose command it was, only that they were Confederate. Anyway, I still thought I wouldn't have to carry a gun."

"So your cousin is with you here?"

With bile rising in my throat, I croaked, "No, he was captured along with a man named Mosby at a train station and is imprisoned in Washington. I tried to get him out, seeing that I was responsible for his capture, but I failed and came back to Stuart."

"Oh, my God," she gasped, bringing her hands up to her face. "I'm sorry, Levon. I'm so very sorry. Why do you feel responsible for your cousin's capture?"

"I got him to stay with me when he wanted to go home. I feel like I must stay until he gets released."

"I don't understand. You are in the Confederate cavalry, yet you don't carry a gun?"

"I do now. I've been involved in the fighting, and yes, the killing too."

Lilly asked, "How could you kill another man when you don't like guns?"

"I don't like guns, but I've faced the wrong end of the gun too. I have done things I regret doing, but I felt I had to, there was really no other choice." Remembering Redmond Burke's words, I echoed them. "A man once told me that I must look at the gun as a tool, just as the blacksmith has his hammer."

She fell silent for a short time, studying my face. "Do you support slavery? You said you were a slave catcher. This I cannot comprehend."

"Lilly, please understand that, at the time, I thought it would help the Confederate cause. My family owns slaves."

"How would owning another man aid your cause? It's just not right," she said pleadingly.

"I know, it was foolish. But now I want to protect my family, our way of life. To make our own decisions. It doesn't have to include owning slaves. I surely wouldn't."

"That is good to hear. But what of your family, Levon? Surely you must miss them. I know I would if I were apart from mine."

"I do miss them. My sisters, my parents, Wilson's family, my brother, Caleb, who surely must be fighting somewhere hereabouts. But if it's anything deeper than what I just said, I don't know. I lost my favorite horse, too. I have suffered losses, but not near as much as others. I cannot let it just keep going on when I can possibly help stop it."

She clasped my head in her hands, and staring at me with her gray eyes, said, "I'm sorry, Levon, for all that you are forced to bear. Being young, as you and I are, should be time spent in carefree youth, yet this damn war seeks to prevent it. But you know one thing. From the time I first noticed you up on the staircase, I saw your sadness, but knew there must be good things in you that others have not seen. You must believe that."

"I'm trying to do the good things, the right things," I replied.

"Let's dance, shall we? Perhaps we can enjoy some of the carefree moments of youth we have been afforded to forget the war."

"'I'd be honored," I said, relaxing.

Taking her hand, I guided her out to the dance floor and we waltzed. Or, should I say, she waltzed while I tried my best to not step on her feet or trip over my own. If she noticed, she didn't say, and that came as a relief to me. Stuart stood nearby, laughing, and referring to an attractive brunette as a "New York Rebel" due to her secessionist beliefs. Apparently, she was a northern relative of the Cockey family, the family we were repaying tonight for their earlier graciousness, and she was quite outspoken.

I held Lilly in my arms, and with her hair smelling of lilacs, my head continued slightly spinning. Holding Lilly as I was, I realized that I did not have this evening in mind when I thought we should take the war into the bosom of the North. This bosom I liked. I had taken Lilly's words to heart, and for tonight, I could forget war's horrors and enjoy my carefree youth. So it went for some time till there occurred a jolt to the peacefulness. Confederate wounded started arriving, so some men lost their dance partners as the women in their gowns warmed to the task of nurses. Fortunately for me, Lilly was not among those pressed into service, and so we continued dancing.

"Oh, Levon, I almost forgot. I must introduce you to a friend of my family who is staying with us. He's from England, you know," Lilly whispered.

"Oh, okay. I'd be delighted."

"But, I want to introduce him to your General Stuart, as well. Do you think that would be alright?"

"I don't know. General Stuart makes his own decisions," I said.

"Chiswell said he would help me with General Stuart," she said, looking through the crowd.

Spotting Chiswell, Stuart, and her relative approaching us, she said, clapping her hands in glee, "Oh good, Chiswell has already made the introduction of Cousin Wales to General Stuart. Here they come."

"Private Lewis, you look very good. Are you having a good time tonight in the company of Miss Greene here?" Stuart asked.

"I certainly am, General. Thank you for asking. May I be of service to you, sir?" I replied.

"Yes, you may indeed. Miss Greene, may I beg your pardon for some time? I would like to discuss an arrangement between Mr. Wales and Levon privately. Would that be okay?" Stuart asked with that charming smile of his.

"Well, of course," Lilly said. "Levon, you won't leave without telling me goodbye, will you?" she asked, briefly batting her eyelashes.

"Oh, not at all, Lilly. You won't leave before I have

the pleasure, will you?" I pleaded.

"I will wait for you," she said simply, curtsying and gliding away, leaving the faint smell of her perfume wafting in the air.

Stuart ushered me out of the swirling dancers, saying, "Let us move to the side of the room for our conversation. Private Lewis, let me introduce to you Mr. Endicott Wales."

"The pleasure is mine, Private Lewis. I'm Endicott Wales," the thin man said in a clipped accent, offering his hand.

I shook his hand and waited, perplexed. He was tall, but rather dainty in manners. His trousers were red and black checkered, much like a laid out checkerboard. He wore a crimson shirt buttoned to the neck, and laced cuffs, all topped off with a black vest, coat, and a tie which some people refer to as an ascot. If not for his pencil thin mustache, he appeared more like a woman than a man. *Oh brother,* I thought, *he does look unusual.*

"If Miss Greene has not told you, Mr. Wales here is a distant relative of her family, all the way from England," Stuart said.

"She said as much."

"But that is not what is important. Mr. Wales here is a British journalist who wishes to document the war."

"Document, sir?" I asked.

"That is to say, he plans to make reports on the war for the newspapers in England."

I shook my head in bewilderment.

"He wants to tell his stories from our viewpoint, the Southern viewpoint. He wants to travel with us. He has graciously asked me if he may accompany us."

"I still don't understand, sir. How am I involved?"

"Not only have I accepted his request, but I have chosen you as his companion."

"Why me, General? There are certainly more experienced men or soldiers under your command to choose from."

"That may be true, Levon, but because of the varied services you have provided me, I believe Mr. Wales will have the full benefit of your experiences and day to day life. You would agree, would you not?"

"I guess so, General," I said glumly.

"Now, understand, I will not permit him to interfere with your duties. Particularly those of a scout, which requires stealth and keenness. You will see to Mr. Wales tomorrow morning and escort him to our column of march. Now, go back to that engaging Miss Greene. I would not want to make her unhappy," he said, his eyes sparkling in merriment.

I broke away to look for Lilly while wondering whether Wales rode sidesaddle or not. I guess I would find out. I found Lilly right away, and she quickly took my arm.

"Is everything all right, Levon? You look upset somehow," she purred.

"It's nothing, really. I guess I'll be serving as an escort for Mr. Wales for awhile. It has made me uneasy," I replied.

"But why, Levon? He is a relative of mine, after all. Distant, to be sure, but still a relative. Do you not like him?"

"No, that's not it," I lied. "I just feel like I've been put in charge of, and responsible for, Mr. Wales. I don't consider myself a real soldier for the reasons that I don't like to be tied to orders, or command others. Don't mistake me, I would follow General Stuart's orders completely, but I like having the feeling I can leave at any time and no one would think less of me. Of course, I would not leave, nor can I think of any instance that would lead me in that direction. I mean, my cousin, Wilson, followed my lead and you know what happened to him. I'm responsible for his imprisonment. But he was family, and Mr. Wales is not. It's that simple."

Slightly miffed, she said, "You make it seem as if he is a child. He is not, Levon, I'm quite sure Endicott can take care of himself. I don't think General Stuart expects you to be some kind of caretaker, and I know that Endicott doesn't either."

"I know, I do. Don't be angry with me, Lilly."

"Levon, don't put undo pressure upon yourself, that's all I'm saying. It is getting late, though, and I should go. I would like very much to invite you to my home tomorrow morning. Will you come?"

"I do accept. I've already been ordered by the general to pick up your cousin tomorrow."

"Splendid. Why don't you come for breakfast with my family? Can you do that, Levon?"

"I don't think that will be a problem. As long as it's not an inconvenience upon your family."

"Don't be silly. They will be happy to meet you," she said, caressing my arm and gazing at me with her gray eyes.

She gave me directions to her house as we stood outside the door of the academy. As we said our goodnights, I quickly leaned toward her and kissed her lightly on the cheek. She didn't seem upset, but just bowed her head shyly.

I climbed up into the saddle and rode slowly back to camp. Upon arrival, I put Climber away, and after making sure he was comfortable, walked to my tent. I sat on my bedroll, removed my boots, and tried to figure out how to sooth my aching head.

I knew I wasn't in love with Lilly, because falling in love at first sight was impossible.

People sometimes spoke of it, but how could that possibly happen? But she made me feel different and I cannot come to grips with what I am feeling. Then, there is the matter of having to take care of the feminine Mr. Wales. In the extreme, it seemed to me to just be short of actually being killed. I was having a hard enough time keeping myself alive and now I had to keep him alive too?

On the good side, so far, our reception had been nice, with no fighting, and I was having breakfast with Lilly's family in the morning. I knew that I best not be fooled, because despite this brief reprieve, things were bound to get a lot hotter, and soon.

Yawning, I took off the officer's tunic and trousers and went into what I can only describe as a troubled sleep. I had dreams, and you know how it is. If you don't immediately awaken from the dreams, you don't remember them, and that's good, but you know they were bad.

I slowly awoke the next morning to the sound of a crackling campfire and the smell of smoke seeping through the tent flap. I put on my trousers and stepped out to be greeted by what, for the most part it seemed, was an always cheerful Chiswell crouched near the campfire.

"Good morning, Levon. Care for a little coffee, would you? Big day ahead for you," he said with a crooked smile.

Grabbing the tin cup filled with steaming, but sour brew, I said, "Yes, I surely need this. What was that you were cackling like a chicken about? A big day?"

"Sure. I heard you got a date at Miss Greene's for breakfast, and you received your first command," he snickered.

"What's that you say? What command?"

"Well, Mr. Wales, of course. I was told he will be

your almost constant companion."

"Oh, yeah, that. Real funny, Chiswell. I don't really want to babysit nobody. I'm not looking forward to it at all."

"We got to follow orders, whether we like or agree with them or not. That's what soldiers do."

"I'm not a soldier."

"In name only, you're not. Stop bellyaching. You must be looking forward to breakfast, though. Made quite an impression on Miss Greene. I thought you would."

"Yes, I like her, but time is short. We will probably be moving out soon, so…" I said, allowing my voice to trail off.

"I understand of what you speak. Get dressed now and don't tarry. I believe Jeb wants to speak with you before you go."

Making my way down to the picket line of horses, I stopped at the general's tent.

"General, it's Levon. I understand you want to speak with me. Do I have your permission to enter?"

"Certainly, Levon, come in."

I pulled back the tent flap and stepped in to see Stuart sitting at a makeshift table looking at some maps.

"Levon, I wanted to talk with you before you proceed to the Greene's place. I noticed a hint of disgust from you last evening regarding the assignment I've given you. I really don't care how you feel personally toward our guest, Mr. Wales, but you may be looking past what benefits he can provide. You remember Endicott Wales is English. Favorable writing may influence England's ideas of us here in the South. England and France's assistance would do a great deal in providing legitimacy to the Confederacy. Do you see that?"

"I hadn't before, General, but I understand a bit of what you say. If his country saw clearly our desires and the purity of them, they may help us, right?"

"Precisely. So treat him well, but don't let him interfere with your activities. I don't want you to be put in danger because you are worried with him, understand?"

"Understood, General," I replied, bringing myself smartly erect.

"Good. Then go enjoy your breakfast," he said, then saluted. He saluted me first! Stunned, I saluted back and stepped out of his tent, then continued toward the picket line.

Already saddled, as all of our horses were nowadays, I mounted Climber and started towards Lilly's family home. The air was clean and crisp, and I drew in a deep breath, enjoying it fully. Lilly's directions were easy to follow and I soon found myself at her front porch. No sooner had I tied Climber's reins to an all too rare hitching post, did Lilly bound out the door with a big welcoming smile and hug.

"Levon, I'm so glad to see you again," she said with girlish excitement.

"You knew I would come. I have to get Mr. Wales," I replied.

"I know, but that doesn't mean I can't be excited," she said with a coquettish pout.

I chuckled at her manner. "I'm happy too. No, really, I am," I said, trying to convince her.

"I accept your apology, if that's what it is. But let's not waste this beautiful morning gabbing out here. Let's go inside so I can introduce you to my family."

We were immediately met by an older man upon entering the house.

"This is my father, Levon. Father, this is Levon," she said, nudging me slightly toward him.

I grasped his hand with as firm as a handshake as I could. "Mr. Greene, I'm pleased to meet you. Thank you so much for inviting me into your home this morning."

He replied with an even firmer handshake. "Good Lord, boy, think nothing of it."

I could see where Lilly's exuberance came from.

He continued. "I must say, you are young, but it is not unexpected by what my daughter has told me." I felt my face warm a bit with embarrassment before Lilly's mother swept in to my rescue.

"Jonathan Greene, shame on you for embarrassing our guest so. Pleased to meet you, Levon. I'm Betty, Lilly's mother."

"Thank you, ma'am, it's really alright," I said, trying to make a stand.

"No, it is not. You are very brave being a soldier and all."

"I was just saying…" Mr. Greene sputtered.

"Don't you start trying to get yourself out of this silly predicament you've gotten yourself into, Mr. Greene. You hush," Lilly's mother said.

"I hope you're hungry, Levon. Thankfully, the war has not taken so much from us yet. My cousin, Endicott, will join us shortly. He is upstairs packing his bags, I believe. Please, come into the parlor and we will have some tea before breakfast. Would that be all right?"

"Yes, ma'am, I would surely enjoy that," I said as Lilly quickly grabbed my hand. I tried to keep my balance because she had surprised me by taking my hand. I struggled to show unconcern as we walked into the parlor and sat down side by side on a couch.

"Pardon me, Levon, and you too, Mother, I'm just curious as to how you came to be in the Rebel cavalry. You must be about the same age as my daughter," Mr. Greene said in a mildly stern tone.

"Father," Lilly protested.

"It's okay, Lilly. He deserves an answer, and I feel

bound to provide it. I'm almost sixteen now so I grant you that I'm young, but not so different than many others that serve the Confederacy. I was originally a, uh, slave catcher," I muttered.

"A what?" Mr. Greene fairly shouted.

"A slave catcher, sir."

"I could not approve of that, son."

"I wouldn't expect you to, sir. But it was for only a short time. I wasn't proud of it. After a time, I met General Stuart and have been with him since. I'm a scout, but have also served as a courier," I said, careful not to mention my visit to Washington. "And a raider."

As Mrs. Greene silently served tea, Mr. Greene continued "What does a raider do?"

"We disrupt and harass the enemy, particularly their supply lines. Have you heard of the Chickahominy Raid?" I paused for the answer that never came. "I was involved in it." I felt Lilly cringe next to me.

"Have you seen fighting, son?"

"I have, sir, reluctantly, at first, but when you are receiving fire, your mind quickly comes to terms with it. To survive, of course."

Arching his eyebrows, Mr. Greene continued his questioning. "Were you forced to kill someone? I would presume you did."

"Yes, sir, I was, and did."

"My God, what this damnable war has forced our young people to do," Mr. Greene said emphatically.

"Yes, sir. I'm not proud of it. But I have grown, and if it is to preserve the way of my life or how I see it, then I will continue. I let the others; the more experienced men, guide me. I trust their judgment. I trust General Stuart."

"He seems like a good fellow to follow. But enough of this talk for now. Here comes Endicott now. Let's gather around the table for some breakfast."

Lilly patted me gently on the shoulder as we made our way to the table. Before me, I saw a feast fit for a king, and sat down, scooting my chair closer. Lilly was right beside me.

A platter of thinly sliced ham steaming in the center of the table set my mouth to water. Scrambled eggs lay next to the platter of ham in a porcelain bowl of its own. To the side of the eggs sat lightly browned rolls in a pan. Placed in front of us, sat glasses of orange juice, ice cubes tinkling against the sides. Maryland hadn't felt the ravages of the war as Virginia had, if this table of food was any indication. I wasn't bitter, but felt a longing for what was lost.

Mr. Greene remarked, "Now, if we can get Mother in here, we can say the morning prayer."

Mrs. Greene came through the swinging door from the kitchen to the dining area with a bowl of gravy with the ladle stuck in it, saying, "I'm here, Father. You may begin the prayer."

After a short prayer, we began helping ourselves to breakfast. There were only a few at the table, Lilly's parents, Mr. Wales, Lilly, and I. I didn't ask Lilly, but assumed she had no brothers and sisters, by the gathering at the table. I didn't want to appear as a ravenous hog, so I looked at Lilly's parents while politely passing the food between us. Hmm, no servants, or slaves neither.

Mr. Greene was of rather average build, not fat or skinny. Of ruddy complexion, his hair was cut short, and he sported an impressive mustache, not like the pencil-thin wisp of dear Mr. Wales. He wore regular black work clothes, a vest that hung unbuttoned, with a white shirt underneath. When I said work clothes, I mean not those of a farmer, but that of a townsperson. Which, of course, he was, being the constable. In spite of his official title, he held the youthful exuberance of his daughter, which I had noticed before.

Mrs. Greene was the lady of the house, for sure. Not unattractive at all, for she possessed the good looks that Lilly had inherited. Her hair tied back in a bun, she wore a simple dress and an apron bound around her waist. She was soft-spoken, but I think her words carried a lot of weight at the Greene home.

Mr. Wales said nothing, he just stared at me as he ate. Did he know I couldn't stand him? Perhaps, but his gaze betrayed nothing.

We made some small talk while we ate. Lilly was noticeably quiet, which made me squirm a little.

Mr. Greene broke the silence with more questions. "So, Levon, what is your General's plan? What I mean to say is, what is next?"

"I don't know, sir. I expect we keep going deep into Maryland. Other than that, I cannot say," I said, pausing from bringing a forkful of egg to my mouth.

"Do you know but cannot say? Some sort of secret strategy, then? You know I am the law here and will not tolerate any lawlessness in Urbana."

"Mr. Greene, I just don't know what Stuart is commencing to do. But I'm certain it would not include any illegal activity outside those acts committed in war."

"So you believe that if the action constitutes an act of war, although perhaps illegal, it is permissible?"

Before I could answer, Lilly stood up and blurted out, "Daddy, please stop it!"

"Wha—what? I was just…," Mr. Greene said.

"Jonathan Butler Greene, you stop your tone. That's enough," Lilly's mother said, her voice shrill. "Levon is a guest in our home and I cannot believe you would treat someone like this with your accusations and all. He is but a boy!"

Mr. Greene mumbled something under his breath

with an air I could only describe as chagrined.

Unsure of just what to do, I looked at a stunned Wales and said, "Perhaps we should go."

Lilly pleaded with me, whimpering, "Levon, please don't go." Stamping her foot, she continued, "Daddy, you will apologize this instant!"

"Jon?" Mrs. Greene added.

"I'm sorry, Levon, I unduly blamed you. Lilly is our only child, and my protective nature has risen. With this blasted war, I have begun to question so much."

"It is fine, Mr. Greene. I mean no harm to Lilly, nor would I bother her with improper intentions. I admit, I like Lilly, but we have only just met. I do not know what tomorrow holds, nor in the weeks or months ahead. I would not involve Lilly in that. But I'm a soldier now, and will continue to be despite other's feelings. If I have upset you, I sincerely apologize."

Mrs. Greene hushed me. "You have no need to apologize, Levon, that is nonsense. I believe Mr. Greene will mind his manners now. Won't you, Jonathan?" she said glaring his way.

"Yes, Mother," Mr. Greene said.

"Fine. Let me bring out some tea after our breakfast. Lilly, could you help me clear the table?" she said softly.

While Lilly and her mother cleared the table, Mr. Wales, Lilly's father, and I, suffered in uncomfortable silence in the parlor.

Endicott Wales, attempting to break the stony silence said, "We will move out today, Private Lewis?"

"I believe that is the general's order."

"Good, very good, then," he stammered.

I tried to control myself. I didn't want to show anger or a lack of gratitude toward Lilly's family's invitation to breakfast, but my hackles had been raised sure enough. I slowly sipped on the offered cup of tea and felt all eyes trained on me, excepting for Lilly, who sat with her eyes downcast and cheeks flushed red, quietly looking at her cup.

I brought my head up, staring directly at Wales. "We must leave now," I said.

"Okay. I must say my goodbyes and get my baggage. I will meet you on the porch."

I quickly said my thanks to Lilly's family as best I could, feeling that, unfortunately, my words lacked sincerity, and walked out the door to the waiting Climber. Lilly, trailing behind me, grabbed my shoulder and spun me around to face her.

Her eyes streamed with tears as she pleaded, "Levon, please do not be angry. My father gets overprotective at times. I know he wasn't judging you, but maybe this whole thing."

"It seemed like he was judging me," I said begrudgingly. "I should be used to it. I, us, the Confederacy, the Union, we are all to be judged, eventually, anyway."

"I know. I just don't want you to think of me badly, Levon," she said, clutching the collar of my tunic.

Holding her shoulders, I looked deep into her gray eyes brimming with tears. "There is nothing you could do that would ever make me feel badly toward you, Lilly, nothing." Right there, and not caring who saw us, I kissed her full on the mouth and felt her snuggle into my arms. Mr. Wales, exiting the house, coughed a warning that he could see us, and we broke our embrace.

I mounted Climber while Wales struggled to lash his baggage to his horse. Lilly clung to my leg. "Will I ever see you again, Levon?"

"I don't know, Lilly. I certainly hope so," I said with all the impassiveness I could muster. I failed miserably. With Wales firmly mounted, and not sidesaddle, I gently nudged Climber and we trotted off.

As we made our way to camp, Wales called out sarcastically, "Well, that went well don't you think?"

Turning in my saddle, I said angrily, "Shut up, Endicott. Others may judge us, but not you. You are a guest of General Stuart and under my charge. My understanding is that you are to observe and report back to your precious newspapers. That is all."

✿FOURTEEN✿

Careening Toward the Bloodiest Day
September, 1862

Sharpsburg

Once we made it back to camp, I walked briskly to Stuart's tent. I admit, I did not show proper respect, nor any military protocol at all, but flung back the tent flap and announced, "General, I have returned with Mr. Wales in tow. Will there be anything else?"

Thankfully for me, Stuart ignored my disrespect and said casually, "Make sure Mr. Wales has suitable quarters, and you relax as well. I'm going with some of my staff to General Lee's headquarters in Best's Grove for further preparation. That is all."

I stalked out and made way to my tent, while Endicott hurried along behind, dragging his baggage.

"You may stay in that tent there. It is filled with supplies so you must make some room. I'll be in this tent right here. Have a good day," I spewed out. I cared not a bit whether he had a good day or not.

The next morning, Stuart returned from Lee's headquarters and relayed his orders to us. The bulk of our army was to range toward South Mountain, a chain of the Blue Ridge Mountains through Frederick. We were expected to guard the eastern flank of our Maryland invasion. General Lee was to be informed of the Yankee General McClellan's movements, and we were to block the mountain passes to protect Stonewall's march on Harper's Ferry. I didn't have to be told how dangerous our work was to be. For a time, the army of northern Virginia would be split, and if Stuart weren't careful, all of us could be devoured by the enemy.

What I feared most in Maryland was the blurring of lines. Who was a friend, and who was foe? In Virginia, it was clearer. It is not to say that there weren't strangers wandering through our camps. Spies or civilians, sympathizers or not, they did exist in Virginia. But if they weren't wearing blue, chances were good that they were right with the cause.

But Maryland was different. Both armies, I knew, had boys serving in them from Maryland. There were acts of kindness and jubilation at our arrival, like at Urbana, but elsewhere there was outright disgust evident from others. You could never be quite sure. Waves of tension swirled throughout the state, bore on the back of every walking human being. I will say that Maryland mirrored the whole land divided.

Stuart split his brigades and command. Munford sat on his right flank near Poolesville, Hampton's brigade in his center outside Hyattstown, and to his left, Fitz Lee's Brigade at New Market, while I stayed close to Stuart. Stuart had told me it was best in light of our guest, Endicott Wales. Throughout the days that followed, couriers delivered messages to Stuart, and their news caused him to pull back to Frederick. I overheard his concern in a conversation he was having with Captain William Blackford, the mysterious soldier I have mentioned before. Mysterious, because he always seemed to be seen for a short time, then he'd disappear. But for this time, he was firmly by Stuart's side.

"I feel that it is best to conform our movements with the main army less we invite attack from the rear. Our brigades have been roughly handled and I do not intend to let General McClellan through those passes and interrupt Stonewall's capture of Harper's Ferry. Would you agree?"

Blackford, having recently returned from his service as a courier replied, "I concur with you, General. But it is the 12th. Do you not think that Stonewall has affected Harper's Ferry surrender?"

"I would think so, but I would not like McClellan to pursue him any further than he already has."

Did I hear him say pursue? I thought we were on the attack, not them. I craned my neck forward to more clearly hear their conversation, but it died away.

So it was that we rode away from our position at Urbana and Hyattstown toward the recently built National Road through the Catoctins on the evening of what Blackford said was the 12th. I think he was mistaken. I thought it was actually the 13th of September.

Stuart sent Fitz Lee to loop around McClellan's flank to find out what he could of the Yankee general's plans, for he was acting quite different from what he had previously. I offered up my assistance to find out for him.

"No, Levon, not right now. McClellan is acting strangely, and you do have Mr. Wales in tow."

I shot an angry glance at the prissy Englishman. If not for him, I would be doing my job. He met my glare with a look of innocence while twirling one end of his moustache. It just made me hate him all the more.

"If Fitz should encounter the Yankees unexpectedly, I want a full brigade to confront them, not just one man. Even if that man is you," Stuart said with amusement.

"Of course, General," I replied, falling into a sulk.

We hop scotched through the South Mountain gorges, first at Turner's Gap, then traveling to assist infantry to where Stuart felt might now be the weakest link of the Confederate line, Crampton's Gap. I will try to maintain the proper chain of events, but frankly, things are happening so fast I can scarcely remember what happened first or what followed what.

One such day, prior to Sharpsburg, Stuart received a man who, according to the pickets who brought him in, claimed to be a Confederate sympathizer. Now, remember, sympathies among the citizens of Maryland were, at best, very murky. Stuart invited me into the conversation along with members of his staff. I stepped into his tent carrying a load of skepticism.

Stuart opened by saying, "Sir, my pickets tell me you may have some information that would be extremely important to know the contents of. Is that true?"

"Yes, General. I was in the Yankee camp on the morning of September 13th past, General McClellan's main column in effect. A dispatch was received by Mac hisself. When that Yank General received the news, he said excited as can be. 'Now I know what to do!' That's what he said," the man replied.

Stuart, seemingly grown stern, pressed the man. "Sir, I beg your pardon. Throughout this war we receive information which not only gives the enemy pause, but us as well. Sometimes it is false or inaccurate, and even, I dare say, deliberate. Do you know of what I say?"

"You don't believe me or you think I'm a spy?" the

shabbily dressed man said with a slight quivering of his lips. *Surely, he is lying,* I thought. *He traipses in here, says he has been in the Yankee's camp and gives a little statement about what he supposedly heard.*

Stuart leaned back in his rickety chair, studying the man. "You admit you were in the Yankee camp, or purport to have been there. Maybe that was what you were told to say. Sir, I am no spy, but a warrior. But this I will tell you. Your story is improbable, and you have given me nothing but a statement that many generals have said. It is not useful."

"General, I beg your pardon, sir," I said. "May I suggest something to say check his tale?"

"Go ahead, Levon. That is why I asked you in here."

I mustered up my best steely gaze and said, "Forget for a moment of what you say the Yankee general said. How did you come to be in the Yankee camp? Secondly, have you ever served in the Confederacy? If so, where and when? Also, what is your name? Surely, you wouldn't be afraid to give us your name?"

"My name, private, is Norris Milhone," he said with a hint of disgust. "I'm from the Frederick area. I'm hearing that some southerners may be arranging a group of irregulars. The term is partisan rangers, I believe. Do these rangers exist as of yet? I am not sure. So, in answer, I have not served in the Confederacy, as of yet. But when I found myself in Maryland and wanting to aid our cause I made my way into the Yankee camp. Maybe it was providence. I wanted to find out what I could and get it to General Stuart."

Taking his eyes from me and on to Stuart, he continued. "General, I understand you would have suspicions of me. But please, General, I can help. When General McClellan got the dispatch, I was very interested in what caused him to say what he did. He also exclaimed, "Here is a paper with which, if I cannot whip Bobbie Lee, I will be willing to go home." I asked around camp, and through some officer's loose lips, I found out. They seemed to think that the correspondence received was Lee's orders. I don't know why they felt that way, but it goes to the heart of McClellan's statement it seems."

Stuart shot erect in his chair and his eyes widened. "Of course, I should have known! For some time I have been surprised by McClellan's quick advance. It has certainly not been his pattern. What you say, Mr. Milhone, may ring with some truth. You will stay with us awhile to prove to me that you can be trusted. Dabney, get this information to General Lee. They may indeed be ahead of us here. Everyone may now go."

A short while after, Stuart, feeling that as yet no heavy Union presence existed at Crampton's Gap, set out south with Hampton toward the Potomac. As we rode, Endicott boldly asked Stuart what was going on. I was shocked by his questioning, but before I could raise my objections, Stuart answered him with nonchalance.

"I'm very happy to accommodate your question, Mr. Wales, and I will. But this is the very last time. In the future, I urge you to know your place. My men, I trust, and tell them everything. But you, you are not a soldier but a guest. You have neither military background nor the need to know my plans. Do we understand each other?"

"Perfectly, General," Wales said meekly. I quickly clasped my hand over my mouth to stifle a snicker.

"My concern is that McClellan may bypass the mountain gaps and seek to relieve the siege General Jackson has placed on Harper's Ferry. I aim to prevent that, for I have infinite knowledge of Harper's Ferry, having arrested the abolitionist John Brown there. Do you find my explanation suitable to you?" Stuart said scornfully. "Good."

I rode past Wales and casually said, "I thought you were only here to report on our cause, not discuss strategy." Endicott Wales, I'm happy to say, remained silent for the rest of our ride to Maryland Heights.

Once we arrived near the Potomac River, Stuart immediately became engaged in conversation with a man I believe was Lafayette McLaws, the area commander occupying the heights.

While Stuart conferred with McLaws, I took the opportunity to dismount and walked to the edge of the heights. I stared down into the valley where Harper's Ferry lay. Maryland Heights lay on one side along the Potomac, while Loudoun Heights on the opposite side sat astride the Shenandoah. I overheard part of the general's conversation and found out that the Loudoun Heights were equally armed by Jackson's men.

The Baltimore and Ohio Railroad, which runs along the Potomac River Valley before making a sharp turn at Harper's Ferry, sat idle as if waiting for Stonewall's attack. I watched the enemy figures below running to and fro. There were a goodly number of them, I thought. They might put up a good fight, but ultimately, I knew they were doomed.

Before leaving back toward Crampton's Gap, Stuart shouted out a warning to McLaws about an unguarded road that led north from Harper's Ferry to the village of Sharpsburg.

Arriving just after dark, it was impossible to miss the mounds that dotted the slopes of South Mountain. Confederate dead. I shuddered with the realization, and next to me, Wales muttered, "Oh my word."

For once, Wales and my feelings were mutual. Our army had been pushed into the valley west of the South Mountain. Stuart turned to me, and with a queer smile, said, "The Yanks may have broken through our defenses,

but far too late to save their fellows at Harper's Ferry."
His voice betrayed the same grimness we all felt.

Spying the young artillerist, Pelham, Stuart's
behavior brightened considerably and we galloped up to
him. Stuart shouted, "Major, I'm delighted to see you. I
heard a report this afternoon that you had been cut off
and surrounded."

Pelham smiled broadly. "We were, but Colonel
Rosser and the horse artillery somehow managed to cut
their way out and keep fighting."

It was in Pleasant Valley near Sharpsburg that we
learned of the surrender of Harper's Ferry and our hearts
again soared. An expected retreated was scuttled for the
moment, and as one body, we wheeled to make battle. I
was the lone rider accompanying Stuart when he met
with Jackson in person. Stonewall requested that Stuart
convey news of the surrender of Harper's Ferry to the
commanding general at Sharpsburg, and we rode off at a
full gallop.

FIFTEEN

The Yankees Called it Antietam
September 17, 1862

The Bloodiest Day

On the morning of September 16th, 1862, after leaving Stonewall, I rode along with Stuart as he led Fitz Lee and Munsford's brigades toward Sharpsburg. Something clung ominously in the air. I had been in battles before, with the Second Manassas being the biggest one to date for me, although I largely watched that one. But today, it felt different.

Even with my lack of military training, I could see that this event, or what the next few days would bring, could very well be climatic. The air fairly hummed, filled with the footfalls of men, the jangling of traces from horses and mules pulling wagons, and the creak of wheels on the rutted roads.

Where once I had heard we were in retreat, today

revealed nothing of the sort. For in the surrounding area, the two armies reminded me of animals in the wild. The predators and the prey, circling, sizing up each other. The only difference was, neither us nor the Yankees resembled the prey. Both armies stood as predators eager to feast on the victims. We pulled up, seeing Longstreet's men drawn up east of the Potomac and west of the Antietam Creek. The Yankees, growing in force, laid to battle along a road that ran past a white washed church of the Dunkers and the creek. At last, the fighting dwindled away for the day, and I began to feel rather small. It was not a feeling of exuberance, for I was scared out of my wits.

Endicott, noticing my uneasiness asked almost sympathetically, "Levon, are you all right?"

Without sting, I mumbled, "No."

I followed Stuart as he shifted us, cavalry and infantry alike, shoring up our left until our lines extended almost four miles. Stuart, although silent in speech, was active in deed. I spent an uneasy night under a light rain, shivering from either the cold rain or my own fear, I don't know which. Perhaps both.

With dawn not yet breaking on that awful day, a man from Fitz Lee's command uttered, "Day breaks, the sun rises. Here stands the Army of Northern Virginia, defiant. There stands the Army of the Potomac, irresolute." He mirrored my thoughts to the upmost.

The fighting began anew as the sun came up and rose in its intensity. Stuart's command was flung piecemeal, and with so very few of his cavalry present to lead, Stuart directed 14 cannons on the ridge of Nicodemus Heights.

I sat in my saddle, seized by uncertainty, until one of the cannoneers fell and I dismounted to take his place. Flinging the reins of Climber at Endicott, I shouted, "Take the horses away from the artillery. Hurry."

Shaken, Endicott said, "Certainly, yes, most certainly." He rode away, leading several horses with him.

The unlimbered guns were a combination of mountain and field guns, and I quickly grabbed a rammer. I waited for the artillerist to pull the sponger from the barrel, and for the ball to be placed in the barrel before ramming it down.

As the sun rose, the rattle of musketry began, and charging through the mist along the Hagerstown Pike came a wall of blue. Stonewall's men, lying in wait in a cornfield, were instantly engaged in a wild fight with the charging line of blue.

I felt rooted to the spot, momentarily unable to move until Pelham's scream to, "Fire, dammit!" shocked me back into the murderous moment as the lanyard was pulled, belching its fire. On and on, I aided the gun crew loading, ramming, and firing the Blakelys and Napoleons, intent on punching holes in the blue attack. The Yankee charge melted into a wall of blue, no longer distinguishable by individual men.

In the cornfield, every stalk was cut short either by a musket ball or a falling body. The air around me was filled with whistling lead and artillery thunderclaps as the Yankees trained their artillery on us. Caissons were split into shards of splintering wood, and the draft horses who pulled them pitched to the ground, whinnying in agony.

Sweat poured down my face, stinging my eyes. I heard the sharp report of a nearby pistol. I wiped my eyes to see a trooper in an act of mercy shooting the horses in the head to end their pain.

The young artillery commander, Pelham, yelled at us to change the range of our guns to fire back at the Yankee batteries that were presently pounding away at us. Firing over a farmhouse caught between the lines continued until Pelham ordered us to stop.

One of my fellow gun mates, Morgan, shouted, "Colonel, we need to stop. There are women and children running out of the house. They're running into our lines of fire."

Along with Pelham and others, I shouted at them to go back to the relative safety of the farmhouse, but they came on, alarmed as they were.

Pelham motioned me and a few others to mount up and ride down toward their flight. "Come on, we must escort them out of harm's way." My horse, Climber, had already been led away by Endicott minutes before, so I just jumped into the saddle of the nearest available horse and galloped down, following Pelham. Approaching a screaming woman, Pelham, in a remarkably calm voice said, "Miss, please, you must go back to the house. Our shells won't harm you."

"No, no! You're going to kill us all," she screamed hysterically.

"No, no, dear woman, our shots fall far from your home. You would be safe there. To continue to do what you are doing will only bring you greater harm. You see, the Yankees have stopped firing, as well," Pelham said, gesturing at their cannons.

I spied a young girl ahead of the others, running toward our silent guns, her little legs pumping furiously and pigtails flying. I kicked my mount's flanks and started after her. Pounding up next to her, I reached down and scooped her into my arms and placed her in front of me on the saddle.

"Let me go! I want my momma! Momma!" she wailed, squirming with all her might as I gamely tried to hang on.

"Quiet, little sister, quiet. I won't hurt you," I said in the most soothing tone I could muster.

She cared not a bit but kept kicking and screaming. My horse snorted, quickly becoming angry with the kicking child and me astride his back. "Look, see? There's your momma right there," I said, pointing at the woman who clung to Pelham's back.

"That's not my momma. That's my auntie," she said plainly.

"Well, I'm sure she is around here somewhere. Let me get you to safety first. Hold on."

"Okay, but I want my momma," she said, sniveling. But she did wrap her arms around my neck and bury her face in my chest, momentarily growing quiet, thank God.

"You stink," she said.

I had to chuckle a bit. I'm sure my clothes reeked of burnt powder, dirt, sweat, and God knows what else. Children are so good at stating the obvious, not hampered by touches of courtesy that we as adults feel.

Once we managed to shepherd the small group to a safer area away from the lines of battle, I eased the little girl down to the ground. The little pig-tailed girl, as quick as can be, ran to another one of the woman gathered there. Aww… back with her momma. I allowed myself a smile, took a deep breath, then wheeled my horse around and started back toward the line of batteries.

Arriving back at the cannons, I noticed that more pieces had been added and now numbered nineteen. Stonewall's men had been battered in the cornfield so that it resembled a rug in a drawing room. A rug of gray-clad unmoving bodies. Stuart and Pelham simultaneously shouted out orders to fire and we poured double canister into the blue masses. It was a relief, surely, for the few of our infantry still alive in that God-forsaken cornfield, for they let out a hoarse roar as the enemy attackers began falling by the dozens and were driven into the west woods.

We were continually forced to move our positions as the enemy cannons searched us out. Upon Stonewall's order, Stuart led a small detachment of us to the enemy's right to figure if it was favorable to an attack.

We rode for a short time until coming upon a farm obstructed by hastily prepared enemy breastworks. Stuart looked at us, sighed, and said to no one in particular, "I believe we have been stopped. There is nothing to be gained here."

We stumbled back to the main body of our army, where I found Endicott and my horse. As the sun began to drop, reports trickled in that miles away, a Yankee attack at Rohrbach Bridge had been repulsed with the arrival of A.P. Hill's men from Harper's Ferry. Unlike any other large battle I had previously seen, each seemingly small skirmish grew into huge fires of fury.

Endicott and I stood wordlessly looking at the miles of carnage that stretched as far as our eyes could see. Smashed weapons and gun carriages, bloody bits of clothing, discarded knapsacks and bedrolls, dead horses, and oh, my God, the corpses of so many men lay rotting on the ground.

The smell of the bodies, vomit, and excrement wafted up to my nostrils. Scores of big black birds circled lazily over the killing grounds before swooping down to pick at the dead meat. Before I could react, I retched. Mouthfuls of foul-tasting bile flowed out, splattering on the ground beside me. I glanced up at Endicott who was holding a lace handkerchief to his mouth. He looked like he was going to follow suit.

Nighttime fell, and an evening's sleep failed to yield any restoration to me. I awoke groggy and in a dark mood, mirroring the darkness of yesterday. On the 18th, we waited for what, I do not know. It was as if Lee was daring the Yankees to attack, but they did not.

I could see the Yankees in the distance, parts of their blue uniforms peeking through the brightly colored autumn leaves of the fruit orchards. They seemed to me no more eager to fight than us, so soon after the hell of yesterday.

A band of the enemy did approach under a white flag of truce with a request to bury their dead, and I'm certain it was granted, for they set to work right away. The day raced through, and before I knew it, night fell again. As the moon rose, a heavy rainstorm commenced. The call to retreat did not catch me by surprise, for I felt certain it would have happened earlier in the day.

Previously, I was confused with the word retreat, but no longer. I had watched the Yankees run at Second Manassas, so I was well versed in the matter, I thought. True, we had taken the war to Maryland, but except for the good people of Urbana, they had rejected the invitation. Demoralized and defeated, we began crossing the Potomac back into Virginia. Stuart kept leapfrogging back and forth over the river, but I did not follow.

I felt the defeat, so after fording the river near Shepherdstown, turned my face to the sky, letting the tears of the angels and the families grieving for the lost loved ones wash over me. I felt a burning in my chest, and thinking I might have a wound, stuck my hand inside my coat to my shirt. It didn't feel wet, and when I pulled out my hand, not a speck of blood appeared. Fishing inside the pocket of my shirt, I pulled out the forgotten photograph I picked up on the Second Manassas battlefield. Damn, if that forlorn little girl didn't look somehow sadder.

 SIXTEEN

The Gaiety at the Bower Initially Escapes Me

I was sick. Heartsick, actually. My very soul felt blackened. After crossing the Potomac, I should have just rode all the way back to Wytheville. Perhaps it was as others had remarked, I was young, maybe too young. But hell, there were drummer boys much younger than I standing in the face of battle. What were the expectations of others upon me? There were not any, as far as I could tell. I liked riding and enjoyed harassing the Yankees on raids like the Great Chickahominy, but jeez, this was wholesale slaughter. The soldiers certainly weren't driven to the darkness any more than me, but maybe they just weathered it better, is all.

While I sat under a lean-to that night, pondering all of it, Endicott Wales, the British journalist, sat quietly next to me, studying my face. "You are troubled, Levon. I can see it," he said.

"I wha—" I said, for he had broken my thoughts.

"Levon, I know we have not spoken at any length. There has not been time for it. But I sense you do not care for me. Is that a fair assessment?" he said.

"I don't know what that word assessment means," I muttered back.

"Calculate, think. Am I right?"

"You are all right, I guess," I lied.

"Exactly," he said. "Care for a cigar? I prefer the pipe, of course." I accepted his cigar while he started packing his pipe. Continuing, he said, "Perhaps your general's orders are not to your liking, but it is an order, as distasteful to you as it may be."

"So?" I challenged.

"And so you do it. At my cousin's house, you indicated as much. You are a soldier so you will follow orders."

"But I'm not, not really."

"You are drawn to the cause, though," he said blowing out a mouthful of smoke.

"I don't know if drawn is the right word for it. I used to think so, but now, now I'm not so sure."

"If you are not drawn, then what? General Stuart placed me with you because you are strong with the cause. At least, that is what he said."

"I don't know. Perhaps it's his expectation. Maybe he was wrong."

Endicott, intent on his questioning, continued further. "Why do you feel his perspective of you is mistaken?"

"I was thrown into this, all of this," I fairly shouted.

"You were drawn into the cause. Drawn is defined as a cause to go in a certain direction."

"Drawn, then, is the wrong word. I, in my foolish mind, thought it was the right direction. Instead of slave catching. Instead of Josiah Wheeler. Instead of participating in the capture of the black man. I felt willing to do some scouting for others who would do the fighting, not me. Maybe I lack courage."

"Okay, let us discuss your feeling that you lack courage for a moment. Who is this man of whom you speak, this Josiah Wheeler?"

"I think I mentioned before that my cousin, Wilson, and I were involved in a group that was loosely defined as a home guard. It was anything but a guard. Josiah Wheeler was the leader because he was the oldest. He wasn't interested in protecting our homes. He was interested in capturing runaways and brutalizing them further. As I watched his behavior become increasingly more violent, I objected."

"Then what happened? After you objected?"

"He turned on me, it seems. I realized later during our last outing that he wished me dead. He sent his assassin; a man named Lo, out with Wilson and I. Lo admitted it to me just before his death."

"Admitted it before his death?"

"Yes, we got caught in a tangle up around Dranesville where he was accidentally kilt. He told Wilson and me as he lay there dying that Josiah wanted me dead."

"So what happened to the delightful Mr. Wheeler?" Endicott asked, his voice dripping with sarcasm and disgust.

"Don't know. Never went back. That's when I decided to join Stuart, and dragged Wilson along with me. Oh no, poor Wilson. It is also my fault he is in prison," I said with labored breath.

"Yes, well, maybe it is as well. Imprisonment is dreadful, but at least he is not fighting."

"I only hope he is still alive. I promised myself I

would stay until he is released. Now I'm scared and not so sure I can even do that. I am a coward."

"No, Levon, you are not a coward. It is correct to be scared. I'm sure all fighting men are. But fear and courage are two different things. I believe you are very brave. You have withstood the greatest danger, that of death, yet you remain. Standing tall through flying shot and shell, bringing their messages of death. You helped man the cannon without question. It was hell up there. Certainly, it cannot compare to what we witnessed in that cornfield, but fearsome all the same. No, you do not lack courage, Levon, you are very brave."

For a time, we did not speak, but smoked. Me on his offered cheroot, and he on his pipe.

"Levon, you know I'm here to report on the Southern cause for the newspapers. Do you mean to tell me you do not believe in the cause? And what of the rest of the Confederacy? Is there no cause at all? I think not. It is that a cause can take many forms. You may have been cast into it, as you yourself say, but something has been ingrained within you. Perhaps it is your cousin's imprisonment which binds you here. But what of the other soldiers? Their cause may be interpreted as the protection of their homes, to fight off the invaders. Preserving their way of life by governing themselves and not ruled by some far off potentate.

I will report to my publishers what I know. There is a cause that I can see. It is as noble as any ever undertaken. I recently received correspondence of a speech given by the esteemed William E. Gladstone, Chancellor of the Exchequer, in which he said, 'We may anticipate with certainty the success of the Southern states so far as regards their separation from the North.' I believe that points to recognition of the Confederacy, at least by my homeland. I intend to continue to promote that. It is, in fact, why I'm here. Levon, let us lay differences aside with the realization that our companionship can be mutually beneficial."

I said nothing, my head down, mindlessly spinning the cylinder of my revolver.

"And, Levon?"

I looked at him through a lank of hair that had fallen in front of my eyes. "Yes?"

"Is it possible you have lost something you are not even aware of? Something you previously had?"

I don't know what he meant, and I was in too foul of a mood to answer, so continued staring at the ground, absentmindedly fingering the hammer of the revolver. I suppose he grew tired of waiting for an answer and wandered away. I continued to cock the pistol until, raising a blister, I laid it down and fell asleep on the grounds of the Bower, the Dandridge family plantation.

Much of Stuart's immediate staff was encamped here, while the rest of the cavalry's line stretched for miles around. I cannot complain, for the Dandridge family were most gracious hosts, and 'twas better to be here than out on the bleak picket lines.

For the rest of September, it seemed like the Army of Northern Virginia was content to reorganize and refit, disinterested in making battle. Apparently, our enemy felt the same way for they made no attacks into Virginia. I was far from ready for fighting, if I was even ever going to be ready again, so I was grateful for the respite. But, forgive me, for I have gotten ahead of myself.

Backing up, it was the morning after our conversation that I awoke and stepped out of my tent into a bright, sunlit day. The ground was still muddy from the rain, and what sky you could see through the overhanging oaks, was blue and cloudless.

I gathered some twigs and attempted to start a fire.

For a brief time, I watched the twigs battle the soggy ground before glancing up. There had been one change in me that I was profoundly certain of for sure. After last night's conversation with Endicott, my irritation with him had vanished. Oh sure, he was still prissy, but he listened to me, and just perhaps he understood me a little more than I cared to admit. Could he help us by his writings? He said he could, and would, so I was in little position to complain.

He was just working his profession, so why could we not ride together, and perhaps he could help. After all, he had guided the horses away during the artillery bombardment and had not protested one bit. He was indirectly involved, and his actions went beyond his job description, certainly.

I went fishing in my pocket for the stub of last night's cigar when, speak of the devil himself, Endicott strolled up.

"Good morning, Levon. I trust you slept well?" he inquired, cocking his eyebrow.

"All right I suppose, and you?"

"Quite fine. A bit wet, but my tent gave almost sufficient shelter. Do you mind if I sit here and try to warm myself by this pitiful fire?"

I looked at the sputtering mess of fire where the twigs gallantly continued their assault on the moist ground. I laughed. "Yes, of course, sit down."

"Let me add this dry kindling and log and see if we can get it sprung to life, as it were. Ahh, yes, there it is," he said, beginning to rub his hands over the growing flames.

We sat on two stumps, pondering the fire, until Endicott exclaimed, "Oh yes, I almost forgot. Before taking leave of my cousin's family, I was able to obtain some very good coffee grinds."

"So, you stole them, then?" I snickered.

Aghast, he fairly shouted, "Of course not. I certainly plan to repay them at some point! The quality is much better than the bitter brew we've had to endure lately. Certainly, you would not refuse these grinds you say I've stolen?"

"Keep your britches on, Endicott. I was having some fun with you, is all."

"I accept your apology. This will be much better," he said, handing me a tin cup.

The mixture of the coffee and smoke of the cigar in my mouth was most pleasant, and I enjoyed it fully. We looked over at the mansion's porch where several members of Stuart's staff pleasantly chatted with what I suppose were members of the Dandridge family.

"I don't understand their gaiety," I said. "I have seen such horrible things. Did they not see the same?"

"Oh, I'm sure they did," Endicott said dryly. "I have a theory about their apparent frivolity, as you call it."

"Gaiety," I corrected.

"Gaiety, then. Remember, Levon, you have not gone through all that they have. By your own admission, you entered this horrid affair after its beginning. How much transpired before you came to be with Stuart, I cannot know. But what they may have endured has hardened them somewhat. What I mean to say, it is possible that what we just witnessed, they have seen before. Perhaps they know it will occur again, so it is better to let go of it for but a short time. To not let go, it seems likely to me, is to invite more darkness. We cannot know how long this will take. Levon, what you are experiencing now is a little of which I spoke last night."

"Meaning?" I said.

"To lose innocence is a hard thing. Perhaps the hardest thing we all have to undergo as we approach maturity, as we grow up. There is not one person alive who does not pine for the carefree days of youth, not one. You might be struggling with it now because of what you have done to this point has been relatively easy. Do not mistake me, you have encountered danger, been shot at, and shot at someone yourself. These are terrible things, indeed, but you have grown from each experience. You are becoming an adult."

"But, I'm young," I protested.

"Older than your years, my boy. Older than your years."

Chiswell fast approached, his visage hard, lips set, and holding none of his usual mirth. He fairly barked at me, "Levon, General Stuart wants to see you, now!"

I stood up and followed him as he stomped ahead, not caring to walk with me, it seemed. It was curious, and I started feeling slightly panicked.

"General, here is Levon," Chiswell said, pulling back Stuart's tent flap. I stepped in. Stuart's face mirrored Chiswell's, hard.

"Sit down, Levon."

"Thank you, General."

"How are you feeling, Levon?" Stuart asked.

"Fine, General."

"Really?" Stuart said, leaning back on a rickety stool.

"Pardon me, sir?"

"Levon, I command many men, as you know. It is impossible for me to know where every man is all the time. You would agree? Do not answer that, for I know your answer. However, since you joined us, you have always been nearby. It is a positive thing that you are, for I can call on you to do many things which need to be executed immediately. Our orders were to cover our retreat, but you were not in sight. Where were you?"

"I crossed the river with the main body, sir," I

stammered.

"Your orders were to stand guard for everyone else. We were to hamper the enemy advance, to provide safe passage for everyone else."

"I have no orders, sir," I said regretting it as soon as I uttered it.

"You damn well do," he said, slamming his hand down on the table separating us.

Furious now, he continued, "That is the problem then. You are either in the Confederate cavalry, or you can go back home."

I began to shrink, and said, "I was afraid. We were in defeat, we had been beaten."

His face began to grow redder by the minute. "We are all afraid from time to time. That fact is undeniable. I am not certain we were beaten. If we were, however, one battle does not a war make. But I need to know that everyone in my command from the lowly cook up to my commanders is strong, will continue the fight! Will continue to victory! Good God, man, where do you stand?"

"Here, I suppose," I said weakly.

"Supposition is not good enough for me, Levon. I must know you can be counted on. I have counted on you before and you have never given me cause to pause. Must I pause now? Decide! Do not use an excuse that you are afraid, or perhaps too young. There are many younger than you who are soldiers. I have need of your services for what is to come, so you must decide."

"I'll stay, General. I will not leave again. I remain at your service," I said, feeling suddenly and surprisingly emboldened.

"Good, Private Lewis. Yes, you are hereby formally in the cavalry. No uniform, no change in duties. And, Levon?"

"Yes, General?"

"Remember, we still need to get your cousin back with us."

Managing a weak smile, I said, "I remember, General. Thank you." That said, I stepped out of his tent and slowly walked back to my own.

There, it was done. No going home, only forward to whatever lay ahead. Endicott still sat by the fire. He stood upon my approach.

"Everything is okay. Am I correct, Levon?"

"Yes, Endicott. I was reminded that I am needed. But, boy, Sharpsburg was really bad. I ain't ever seen nothing like it. Or, at least, not to us."

"So you met with General Stuart. How did it go? Mind you, I'm not asking you about military strategy, which I doubt was discussed anyway, and as you so adamantly pointed out to me previously, strategy is none of my business. I'm asking you for your continued part in this."

"I'm staying put. Soldier on. Soldier…it's funny," I said with a chuckle. "General Stuart said I'm formally in the Confederate cavalry now."

Endicott gazed at me. "A soldier. Commitment, it is an adult responsibility. I thought it was in you."

We spoke no more that morning by the fire. It was in the afternoon that I saw Hampton, von Borcke, and a few others ride toward a hunting range I heard was nearby. The next few days were quiet for me, while the parlor games and what I heard were fabulous meals, continued to occur inside the Dandridge's palatial mansion. I felt no part of it, nor did I wish to be. But that was about to change.

It was in the late afternoon of about October 1st, as I recall, I happened to run into Chiswell, who had returned to his jovial self.

"Hello, Private Lewis," he boomed. "I heard you really are one of us now, congratulations. Now you can participate in drilling and the like," he said with a hint of sarcasm.

I smiled a bit ruefully. "Yes, now I can join you in all those enjoyable things."

He reared his head back in mock astonishment. "You've had nothing to do. Do you not think I have noticed you moping around here like a hound that has been caught sleeping in the hen house while the fox got the whole coop? Tonight, we're going to accompany Jeb to General Lee's headquarters. I think he's afraid others will think he is enjoying himself too much after that mess at Sharpsburg. He's going to take the banjo player, Sweeney, and some other musicians down to Lee's headquarters to give him a serenade. You and I, and a few others, are going along. Endicott, too, if he so desires."

Endicott piped up, "That sounds splendid. I'm in need of some merriment. It has been quite long since I have been amused."

Chiswell looked at me. "All right, it is settled then. We will leave in an hour or so. You best get your pressing affairs in order." He walked away laughing.

We rode away from the towering oaks of the Bower later that evening toward Lee's encampment. The moon hung low and bright, providing at least a dimly lit path all the way. We were kept warm and in good spirits the whole time, more than likely due to the jug of rye that was passed from man to man. I partook of a gulp myself. Now, it wasn't a shot of courage and I didn't choke on it, either. It burned good. Upon arriving at Lee's encampment, we all dismounted, tying our mounts to the picket line.

General Lee didn't come out right away, so the

musicians just played away, and Stuart did a hilarious jig around one of the fires. I must admit, the man does know how to have a good time. Now, we all knew Stuart didn't drink, but I recall that much of his amusement seemed to come in the company of women. There weren't any women here, but there he was, dancing and laughing along with the others. I stood there in a bit of a blur, no doubt from the rye, and just watched. Endicott was there too, right beside me, in fact, watching Stuart with a bemused smile on his face. Lee finally appeared, and glancing around at the scene in front of him, remarked, "Gentlemen, am I to thank General Stuart or this jug for the fine music?"

We all chuckled in response. Stuart remarked, "Well General Lee, pardon me, but you know I don't drink. I find the music can be quite soothing. Soothing the savage beast, I believe is what is said."

"You mean that jig I saw you performing is soothing? I cannot be that old."

"Ah, you caught me, General," Stuart said with a hearty chuckle. "Oh, this fine music can be either soothing or invigorating. The choice is in the listener."

"Well put, General, well put."

These visits were frequent in the first days of October, 1862, but Stuart did not confine them to Lee alone, but Stonewall as well. I don't know why Stuart and Stonewall got along so well, for they seemed so different.

Stonewall was a pious man who neither smoked, drank, nor played cards, and seemed always to be dressed in a drab plain uniform that held no trappings of the military pomp that Stuart seemed to relish. Men that serve in his brigades say he prefers not to fight or march on the Sabbath, but when engaged, is rushing the fight.

Now Stuart, oh, what can I say about Stuart? Yes, he didn't drink, just like Stonewall, that is well known. But he embraces all the pomp the military life affords, or rather, that of a medieval knight as he proclaims with his capes, plumed hat, and golden spurs attached to polished knee high boots. He would never be described as drab. He is flamboyant. So much so that he sometimes irritates other generals. Not so with Stonewall, though. He has known Stonewall since the John Brown affair in 1859, so that is perhaps where their friendship began. Perhaps what bound them together so tightly was that they both loved the fight.

The fondness they felt for each other was never more evident than during an incident that occurred just the other evening. A clamor arose around Stuart's tent, and since I was close, I wandered over. Stuart had just finished proclaiming, "This will make Stonewall the most nattily attired general in the whole army!" while holding a brand new coat with gold braids and lace. He also stood admiring some new trousers and boots from other admirers of Stonewall. The outfit was topped off with a rather smart hat, if I do say so myself. I giggled, and Stuart just beamed. "We must ride over to Stonewall's tonight to present it to him."

We rode over later in the evening. I hadn't exactly been invited, but nobody set to complainin' when I tagged along. We arrived at Stonewall's camp to find him asleep. Curious I was, that Stuart did not seek to awaken him but just crept into his tent. When several hours went by and neither of them appeared, I just bedded down for the evening.

Early the next morning, Stuart joined us at the fire with a slight smile on his face, betraying nothing, Stonewall still did not appear. When Stonewall finally did emerge, Stuart nonchalantly asked the crusty general if that night's sleep had been restive.

I will never forget that moment for as long as I live.

Portraying the same nonchalance as Stuart, Stonewall replied that it had, adding, "But, General, you must not get into my bed with your boots and spurs on and ride me around like a cavalry horse all night." I burst out laughing, as we all did. Stuart ended up spitting out his coffee as he erupted in laughter, as well.

When the laughter died down, Stuart made a great show of presenting Stonewall with his new uniform. Stonewall seemed to shrink to the size of a small boy as he kicked at the dust with one boot, and hanging his head, stammered out an embarrassed thank you. Embarrassed? The great Stonewall, a leader of the fiercest fighting force around? Don't that beat all?

The Yanks did finally get some gumption, and crossing the Potomac opposite Shepherdstown, attacked Rooney Lee's command near Martinsburg. Furious, Stuart pounded out, arriving too late, as the Yankees were busy re-crossing the river. We returned to the Bower, but the relaxation was short lived from what was to come.

SEVENTEEN

The Chambersburg Raid
October 8th — 12th, 1862

Before Stuart left for another meeting with General Lee, our camp was already awash with rumors. Some said that another raid was afoot, while others said they weren't certain if it was another raid, but something big was about to happen. I don't know what caused them their feelings for I felt nothing at all. Stuart returned shortly and went straight into his tent.

It grew late, and I was about to retire when Chiswell rousted me. "No, no, Private Lewis, no sleep for you tonight. Jeb has received orders from our General Lee to raise some havoc in the north. Lee told Stuart to take his best horsemen; the number has been bandied of about 1500, to damage some of the Yankee General "Little Mac's" communications. You are among the best horsemen around."

"What makes you say that?" I said in mock incredulity.

"Now, Levon, I've known you about a year or more."

"So?"

"Word spread around camp, although I don't recall who I heard it from particularly, but that you won the Wytheville County Fair races last year. That right?"

"That's so, but nobody was shooting at me then," I said simply, stating the obvious.

Chiswell drawled, "It has been my experience that horses, once exposed to gunfire, adapt to it to some degree so that shouldn't be a problem."

"Well, my prized horse, Sol's Mistress, never did cotton to the shooting too much before I lost her, but Climber seems to do all right with it, although we have been shot at rather sparingly."

"See, it appears that I am correct."

"So it appears."

Even though it was past midnight, the sounds of a fiddle, banjo, and bones struck up over close to Stuart's tent. I looked at Chiswell quizzically.

Chiswell smiled and shrugging his shoulders. "It's a farewell serenade for the ladies of the Bower. You know how our general is."

I gave him a quick smile. "Yes, I do. I do, indeed," I said, and went to gather my belongings, saddlebags, and such, and fetched Endicott. Endicott was half asleep when I reached him, and I had to shake him quite violently to wake him.

"My word, boy, what is the meaning of this that you should stir me at this ungodly hour?" he said rather gruffly. I should say that gruffly for Endicott was rather mild when placed next to other men. But it was different from his usual speech.

"C'mon, now, Endicott, adventure awaits," I said in newfound gaiety. "We're gonna do some disruptions to the Yanks, although Stuart's plans are rather cloudy to me, almost like secretive."

"Well, fine then, chap. I shall gather myself together this instant and present myself shortly. I will meet you at the horses then?"

"Exactly," I said over my shoulder as I hurried off. I needn't have hurried because we didn't leave till noon, but nobody got much of any sleep. A hum was in the air that fairly shook the leaves of the oaks as we saddled up. I think we all shook a little too. Of course, we all didn't leave at noon, and that caused me a bit of indecision. Columns moved out with a shout, but I didn't know what to do. Stuart wasn't with them, and he had told me to stay close. Hell, he hadn't come out of his tent, and the troopers disappeared through the oaks. Endicott and I just stood there shifting our feet uneasily.

Finally, Stuart emerged, not even batting an eye. His orders had caused a stir, and yet he had an air of nonchalance. His behavior irritated me some, but he was the general, and what he says goes. So, Stuart with his staff, Endicott, and me trotted north to Darkesville and picked up Grumble Jones' brigade. On the road to Hampton's camp at Hedgeville, we picked up Fitz Lee's men, and then Hampton's when we got there. The army grew, along with the excitement, and a tinge of uneasiness. I don't know about the other riders, but I weren't eager to traipse back into Maryland, no sir.

Hedgesville became the rendezvous spot prior to us crossing the Potomac at nearby McCoy's Ferry. Stuart gathered us all around, roundabout 1,800 of us, including four of Pelham's guns and their crews. Glancing around, it seemed this bunch contained more men than went along on the Chickahominy raid. Then Stuart's aides began reciting his orders.

"Soldiers! You are about to engage in an enterprise which, to insure success, imperatively demands at your hands coolness, decision, and bravery." I flushed hot with pride and straightened myself erect in the saddle.

"I expect implicit obedience to orders without question or cavil, and the strictest order and sobriety on the march and in bivouac." I stifled a chuckle as I saw a number of troopers stuffing flasks deep in their saddlebags while others just poured the contents on the ground. Rather regretfully, I might add.

"The destination and extent of this expedition had better be kept to myself than known to you. Suffice it to say, that with the hearty cooperation of officers and men, I have not a doubt of its success. A success which will reflect credit in the highest degree upon your arms. The orders which are published for your government are absolutely necessary, and must be rigidly enforced."

Now, I like nothing more than a raid, if that was what this was. Never a lot of fighting, but a great deal of looting, and may God strike me dead for my sin, but I did enjoy looting. Was not looting theft at its most base? But taking new boots or other articles of clothing or enjoying the sweet taste of a peach, was it really wrong? I was merely taking what the Yankees always seemed to have in plentiful supply, and we did not. I could wrap my mind around the fact that it wasn't really wrong. After all, it was a time of war.

But I shivered a bit when I thought it might be in Maryland. Certainly, it wouldn't be back in Maryland, would it? My stomach did flips when I thought what could await in Maryland, and the flipping was for two widely different reasons. Fear it was. Sharpsburg was horrific, and then there was Lilly. To get over both of them was proving difficult. I wanted to forget

Sharpsburg, but not Lilly, yet, they were both unsettling.

Endicott spoke up, breaking through the fog of my thoughts. "Levon, are you all right?"

"Oh, yes, I was just thinking of something, is all."

"I think Stuart is breaking up the brigades and issuing additional orders, you better go over."

"Of course," I muttered.

I wandered over to Hampton's brigade to hear the orders that followed. A third of each brigade's command was detailed to seize the property of the citizens of our enemy, especially horses, while the remainder be in readiness in case of attack. Receipts were required for citizens whose articles were confiscated. Magistrates, postmasters, sheriffs, and the like were to be arrested to be held as hostages for imprisoned Confederate citizens. The last of the orders brought a sigh of relief. The seizure of private property in Maryland was prohibited. I was a bit confused, though. We were going to cross the Potomac and smack into Maryland. What then?

Although Stuart's plans were shrouded in secrecy, I felt a bolt of lightning shoot through me, and I was eager to get started. I trusted Stuart, as we all did, and so whatever he led us to do, I would follow. Endicott and I began to bed down for the night, however. At least I did, because Endicott was busy scribbling on paper by the light of a dying fire.

Back in the saddle before dawn, we began marching toward the Potomac. I was able to attach myself to the advance guard commanded by Colonel M.C. Butler of the 2nd South Carolina Cavalry as we routed a picket of Illinois cavalry posted on the river's edge with nary a shot. I sat on the opposite bank of the Potomac, smiling in satisfaction as the main body splashed across.

Upon crossing the river, Stuart guided us left toward the Pennsylvania line, eight miles distant. I fought off the ghosts of my Maryland fears because it was apparent we wouldn't be in this state too long. I smiled in relief.

Still, early in the morning, we crossed the familiar National Road west of Clear Spring, Maryland and easily captured a signal station, although a few Yankees did escape. I overheard Stuart in conversation with someone saying that it best we keep moving since McClellan would now certainly be alerted to our presence by either the cavalry that we scattered on the edge of the Potomac, or the signal station escapees. But Stuart's face remained unchanged with his look of nonchalance, simply stating a fact.

As we surged across the Pennsylvania border, I could not contain my joy. It erupted from my mouth, joining everyone else in our party's cheers and shouts.

Announcements of further orders spread through our ranks. "We are now in enemy country. Hold yourselves for attack or defense, and behave with no other thought than victory." These words bounced among the bobbing heads of the horsemen. Endicott had been wearing a slight smile on his face ever since we had started our chorus of shouts and cheers.

"So, Levon, it seems your spirit has risen along with these other fellows," he said.

"Yes, it is good to carry the fight on to the Yankee's country. I do hope that it does not turn as Maryland turned out though."

"From my viewpoint, it seemed like the battle at Sharpsburg was rather thrust on you and the Confederacy. Perhaps if your General Lee's orders had not been, how do I say this delicately, obtained, then you may have had the opportunity to deal with your Northern counterparts much differently. You were put on the defensive, much as a boxer would be trying to survive to the end of the round. But here and now, you are on the offensive, or so it would seem. To continue using the sparring match as an analogy, you are attempting to throw that punch that would knock out your opponent. The keen eye says that this is a surprise, and hopes that it will remain so."

Rubbing my chin in thought, I said, "You seem to be on to something, Endicott. I think Stuart will keep up a rather brisk pace to keep beyond those damn Yanks, who surely know we are abouts anyhow. For me, since this is a raid, I don't expect any large battles to erupt. Mostly dealing with civilians, I think. We may disrupt communications, surely gather horses, which we surely need, and strike some fear into Abe and their capitol. But horses we surely do need, for they are plumb wore down. Even my Climber here," I said, patting my horse on his flank, "suffers from greased heel, so we need the horseflesh."

I'd no sooner said that when I was detached, as were a large number of others, to round up and seize horses for either the cavalry, or for the weaker ones to pull wagons. I rode along with Chiswell as we set to work. The intermittent rain had forced the farmers into their barns, so sometimes it took no more toil than riding up and herding the horses out. Other times, it was simply amusing.

Chiswell and I came upon an old man driving a sorrel mare attached to a cart, and when informed we would be taking his horse, he got angry. He shouted in protest, "I know for a fact, you two, that the impressment of horses is forbidden on orders from Washington. That is the law and I don't care if you are in the military or not. You cannot lay aside the law of the land."

I piped up, "Sir, that would be so if we served the Union. But we do not, so you must kindly turn over your horse to us now."

The old man showed only a hint of disbelief. "Don't try that on me, young man. The rebels wouldn't dare come this far, plus, they would be wearing gray, which you two most certainly are not." Glaring, he continued, "I don't want to spend any more time in such foolery, plus, I'm getting wet. So I will take my leave."

"You may do so, sir, for we wish you no harm. However, your horse is going with us," Chiswell said plainly.

Now the old man set to cursing a blue streak, if you'll pardon the pun, as I unhitched the sorrel from his cart and began leading him away. Chiswell snapped a salute to the man, bade him good day, and we rode away.

At a farmhouse, the owner pleaded with us as I began rounding up his horses. Chiswell, now not amused in the least replied, "This is what we call making solid Union men feel the war."

We charged into Mercersburg, noon time, putting fear into the astonished citizens, but I did no physical damage, nor did anybody else I know, fairly as a fact. I continued with my duties collecting horses, while others did a brisk business with the stores, buying hats, boots, and other clothing with good Confederate money. I did feel a slight pang of sadness when I looked into the faces of the mute townspeople. They said not a word as we looted their town, but looked on in wonder, surprise, and fear. But that pang quickly disappeared when I knew the Yankees had caused much more suffering upon our people.

I lost track of Endicott during that time, being involved in my duties as I was. When we met again on the march out of Mercersburg, he told me he had bought nothing and hadn't disturbed anyone either. I believed him, why would he? He is not fighting for a cause, and is not expected to. Before leaving the city limits, Stuart chided himself for not having me cut the telegraph wires knowing that word may have gone out on our activities. I watched him hurriedly confer with members of his staff, and shortly thereafter, he remounted and began anew.

We were not harassed at all, and by 7:00 pm, we halted outside Chambersburg, Pennsylvania on a moonless and rainy night, October 10th, 1862. I was ordered to join a detail of the 2nd South Carolina to ride out under a flag of truce to demand the surrender of the town.

Leaving Endicott, I passed by Stuart, who muttered under his breath, "Be careful, men, for I fear a trap." We cantered into the center of town, meeting a delegation of terrified citizens who shuffled toward us, downcast.

When they asked for our terms, Hampton replied flatly, "Unconditional surrender."

He promised them that their personal possessions were protected, excepting for those of a military necessity. A military necessity meaning horses, mules, clothing, food, and weapons were going to be ours. I smirked gleefully, unable to hold in a bit of hostility. Once again, we were behind McClellan and were seizing a good deal of his supplies. A victory, perhaps, but without a drop of blood was surely as sweet as the taste of watermelon on a sticky humid night.

The citizens had no choice, glumly surrendering their town, and by 8:00 pm, we had a firm hold on it. I watched with curiosity as one of Stuart's most trusted scouts and guide, Hugh Logan, chatted with a dapper man who was among the delegation of citizens who had met us.

It wasn't that they were talking that was so curious, but the manner in which they did so. Everybody knew that Logan was Pennsylvania born and had lived in the state for a large portion of his life. Off to the side, they seemed to be relaxed and at ease with each other. It was almost as if they were conspirators in some plot they didn't want any others to know of. I wondered whether perhaps it was all very innocent, and they had known each other long before the war that now divided us.

My curiosity was cast aside when Stuart rode in leading the main body into the town square. Very few of the residents would admit to holding office in town, so it took some time before a few minor officials reluctantly admitted their positions and were placed under guard. They would later be exchanged for Confederate prisoners held by their military. All of us spent the next few hours ransacking the stores and warehouses, and of course, collecting horses.

I joined dozens of other raiders in one store, availing myself of all new clothes, for mine were worn or wet, mostly both. I say raiders because that was surely what we were, and there was no longer any doubt. I stripped myself naked right there in the store, being unashamed at all while I pondered the meaning of a raid. This, like any other undertaking, was held under the guise of a military action. I slipped on the red underclothes. I guess some will argue if what we do is necessary. It does not involve killing, but if it damages the enemy, how can it not be necessary? The Union has what we need and I do not see it as wrong to take it. I cinched up blue trousers and went looking for a tunic that would fit. The Yankees have done the same to us and most of what has occurred has been in our country.

So it was as Chiswell had told the complaining farmer, "making the solid Union man feel the war." I found a tunic, overcoat, boots, socks, and a new carbine. The new rifle was one of them repeatin' ones, and I admired the power and polish, for it was unused. I walked out of the store feeling satisfied and met Endicott, who stood solemnly on the walkway. Together, we walked to a bank that stood open. There, Colonel Butler and a few of his men were talking to a cashier who stood in front of open drawers and the vault. They lay empty and the cashier, gesturing excitedly, told Butler that all the money had been spirited away.

"So, you can see, sir, all the money has been removed," the cashier said.

"So it has, and why would that be?" Butler said nonchalantly.

"Well, sir, to keep it secure, of course. We received warning from Hagerstown that you might become active up this ways. Now, while I'm somewhat shocked that you are indeed in town, I have proof that I was prudent to do what I did."

"Indeed, sir. I am satisfied with your explanation of the events which I will relate to General Stuart. If there is nothing else, I will—" Butler was cut short by the cashier.

"Sir, I appreciate your courtesy. May I at least provide you and your men some food as thanks?"

Butler replied, "That is quite gracious, sir. I wholeheartedly accept." As the cashier's womenfolk began to bring out food, Endicott and I took our leave.

We walked aimlessly for a time, getting soaked by the rain all the while. I didn't know quite where to go. We had bivouacked throughout the town, and just outside, as well, so there were many places we could seek out shelter, but I couldn't reason in my mind of where that might be

Endicott broke our silence with his question. "Where to now, Levon? Where should we go? Perhaps we should conduct ourselves toward General Stuart. He may have further orders for you. Would you agree?"

"Yes, you're right, Endicott, of course. Let's mount

up and see if we can find him." Riding through the raw wind and rain, we came to a farmhouse that was being occupied by what must have been twenty or more fellow raiders.

"Maybe he's here. I see some officers about, let's check," I said, dismounting.

"Lead on, Levon."

Nodding to a couple of troopers on the porch, we entered the farmhouse. Inside the cozy parlor, and warmed by a crackling fire, sat several troopers and the mysterious man I'd spied talking to Logan when we entered town. Various periodicals lay about, naturally, all Union, including newspapers from New York and Philadelphia. Prominently featured were also two local newspapers, as well as the Chambersburg Franklin Repository, and Juniata Sentinel. An uneasiness came upon me, from where, I do not know, and only eased a mite when the mysterious man offered us coffee and a seat around the circular table.

I expected Endicott to decline, choosing the ground coffee he had brought along with him. But when I glanced his way, he had turned the pouch upside down, showing it empty of its contents and smiled wistfully. We spent most of the night discussing our differing views with that of our host, while Endicott and he also talked about the various printing and newspaper practices of the times. I quietly sipped my coffee, enjoying the warm pleasant atmosphere that shielded us from the raw weather outside, and as the evening progressed, my caution waned.

Our host was very cultured and it showed in his mannerisms. As Endicott and he conversed, I knew he was intelligent, and when they talked in detail about the printing business, it went right over my head, you know. When Endicott stood, politely asking our host if he could spare some tobacco for his pipe, our host simply pointed to a tin box on the mantle. Endicott and some of the other pipe smokers generously filled their pipes with Killickinick, and after our host's assurances that he did not find smoking offensive, they all lit up simultaneously.

When Endicott sat back down, momentarily satisfied and thankfully quiet, for that man could talk, we steered the conversation back to our interests. The war, I felt, an issue which I could intelligently speak of, came back up.

Someone's staff officer said, "Surely you must agree, sir, that your country has had little to no success against ours."

"To this point, I would agree. However there is no hope for the unity of the North unless it has asserted its military mastery over the South. To be defeated by inferior numbers would simply demoralize and disintegrate the North. If, instead of a republic, we are to break into principalities, then its promotion is anarchy. The North cannot allow the South to leave."

I was set to object about halfway through his statement but stopped short when his last words rang of some sense. If what we ultimately would achieve through our victory was no government, then would we really accomplish anything? It set me brooding right away while more raiders entered and left, then the talk moved on to the Emancipation Proclamation.

I answered my own question not soon after. But, of course, we did not fight for any government at all, but only the right to govern ourselves. Yes, the republic might be less loosely joined if we were all to be reunited as the host had said, but if the Confederacy was a nation unto itself, would it not still be a united republic? Endicott and I decided to take our leave, but I cannot for the life of me think why. We would leave the warm comfort of this man's home to enter the brace of oncoming winter? I guess it was the polite thing to do, and besides, we were the enemy. As we walked out the door, I had to admit that our mysterious host had been as gracious as most of the finer Southern homes I had visited in my youth. Home, would I ever see it again?

Endicott and I found a suitable place in the man's yard and bedded down among brothers of ours who were already there. Awakening the next morning, and after a short breakfast, we once again went to seek out Stuart. The ransacking of the stores and warehouses lying amid the red brick houses of Chambersburg continued in earnest.

Just by chance, we encountered Stuart astride one of his horses, Skylark, in the middle of the town looking slightly annoyed.

"Ah, there you and Mr. Wales are. I'm glad to have you about. I may have need of you soon. I have just been informed that we have failed to destroy the bridge over Conocheague Creek being that it is made of iron and not wood. We must leave this lovely little town, because I'm quite sure by now that Little Mac has been alerted to our presence. Apply the torch!" he shouted, and the government depot, railroad machine shops, and a warehouse stocked with ammunition, quickly burst into flame. The sound of the exploding ammunition trumpeted our departure from the town, and I'm aware that the citizens surely sighed in relief.

What Stuart did next clearly perplexed me because it didn't make a lick of sense to me at the time. He directed us east out of Chambersburg toward Gettysburg. I thought we would just go back the way we came. My confusion was cleared when Stuart motioned Captain William Blackford, Endicott, and I to ride alongside him.

"Blackford, I want to explain to you my reasons for selecting this route; and if I do not survive, I want you to vindicate my memory. "Scribe," he said, pointing at Endicott. "I wish for you to hear me as well, so that what I say is not translated or perverted either, but to be doubly noted."

Endicott replied rather solemnly, "I understand, General."

We halted and he pulled out a worn map before continuing. "You see, the enemy is sure to think that I will try to re-cross above, because it is nearer to me and further from them. They, I assume, will have all the fords strongly guarded in that direction, with scouting parties on the lookout for our approach so they may concentrate to meet us at any point. They will never expect us to move three times the distance and cross at a ford below them, and so close to their main body. Therefore, they will not be prepared to meet us down there. Do you understand what I mean? Do you think I am right?"

Blackford said, "I understand, General. I, for one, do not doubt your command of the situation. If it should need to become known because of necessity, I will recite exactly what you have said. Beyond that, I believe your choice is wise. I think I speak for all in this command that you have our complete trust."

Stuart briefly looked at me and I nodded my agreement. "Let us continue then," he said, and we rode on. Stuart ordered the advance guard to turn right toward Hagerstown to mislead the enemy. We rode several miles, veering southward toward Emmittsburg, Maryland. Unlike scant days ago, I was actually relieved to cross back into Maryland. Closer to safety, I suppose. Stuart issued orders to stop collecting horses once back into Maryland, not only because we didn't want to create any havoc, but our train of captured horses stretched several miles as well. Stuart continued guiding us with caution, admonishing the column to keep together and the advance guard to watch for solitary figures on the road, lest there be spies about.

We reached Emmittsburg before nightfall, where we enjoyed the hospitality of the pro-Confederate citizens of the town. I hurriedly dismounted and was given food and water. Even my horse, Climber, was watered. The reception was brief for we had to keep moving. A little boy ran up to me, snatching a button off my coat before dashing off.

Stuart learned from some of the Emmittsburg citizens that less than an hour before us a company or two of Union cavalry, known as Rush's Philadelphia Lancers had come through town in search of us, of course. We angled southward as if headed towards Frederick. Another ace from the stack of cards Stuart played to throw off our pursuers. Pelham and Southall captured a Yankee courier whose dispatches indicated that a strong Union presence lay in Frederick, while Union General Pleasanton with 800 troopers was moving northward along the same road we were now on!

Stuart, seemingly without a care, at least to my eye, simply returned to our original route running through Rocky Ridge, Woodsboro, Liberty, New London, and New Market, all well east of Frederick. We struck out on the road toward Woodboro when another amusing incident occurred on a trip that was full of such moments.

I was riding along with Stuart and Wales near the head of the column when we ran smack dab into a buggy driven by a Union officer going in the opposite direction. Enraged the officer yelled, "Get out of my way. Move to the side and let me pass."

Stuart and I rode up and reined in, Stuart clearly bemused.

The Union officer bellowed, "You are in command of these men?"

Stuart replied simply, "Yes, sir."

"Well get them out of the way. I'm a recruiting officer and I'm on the way to fill my quota."

Stuart leaned over and whispered in my ear "I never dreamed that the blue uniforms we are wearing would present themselves as a treasure so quickly, or at such an opportune time. Take over his reins." Hopping down from Climber and jumping on the bench alongside the officer, I jerked the reins out of his hand.

The Union man howled, "What are you doing? This is an outrage."

Stuart rode up close, and smiling broadly, said, "You are now a prisoner of mine. I'm Jeb Stuart, and you will now have to recruit Confederates for your precious Little Mac."

We rode some ways, the stunned Yankee beside me not uttering so much as a peep. Not wanting to ride in the buggy any longer, I bribed Endicott to take over and he happily obliged.

With some of our party who were natives of the region guiding us, we passed through Hyattstown which, incidentally, was only a few miles south of Urbana. Stuart again reined up and motioned for Captain Blackford, Endicott, and I to drop out of the column and join him on the side of the road.

Stuart, with a characteristic sparkle in his eye, for he was never uncharacteristic when speaking of women, asked Blackford, "How would you like to see the, "New York Rebel" tonight?"

Blackford, taken aback, said, "Well, of course. That would be delightful."

Stuart turned his attention to Endicott and myself. "Levon, I seem to remember that you were quite enamored of a certain young lady, one of Mr. Wales's cousin's family. I believe her name was Lilly."

"Well, I, uh, I mean," I sputtered.

Laughing, Stuart continued. "It's okay, Levon. I will give orders for Mr. Wales to be divested of the carriage and given a horse so you two can visit the family. Mr. Wales, you have no objection, I presume?"

"Not at all, General. You are most gracious to ask," Endicott replied.

"It's settled then. Give the buggy to the wagon train and I will have one of our captured horses saddled up."

Not much later, the four of us galloped west away from the main body toward Urbana. "Now, Levon, you and Cousin Endicott will have just a short while before returning to the column. You will be able to find them, I'm sure," Stuart said over his shoulder as he and Blackford trotted through Urbana. Endicott found the Greene household and we reined up in front of the darkened house. It was just about midnight, I figure.

"What do we do now?" I asked.

"We will knock on the door, of course."

Endicott dismounted and walked to the door, rapping on it rather loudly, I thought. Not but a short moment later, I saw the shadow of a lit candle dance behind the closed curtain. From the upstairs window, Mr. Greene peered out and growled, "Who goes there?"

"Cousin Endicott, Jonathan, and I've brought along a friend."

"A Union soldier, Endicott?" I had forgotten that I wore the full uniform of a Union soldier.

Endicott laughed. "No, nothing like that. It is Levon, is all. He just had a…" he said with a cough, "change of clothes." I heard Lilly's voice float down from the upstairs, "Did he say Levon, Daddy? Did Cousin Endicott say he brought along Levon? I must see him. Is it okay, Daddy, please?"

"Yes, child, you may, but bundle yourself up. I don't

want you to catch a chill from the night air, unless they can come in."

"I'm afraid not, Mr. Greene. We must be going back to the main column's march. We can only stay awhile," I said more coolly than I had intended.

In an instant, Lilly was rushing out the door, ignoring Endicott and running right up to me. She grabbed my leg as I was still mounted and murmured, "Oh, Levon." Suddenly, I felt lightheaded.

"Lilly, it is so good to see you again." It was all I could muster, trying to remain the gallant warrior. For several moments, we said nothing, but stared into each other's eyes.

"I was so afraid for you. We heard of the terrible fighting at Sharpsburg. I was worried you would be hurt, or worse," she said, her gray eyes slightly welling and bottom lip trembling.

Taking her hand in my gloved one, I said, "It was the most terrible thing I have ever seen. It is my wish to never see so much carnage again."

"But, Levon, you have fought before," Lilly said.

"Fought, yes, and there was bloodshed, and undoubtedly there will be more, but…"

"Yes, Levon?"

"It was the most savage slaughter I have seen, and although I am physically unhurt, I have trouble ridding it from my thoughts."

As her gray eyes bored into mine, she asked somewhat acidly, "So, what are you doing now?"

"We are coming back from another raid. We went all the way around McClellan again," I said stiffly.

"Did you not kill this time?"

"We did not! We ransacked stores and grabbed horses, and generally scared the bejesus out of some of the town folk of Pennsylvania, but that is all. I did not kill anyone."

"I'm sorry, Levon. But when will it all stop? When will you stop?"

"When we are free to govern ourselves, and only then. But, Lilly, must we be so harsh toward one another?"

"You're right, Levon. We should not be so toward one another. I'm sorry, but I'm so afraid for you."

"Do not worry, my lo…," I stopped in mid-sentence, mindful of what I had almost said.

"What, Levon? What did you say?" Lilly said a little breathlessly.

"Nothing, I said nothing. Endicott we must go. Come on," I shouted, starting to wheel Climber around.

"Levon, don't you dare pull away from me like that!"

"What?" I began to ask when Lilly, clinging to my leg, reached up, and grabbing my face in her hands, kissed me.

"Lilly, your father is right there." And indeed, he was on the front steps glaring at me.

"Blast my father, Levon. You will see me again," she commanded, stamping her foot for emphasis.

"That I will, with orders like that," I said, smiling at her demeanor.

"But we must go now, Endicott," I continued.

We departed from the Greene family and headed back to the main column. Reaching the column only eight miles from the Potomac River, I began to get rather sleepy. Our entire party was fighting fatigue. Hell, I rode past several troopers asleep in their saddles. Stuart, however was tirelessly talking to Confederate sympathizers and scouts who were familiar with the area, darting from one road to another, mindful of what I believe he thought were the yet unseen Union pursuers. We rode all night until finally meeting the enemy at 8 o'clock on the morning of the 12th.

A band of Yankee cavalry watched us approach, coming out of the woods near Poolesville.

I was curious as to why they weren't attacking us on sight. Of course! Once again, I had forgotten that we were still wearing the blue overcoats, so they thought we were fellow Union cavalry. Stuart, noting their hesitation, screamed, "Charge!" And I galloped along with the 1st Virginia towards the surprised Yanks. They did the only thing they could and quickly scattered.

Stuart ordered Colonel Butler, manning one cannon and a detachment, to act as the rear guard as the main body started across the river. I kicked Climber's flanks and lurched forward, splashing over the Potomac, which was no more than a stream at White's Ford. After making it across, Stuart became visibly agitated, which I have said before, is rare for him.

Stuart shouted, "Blackford we are going to lose our rear guard!"

Blackford responded, "How is that, General?"

"Why, I have sent four couriers to Butler and he is not here yet, and see, there is the enemy closing in behind us!"

"Let me try it!" Blackford shouted back.

Stuart extended his hand. "All right, and if we don't meet again, good bye, old fellow."

With that, Blackford sped off. I just sat there, dumbfounded. I should have gone in Blackford's stead, for he was too valuable for Stuart to lose, but they had made quicker decisions and I was too slow to follow. Time slowly crept by until suddenly, Butler, his men, and that lone cannon came splashing across as the bullets of both Yank cavalry and infantry whizzed over their heads. Some of our artillery pounded away at our pursuers as everybody made it across to the Virginia side of the river.

We all broke out cheering at our success, even Endicott, who was politely clapping. I smiled at his behavior. What a strange man. Only an observer, he felt more like one of us. Riding gaily to Leesburg where we camped, I thought of what our entire raid had accomplished.

Over a thousand horses, about, um, 30 or so civilian prisoners, over 300 enemy soldiers paroled, property in the form of clothing and weapons, and a great amount destroyed as well. The Richmond Dispatch later trumpeted, "All honor to General Stuart and the brave boys that assist in upholding his banner."

Camping at Leesburg that evening, and then heading back to the Bower, the views of the raid varied widely. I shared the view of many others who said it was the greatest of all time, while others dismissed it as pure foolishness. One of the troopers in the 3rd Virginia, who coincidentally had not participated in the raid, remarked that it was just another one of Stuart's foolish raids that resulted in more horses being broken down than captured, and even Wade Hampton added that the raids to be no more than glorified horse raids with little military importance. Hampton has always been at odds with Stuart, and I pledged to never ride under his command.

 EIGHTEEN

Winter Brings Sorrow

The Fredericksburg Line

My mind was heavy with thoughts that whirled around in my brain as we made our way back to the Bower. I didn't realize how fleeting was the time that I must come to grips with them.

Lilly Greene was upmost in mind simply because I could not figure out why she affected me so. When I am in the presence of her gray eyes, it is hard to catch my breath, and my tongue seems to be tied up in knots. Certainly, I couldn't be in love with her, for God's sake, I barely know her. But yet, from time to time, she comes to mind, and as I watch the brilliant artillerist Pelham romance Sallie Dandridge once we were back at the Bower, it just seems worse. Envy, I guess.

"Why is it, Levon, that when you are with my cousin Jonathan's family, and particularly his daughter, Lilly, you revert to the shy schoolboy you must have been prior to joining Stuart?" Endicott inquired one day as we strolled through camp.

Faking ignorance, I replied, "What do you mean by that?"

"You act like a boy wearing short britches rather than trousers, or are you trying to act like a man of few words, which most assuredly you are not?" he said, goading me.

I felt my face grow hot under his attack. "I—I just can't," I said, embarrassed.

"Look, my boy. It is apparent to me, as it must be to others as well as her, that you are somewhat smitten with her. Why can you not express yourself in some small way?"

"Because, what will people think of me? They will say, 'He is too young. He doesn't know her, or she him.' Besides, it would not be proper!"

"Proper?" Endicott fairly exploded. "Levon, love is not proper. In fact, love is beyond description of any sort. Scholars, poets, musicians, and more, down through the ages have been unable to define or describe it. Did Cleopatra not love at first Julius Caesar, and then Marc Antony? Did Paris not love Helen of Troy, or did Sir Lancelot not love Queen Guinevere? Who can truly say? Who can truly question it? It is preposterous!"

"I—I…" I stammered.

Once again, Endicott cut me off. "Has it not occurred to you that sweet Lilly has feelings for you, as well? She showed it to you. She opened her soul to you and you quickly rebuffed her. But I heard you almost utter it in the doorstep of my cousin's house. You began to utter the word love before stopping yourself. What is your defense to that?"

"I have no defense to it. I admit I almost said it. But I did not." Then, partially lying, I said, "I have more important things to attend to."

"We will re-examine it, I say."

"Re-examine it on your own time. Once again, I have other worries."

I left Endicott there and proceeded to the corral to check on Climber, who had been limping badly on the way back from the raid. Sores erupting on his forelegs from the "greased heel" affliction had staggered him, and truly, many of the horses were played out.

Approaching Climber, I stroked his flank and muzzle. "Poor boy. You have done so well for me. What will I do with you?" That damn horse just looked at me with mournful eyes as if in understanding, and saying I had done my best.

"Sir?" I turned to see a small boy with tousled hair standing next to me.

"Yes, boy?"

"Sir, your horse is sick, as you can surely see. I can heal him, sir, and you can ride another."

"Really? What makes you think you can heal him? Do you have magical powers or something?"

"Magical, no. But living here, I have watched my father treat a good number of horses. As you can see, our family has the finest horses, and you can have your pick of the herd you brought in," the boy said as he chewed on a blade of grass.

"What makes you think I can just pick a horse out of those captured?" I asked.

"Well, now, I know you didn't bring those horses along to just have them feed on our grain. Plus, I heard some of the other soldiers say they had to turn out their mounts, so I guessed you could do the same. You are one of General Stuart's men, aren't you?" he said, sizing me up.

"Yes, I'm one of General Stuart's men. So, do you see

any of the horses we brought in as fitting for me? You having a keen eye of horseflesh," I said somewhat sarcastically.

Ignoring my sarcasm, or perhaps not catching it at all, he pointed down the picket line at a long-legged bay. "She seems to have a lot of spirit. She's been kicking up a ruckus the whole time she's been here. I bet she's fast, too."

"I'll take your advice. She seems, at first glance, to be a fine choice."

"Mister, you don't need but one glance. I'm taking your horse out of this line and taking him to the barn." He departed without another word, leading Climber by a tether. I walked over to the bay, and patting her on the rump, introduced myself to her, as much as you can introduce yourself to a horse. I walked away satisfied I had found a new mount. The horse cast a look of disgust my way as I walked away.

In the early dusk of the evening, I found my way to Endicott who was talking with none other than Hugh Logan, the Pennsylvania born scout. It was a proper time, I think, to question him about his curious behavior in Chambersburg.

Endicott hailed my approach. "Levon, where have you been?"

"I was acquiring a new mount. Climber is played out. What are you two up to?"

"I was having a pleasant chat here with Mr. Logan, having never formally met. I remember him from the raid, but that is all. I'm familiar with his face, but not his name or the make of the man."

"The make of the man, you say, Mr. Wales? What a peculiar thing to say," Logan quipped.

"Oh, I don't think it is peculiar at all," I said. "It is important to know what a man is all about, Logan," I said, trying not to squint suspiciously.

"What do you mean by that?" Logan snapped.

"I found your behavior in Chambersburg somewhat peculiar, that's the word you used, but I found it, well, curious."

"What are you getting at Levon?" Logan bristled.

"What I'm getting at is that you seemed quite friendly with one of the citizens from the delegation."

"It's none of your business, Levon. Leave it alone."

I ignored him and pressed on. "Come to think of it, Endicott, you were rather friendly with that gentleman when we were in his parlor that evening not two days shy."

"Did you forget that we drank his coffee, smoked his tobacco, and stayed out of the raw winter weather? It would have been impolite to be anything but completely friendly to such a gracious host."

"You are right. But you talked about the printing business as if you were fast friends. It's curious, as well, but, Logan, I don't remember you being in the parlor. What is your bond with that man?" I said, jabbing my finger at him.

"I said, stay out of it," Logan said, taking a menacing step toward me.

"My word," Endicott said in astonishment, raising his fingers to his lips.

I shrank back. "What's going on? What are you afraid of, Hugh? Who is he?"

Logan answered gruffly, "What I know can get people hurt or killed. It might get me killed for not identifying who he was right then."

"Well, who was he? Surely he couldn't be that important that you knowing him would get you killed. You got to agree that there is way too much pointless killing going on."

I stole a glance at Endicott. "What is he talking about? Do you know who that man was?"

Smirking, Endicott said, "I have a good inkling of who he was."

"Did anyone else notice me with him, Levon?'

"I don't think anybody else noticed, no."

"All right. I will tell you who he was, but not a word to anyone else ever. I will slit your throat if it gets out. Do you understand?"

"Not a word," I said, shuddering.

"He is Alexander McClure." I heard Endicott sigh.

"Why is he important?" I asked.

"Not only is he the editor and publisher of a few of the local newspapers, but also a Union officer. If others in our raid had known who he was, he would have been arrested with the other town officials."

"And, Endicott, you knew who he was?"

"As I said, I had an inkling. A few of the papers had a name under the masthead. When we talked so intelligently about the printing business, I felt somewhat certain it was him."

"But why didn't you say anything, Hugh? You said yourself that not revealing who he was could get you killed?"

I saw Hugh noticeably relax. "Before the war, Mr. McClure helped me through a legal matter. Besides, being an editor, he is also a lawyer. I feel that I owe him some courtesy. I told him; no, I promised him, that I would protect him."

"Oh, Hugh. Oh well, it is of little or no importance, not really. I will keep my word. I will not say a thing."

"Thank you, Levon, Endicott," he said with a nod. "I bid you two good night." As he walked away from the campfire, my concerns of the last few days went with him.

On the 30th of October, 1862, following Lee's orders, Stuart led us toward the Yankees who had crossed the Potomac heading toward the Rappahannock. Stuart was both deliberate and decisive in preventing the enemy from driving a wedge between Stonewall and Longstreet, who were to come together below the Rappahannock.

Now, I don't pretend to know what is in the minds of those at the top of both armies, but it seems to me that they were both itching for a clash that would dwarf Sharpsburg. Stuart, as he often does, eagerly provided the match that would grow into a raging inferno. Starting on the 31st of October, riding with Stuart, who was commanding both the 3rd and 9th Virginia, we ranged east from Snickersville pouncing on one of McClellan's exposed outposts at Mountsville, and rolled them up with little resistance. While kept busy rounding up the prisoners at Mountsville, Pelham and his support engaged in an artillery duel at Aldie.

The fire grew into the expected inferno on November 2nd, when we were attacked near Ashby's Gap Turnpike, between Paris and Upperville, while covering A.P. Hill's front. As fierce fighting broke out over a field broken up by stone fences, Stuart ordered me and other scouts to find out what we could of the Union advance. How large was the advance, and where was it coming from.

I put the heel to my new horse that I had named Spirit, and dove into the underbrush and pines. I carefully picked my way through the trees as the long ago spoken words of Redmond Burke flooded into my head. Hear what others cannot. See and understand what presents itself when viewing the enemy. Are they dispirited or eager to fight?

After picking our way through the trees for what must have been a half hour or so, I heard it. The sounds of horse hooves pounding along a road. It sounded like a large body, and moving very rapidly. I eased closer for a look, stroking Spirit's muzzle to sooth her, and hopefully prevent her from snickering out a welcome.

Through the trees, I glimpsed the color of the uniformed riders. They were blue, no doubt about it. I eased Spirit around and made my way back to Stuart at a full gallop.

"General, there's a long line of Yank cavalry coming from Leesburg," I shouted to Stuart as I reined up.

"Damn them Yanks. We must withdraw."

Oh, we withdrew all right. But Stuart's Horse Artillery made our pursuers pay a heavy price. Upon my news, we withdrew to Middlesburg. Camping near Ashby's Camp, I joined Stuart in riding over to Stonewall's command for a meeting on our next move. Stuart immediately joined Stonewall in his tent. What they discussed, I don't know. Left outside, I remained mounted, shivering under the cold wind that blasted the area. I tugged up the collar of my overcoat and pulled a slouch hat low, leaving only my eyes exposed.

After an hour or so, Stuart left the tent and we returned to Barbee's Crossroads in silence. Stuart's gaze glowed orange as he became enraged after receiving a message that McClellan had slipped behind us, and now occupied Warrenton.

"To hell. They have more horses, more munitions, and more soldiers than we! Always, they keep coming, but I will not, for one instant, believe they will outdo us. Each man in our army is worth 10 of theirs. I will not be embarrassed or outfoxed!"

Endicott and I experienced a catch in our throats during Stuart's brief tirade. Stuart's command was scattered, and when we regrouped at Orleans, found that McClellan's occupation of Warrenton was false. Stuart returned to relative calm and our columns crossed the

Rappahannock on the Waterloo Bridge, as we made our way to Culpepper where Lee's headquarters were located.

Endicott wandered off, leaving me to take care of our horses. My new mount, Spirit, had performed rather admirably. Sure-footed when we had picked through the trees where I had sighted the Yankee cavalry coming from Leesburg, to the long stride shown everywhere else. I have to admit, I have been lucky with my mounts. Riding Sol's Mistress was like riding on a cloud, an effortless, easy gait and manner, while Climber had a short choppy stride that had been just the thing when I eluded the enemy patrol on the way to Longstreet. Spirit was true to her name. Hard to handle, sure, but when there was a job to do, she sure knew it was and went right to work. I brushed her down, and putting a blanket over her, went in search of Endicott, and hopefully, a warm tent. Approaching Endicott, I saw with dismay that he was not in a warm tent at all but out in the awful weather, standing with two gentlemen I didn't know.

"Ancient mariners refer to it as the calm before the storm," I heard him say as he gestured across the way.

"Indeed, that would seem likely, Mr. Wales. They seem to be glowering at each other over the river," one of the gentlemen replied.

"Enough of that for now, Francis. The young man I've been speaking of is here. Levon, I would like to introduce you to two of my associates in the editorial business. This man on my extreme left is Francis Lawley, a reporter for the Times of London." Mr. Lawley extended his hand and I shook it politely. "And this cad here is Frank Vizetelly, an artist and correspondent for the Illustrated London News."

"Cad, you say, Endicott? I don't believe I've earned that moniker," Vizetelly said with a grin. "Mr. Levon Lewis, I presume," he continued shaking my hand.

"I am, sirs. I'm sure what little Endicott has told you about me is mostly enlarged, and likely untrue."

"Not at all, young man. He says he is blessed with the opportunity to watch you grow into the proud soldier of the Confederacy we see before us," Lawley snorted.

"I don't know about that," I said, hanging my head with embarrassment.

"Mr. Lewis, to grow in such a remarkable time is nothing to be embarrassed about," Lawley said, noting my behavior.

"I guess not," I said weakly.

Endicott interrupted. "What I wanted to let you know, Levon, is that I have been communicating with these two and they have published flattering reports of Stuart back in England. They feel certain, as I do, that your Confederacy is soon to be recognized by our country. In addition to our praise of Stuart, these two gents have been effusive, not only in their praise of Stuart, but General Lee, who they are accompanying, and your cause, as well."

"Effusive?" I asked.

"Telling everyone," Endicott said with slight disdain. "Anyway, these two gents have told me that General Stuart has been so appreciative of their flattering reports of him, well deserved, I might add, that he has furnished them with the buggy that the Union officer was only too glad to loan us. You do remember the buggy of which I speak, do you not, Levon?'

Laughing heartily, I replied, "Yes I do. Gentlemen, it has been pleasant speaking with you, but I believe I will get out of this weather and into the tent.

The cold that followed the next morning was not the kind that could be warded off by donning more clothes. Chiswell was walking toward me with a rather grim look, and Endicott strangely just seemed to drift away from our tent.

"Hello, Chiswell. I'm glad to see you. With everything that has been happening, I have not had time to catch up with you," I said cheerfully. His dark look did not change one bit. "What has happened, Chiswell?" I said.

"Come with me, Levon, let us walk awhile," Chiswell said, placing a brotherly arm over my shoulder.

"Redmond Burke has been killed," Chiswell said. I winced as if I had been shot myself.

"This cannot be. How did it happen? What happened?" I cried with the feeling of the wound to my heart.

"He and his sons were ambushed on the evening of November 24th on their way back to Stuart. Believing they were safe in Shepherdstown, they stopped at a house for the night. He was betrayed by Union loyalists there. His loss is felt as deeply by all of us who have served with him, as it is by you. I wanted to be the one to tell you. I know you and your cousin, Wilson, considered him your teacher."

"Yes, we did," I said quietly.

"You do still think about your cousin, don't you?"

"Sometimes, but not enough I think. We have gone through so much since he was captured. I don't know if he is still alive or free."

"Hmm," Chiswell said. "Let me talk with Stringfellow who has some dealings with 'the secret line.' Perhaps through his contacts in Washington, he can find out how your cousin fares."

"By talking to Sil Burrows?" I exclaimed.

"Who?"

"Sil is a girl who visits Old Capitol Prison. She spies on the Yankees and tries to help the Rebel prisoners. She helped me when Wilson and Mosby were captured."

With a queer smile Chiswell ended our conversation. "Perhaps."

I wandered rather aimlessly through camp in a daze until I was almost on top of Stuart's tent. I don't know if I planned to talk with him, or what I was going to say. It is to say, I was not even really aware of it. But a sob from inside the tent stopped me.

A voice, clearly Stuart's, said, "I will never get over it, never."

Beginning to turn away, I was startled when one of Stuart's aides, Captain Cooke, emerged, dewy eyed. Of course, I don't know what had sent me towards Stuart's tent in the first place, and I'm sure Cooke thought I might have been eavesdropping.

"Private, what is it I can do for you? You cannot see General Stuart right now, if that is your intent," he said.

"I'm not quite sure why I'm here, sir. I truly don't. I've just heard of Burke's death, and, sir; I'm quite struck by it."

"So have all of us, young man. Stuart, although, feels it as deeply as any. It is his burden to be touched by the bird of sorrow twice."

I arched my eyebrows in question. "Stuart has found out that his daughter, little Flora, has died. It is as if God has sought to test Stuart's strength of faith. You know, we all are tested, and always will be, at least as long as this persists. But you can plainly hear that our General is too grief stricken to see anyone right now."

"I understand," I mumbled, then staggered away.

The days tumbled onward in a somber blur. Of course, the death of Burke was felt only by those who knew him in Stuart's command. But the general mood of the Army of Northern Virginia hung in the air and mingled with the fog. It didn't seem so bad in the cavalry, except for the shortage of suitable horses, but to ride through the infantry painted a picture that was far more bleak. Our soldiers resembled forlorn scarecrows run down with sickness, lack of food, clothing, and foremost, maybe, lack of rest. But here, we all were massed above the river and the town of Fredericksburg, showing every bit of defiance that could be summoned against the better fed, better clothed, and a larger number of foe on the opposite shore.

One morning, several of us who had been acting as pickets and scouting the Union advance, took many of the horses down to the river's edge to water them. Many would ask, is it not dangerous since you are surely in range of a musket shot? Strange, it would seem, that men bent on killing each other would at times refrain from doing just that. Sometimes a flag of truce would accomplish that, such as when the litter bearers came to pick up the bodies of the dead and wounded, but other times such as this, it was simply understood.

I jumped down off of Spirit and led her and several others to the river's edge where they immediately dipped their heads to drink. Pulling erect, I looked at the men in blue across the way. Their stares were not filled with hate, just placid. A couple emerged from wherever they had hidden and approached.

"Hey, Johnny Reb, I hope you are going to be so very gracious when we come into your homes in Richmond."

"I don't live in Richmond, Yank, and as for being gracious, I think I speak for all of us when I say we will be as gracious as can be with you in chains."

One bearded Yankee, leaping from rock to rock that protruded from the river's surface till he was several feet from the far bank, laughed in response. "Well now, Reb, is that any way to treat us who come to save you from your evil ways?"

I laughed back, "Save us from our evil ways, huh?

You boys invaded our country, and the only way you'll see Richmond is when we capture you."

We then just stood there real genial like, really.

"Want to make a trade, Johnny Reb?"

"Trade what?" I asked.

"I sure could use some fine tobacco of yours for my pipe. What do you say?"

"I don't have any, but perhaps one of the others does. Walt, you got any tobacco we can give to our friends in blue?"

Walt replied, "Give them Billy's some of my tobacco? What are they gonna give us in return?"

The Billy replied, "How about some coffee? Would that do?"

"And a newspaper or two?" I piped up.

"Now, Johnny, why would you want some of our newspapers?" the Billy said suspiciously.

Mustering as much indifference as I could, I replied, "I want to know what you all think, is all. Can't say I figured it out just yet."

"I don't need any damn Yank reading material, Levon." Walt hollered.

"Oh, c'mon Walt. I'll pay you back."

Walt finally agreed with some grumbling.

"Got a deal, Reb?"

"Got a deal," I replied.

"I got a small little raft I put together here. How bout I send you some coffee beans and periodicals in a burlap sack, float it over to you, and you float some of that fine tobacco back across?"

"That'll be fine." He pushed his little makeshift raft toward me. It bobbed on the gentle ripple of the current and I was able to grab hold of it while standing on two rocks. I exchanged the burlap sack with Walt, and he gave me a small pouch of tobacco.

"Now, don't get it wet, Johnny. It doesn't light real easy," the Billy chuckled.

"All right, all right, I'll wrap it in my coat." I shed my coat, wrapped it around the pouch of tobacco, and gently pushed the raft back toward him.

With the butt of his rifle, the Billy guided the raft back to himself and eagerly reached into the pouch. Cradling his rifle in the crook of his arm, he fished his pipe out, stuffed and lit it.

He drew in a long smoke, then exhaled it slowly. "Ahh, there isn't nothing finer on all of God's green earth."

I fished one of the periodicals out of the bag as Walt examined the beans, and there it was.

MCCLELLAN TO BE REPLACED was emblazoned across the front page.

"Hey, Billy," I said. He met my gaze. "Going to replace your general, huh? You tired of us embarrassing you so?"

"What? Hey, wait a minute, you aren't supposed to see that! I want it back."

"Sorry," I said with a wink. "A deal's a deal. See you again when you try to cross the river."

Walt and the others all broke out laughing as we mounted up and guided the horses back to the comfort of our lines.

Seeking to break through the doldrums of my own mind, I cajoled Stuart into allowing me to accompany part of the 9th Virginia on an attack across the river. On the first of December, we slipped down the river near Port Royal, and crossing on flatboats, surprised a cavalry unit of Pennsylvanians. Spraying gunfire when they reached for their weapons, we killed a few and captured nearly 60. We crossed them over on the flatboats, forcing their horses to ford the icy stream. For about the next two weeks, we just rode up and down our infantry lines.

One such morning, everything changed. A few of us, including Walt, had gone down closer to the river and watched the Yankees who were hard at work erecting pontoons to cross the river. *Damn,* I thought, *they are going to try it. They are going to try to reach Richmond, but first they'll have to bust through us right here.* We rode past a group of generals, including Lee, Longstreet, Stuart, and the recently nattily attired, Stonewall.

Walt cackled, "Every time I see Stonewall all gussied up, I just can't contain myself."

"I know what you mean. I still can't get used to seeing him that way. You should have seen him the night Stuart presented him with that new uniform. Crusty he is, but boy, he was truly embarrassed that night."

Walt replied, "What I would have paid to see that. Let's stop and get some food. There is a commissary nearby." We reined up and put the wet mounts on the picket line. Mud splattered and laughing still, we went on our search for that commissary. I was making my way until I met the gaze of an infantry man. It was my brother Caleb!

"Caleb, is that you? Is it really you?" He answered that it was, and I rushed to embrace him.

"Caleb, I didn't know if you were still alive. We're losing a lot of soldiers, Caleb, and since I hadn't seen ya, even though Stuart's cavalry hovers around Jackson's command, I thought you were gone. Not that there isn't a ton of us, but..." I gurgled.

He answered me coolly, telling me he had been wounded at Sharpsburg, carted to Richmond, and now was back here.

"Well, it's like what I've been telling you. We're getting the hell beat out of us, although those Yankee horse boys aren't giving me or any of us any cause for concern, right boys?" I yelled at our group, quickly wiping a tear from my cheek.

Walt replied, "Yeah, you're right, Levon. We're going down some ways and get something to eat. You catch up with us later, okay?"

"Sure, sure. Caleb, do mother and father know you were wounded? Did they ask about me?" I asked him, studying his face.

He told me that someone's brother had ridden out to our place and told them. Our neighbor, Thom, had lost a leg in the same battle as him.

"Whose brother?" I said, puzzled. I couldn't remember our family knowing anyone in Richmond.

"Hannah was a woman I met in the hospital. We spent some time together, and Hannah's family put them up till I moved out with these boys," Caleb said, gesturing to a bunch of country boys behind him. "When the war is over, I intend to make her my wife. Her brother rode out, found the farm, and delivered the letter while I was laid up."

I tried hard to hide a smirk. He gets wounded and gets a girl. Doesn't that just beat all? "Well, you found yourself a woman and only lost an eye?" I said, pointing at this patch. "Damn, the odds are working in your favor. How is our fine capitol?"

The next couple of minutes of our conversation got rather murky because Caleb, for some reason, had got his hackles up. He started yelling at me how the capitol and farm were both suffering, and all the slaves had run off. I didn't tell him about the Hoodoo ritual, or the slaves behavior that Wilson and I had witnessed. Hell, I hadn't even told him about our cousin's family being there. He said our father was worried about losing the both of us.

Caleb said, "He was rather vague on how you became involved except for telling me in a previous letter that you had enlisted in the cavalry."

"Uh, Caleb, I didn't really enlist, at least, not in the typical sense," I said, which was true. "Father said I was way too young, and he needed my help with the farm, but I ran away and prodded these guys to let me join up," I continued telling only a partial truth. Maybe my parents hadn't gotten the letter I'd written explaining the matter.

Caleb kept on his hollering, "As what? How can you help us?"

"Scout, as a scout," I said, briefly telling him some of my duties.

"But the land, Levon. What about our farm?"

I shouted back, "Look, Ca—what are you doing? You were at school, at least, our parents thought you were. But you're here. I'm bettin' you feel the same as I do."

"What's the use if we can't use our farm as we see fit? What's the use if we don't really own the land? That's why I'm here, to fight to keep what's my own."

"And just exactly what do you think I'm doing here? You think I'm on some monthly jaunt?" I shot back.

One of the country boys my brother was with, sauntered up and said, "Caleb, you did find one of your lads, eh?" His words burst forth from the forest of his beard with an acrid smoky smell. Too many cigars, I figured.

Caleb replied, "Ah, no, Sim. This here is my brother, Levon, joined up with the cavalry." I shook his bear like paw when extended.

The giant asked, "You is in the cavalry? How come you don't carry no sword?"

I laughed at his simple question. "Not all of us carry swords. Plus, I'm not regular cavalry, I'm a scout," I said, forgetting that Stuart had placed me in the cavalry as a full soldier.

The giant went on and on about his lack of brains, his brother with him, and that his brother and mine had done some quarreling. The giant then asked Caleb to go, and I bid them both a hurried farewell because my empty stomach had begun to pitch its own spirited battle.

The bombardment of the town of Fredericksburg rose in intensity, causing me to pause and look back at Caleb. He stood right next to—my God, Parson Tyme! He was the parson who served Wytheville. What was he doing here? I swear I could see right through him like he was a vision or ghost, or something. He stood there in his white shirt, ecumenical collar, vest, and long black cloak, his head bare.

With a red wound staining his shirt, he stared at me, swallowing me with his gaze. From the bottom lids of his eyes, fire flickered. Stick-like soldiers of the Confederacy charged towards me with arms outstretched, and eyes wide with fright. He swung a gold pocket watch back and forth, back and forth. With a tilt of his head and mouth yawning wide, a flock of blackbirds flew from his mouth and rose into the air, bunched together as if they were one.

I rubbed my eyes, certain that they must be playing tricks on me. When I opened them again, both my brother and the vision of Parson Tyme had vanished. What did it mean? Had I really seen Parson Tyme? I arrived at the commissary wagon, and after getting a tin of hard tack and some greasy bacon, joined Walt and the others, but said nothing. If I had told them what I thought I had seen, they would think I had gone plain crazy. Maybe they would be right.

After the meager meal that did little to stifle my stomach's battle, we rode back to Hamilton's Crossing where Stuart's command was stationed, and watched. There was little we could do.

Yankee cannons reduced Fredericksburg to nearly rubble, where only a few church spires and chimneys stood in relief. They succeeded in driving out, what I was told later, were Mississippi sharpshooters, and came over on the pontoon bridges they had built.

In their glee, the enemy ransacked the town, destroying what had not been destroyed by their cannons. At least that was what they seemed to be doing, for I could not see clearly, being some distance from them. Sitting atop Spirit, all I could do was watch, as we all did, just watch. Can't say I blamed their ransacking, I had done the same, but at least I was polite about it. Unable to stomach anymore of their hostile hooliganism, Endicott and I turned in for the night.

With wagons creaking and the shuffling of feet, many feet in the town of Fredericksburg conspired together, producing an uneasy sleep. I couldn't see them, none of us could, but we knew they were there, cloaked by the fog.

I tossed and turned, and finally gave up altogether. No sooner had I tossed off my blankets and stepped through the tent opening than the sharp report of two cannons welcomed the dawn. It was the 13th of December.

Once again, a collection of generals stood on a knoll peering into the mist. The fog began to lift and the town below came alive with Yankees marching toward the open plain. The ruins of the town, and the open ground before our lines, teemed with the color of blue. If it hadn't been for the fact that it was Yankees, the sights and sounds would have been glorious. Drum rolls and bugle blasts filled the air. They came on in their starched blue uniforms, their banners rippled in the wind, and their bayonets gleamed in the sparse sunlight.

I watched Pelham charge to a stand of cedars that

stood at the junction of Massaponax and Old Richmond Stage Road, with two gun crews toting a Blakely and a Napoleon 12 pounder. He began to pepper their flank and whole ranks folded. But, to their credit, they closed their ranks and, I thought with a laugh, soldiered on. Pelham shifted position every time the Union guns tried to seek him out. One gun was put out of commission, because I saw the explosion. Stuart began to implore Pelham to withdraw.

"Go now, leave, you gallant man. The enemy will be upon you," he yelled, and then stopped short, realizing with a smile that it was useless. Pelham could not possibly hear him from that distance. He ordered messengers to ride out to Pelham's position and deliver the order to withdraw. He ignored them for some time before finally relenting. I was told his ammunition had run out.

Although I was mounted, all I could really do was watch. I'm sure Stuart felt it was no place for cavalry, and he was probably right. The Yankee cannons pounded the ridge below Marye's Heights with little effect. Fact is, they was shootin' blind because they didn't really know where our cannons were. When Longstreet's cannons finally did open up, the Yankee's accuracy improved, for they trained their sights on the smoke belching forth.

Thousands charged across the open plain. They closed to a couple hundred yards, I figure, when Stonewall unleashed his fury. Cannons roared to life, and our infantry rose as one from hiding spots behind stone fences and a sunken road, feeding volley after volley into the wave of blue. This time, the Yankees didn't close ranks. Line after line crumpled to the ground, and those that remained standing, stopped and quickly shrank back. What followed was attack after attack, and they all were like the first, fiercely beaten back.

But unlike the first two attacks, the following attacks did not surge forth, but scrambled over broken bodies or tore away from the grasps of the wounded from previous charges, who pleaded with them to go no further into the depths of hell we welcomed them to.

Endicott and I rode toward the back of one line of riflemen. Just prior to one of the fifteen attacks, an emerald green flag with a gold harp appeared, causing one of my countrymen to mutter, "Oh God, those are Meagher's men. They are coming!"

A slew of unintelligible shouts erupted from both sides. I cocked my head in wonder and looked at Endicott. He answered my question before I even asked it. He had the uncanny ability to realize when I had a question, and then simply answer it.

"Meagher's men are the Yankee's famed Irish Brigade. Your men and theirs are exchanging Gaelic obscenities. Their battle cry, which you hear rising and falling through their ranks, translates into, Clear the Way."

Directing my gaze to another flag that fluttered among their ranks, he spelled out the words, "riam nar druid o sparin lan," translated, it reads, "we will never fly from the clashing brigades." It seems to me they intend to follow that oath. It's curious that they would fight together in the Old World, but fight against each other in another," he added wryly. They did not fly, but the outcome of their charge was the same, they had failed.

The sun set slowly and their attacks ceased. Those Yanks who could retreat, did so, staggering to the unfinished railroad grade on one side, or the few homes left on Plank Road on the other, or back altogether to Fredericksburg.

There was no silence, however. The broken ranks of blue littered the field, writhing and twitching, screaming for water, their mothers, or just plumb deliverance from their pain. The freezing weather did nothing to quiet them, but only increased their pitiful screams.

I did not have the stomach for it. I could not harden my heart to it, but still did nothing. True, we suffered too because we had dead and wounded that lie in the sunken road, but the plain below looked like a giant swath of blue cloth had been spread out over the entire area. We cried, and some particularly merciful souls carried water out to the suffering men.

For the next few days, there was little fighting except for the occasional desultory cannon ball. The day after the battle, the landscape began changing. The carpet of blue held splotches of pink and black. Flesh! The bodies had been stripped of their clothes to comfort those still living. I heard some of our soldiers complain that the coats weren't suitable to wear since they had too many bullet holes through them. The groans began to dim as minute by minute, and hour by hour, raced away. The wounded simply froze to death, their wounds unattended. The 15th of December, dawn broke to find not a living Yank in sight.

I accompanied Stuart, Endicott, and his two fellow correspondents, Mr. Lawley and Mr. Vizetelly, onto the battlefield.

Limbs torn from each other, bodies torn apart, some missing an arm, another both legs, and yet another, no head at all. Those with heads still attached stared sightless, yet wild with fright. Still others had bodies swollen to twice their size, or blackened to resemble the colored man. Spirit cautiously picked her way through the carnage, her hooves making a gentle sucking sound each time she lifted them from the ground thick with blood that resembled syrup. She shied away, backing up, snorting and neighing whenever we encountered a dead horse or mule. I leaned over, unable to stop my retching which splashed into an open skull. Oh God, I'm sick.

One of Endicott's fellows, I think it was Mr. Lawley, exclaimed, "I have seen Solferino, and many of the battlefields in Italy, but none have rivaled the grotesque carnage displayed here."

Through bleary eyes, I again looked at Endicott for his explanation. "My esteemed colleague refers to the 1859 battle of Solferino and San Martino. A French-Sardinian alliance fought with an Austrian army. Many estimate there were 300,000 pitted against one another, but I do not know. I wasn't there."

To say it defied all imagination would be incorrect, only that it defied mine. What others thought, I cannot say. Even though I had not killed a one during those three bloody days in December, when I looked at my hands, they looked as if they were stained with blood.

That evening, the sky showed bright, with bands of green and red from earth up into the heavens.

NINETEEN

Dancing Along the Rappahannock

The Death of Pelham

Admittedly, I finally succumbed to the somberness and sickness that enveloped our lines like the fog that December in Fredericksburg. A bitter cold with little shelter, and the lack of food, simply added to the misery. Perhaps it was the weather, or the carnage of the last two battles, or the unsettling vision of Parson Tyme. I do not know. After days of coughing up mucous and slogging through the slush feeling like I was carrying a sack of cannonballs, I took to bed, as it were.

It was not a feather quilted bed covered in blankets with the warmth of a crackling fire in the hearth being tended to by your loved ones. No, sir, not even a damn cot. My bed was a burlap sack laid over a patch of rocky ground, with me swaddled in blankets and bit of clothing like a newborn babe. Our threadbare tent provided the shelter, and instead of the tender mercies of family, it was Endicott who served as my nursemaid!

"I hope it's not cholera or typhoid, but I'm not a physician. It is probably no more than a common cold. Of course, it is to be expected. For several days, you wore no jacket or overcoat, and as you well know, the weather did not sufficiently warm," Endicott scolded me as a mother would a careless child.

"Oh please, Endicott, not now," I moaned, feeling my head beginning to throb, but he kept right on.

"Levon, you are a puzzlement to me, to be sure. Sometimes, before my eyes, you seem to leap into maturity, and just as quickly, hop back into childhood. It is truly a puzzlement," he clucked. "I have taken the opportunity to brew a tea with a mixture of rye, thyme, and sage that I was able to procure. This may ease your congestion. So pardon me, if you will, so I can continue with its preparation outside." Not much later, he came back in through the tent flap and offered me a steaming cup.

"My, it is quite cold out there, but this should warm you up, and ward off your respiratory problems, as well, so drink up," he said, shaking off the cold and clicking his own cup against mine.

Inhaling deeply, I took a long gulp of the tea. Bitter, it was, and I winced at the taste and its scalding heat. Endicott, noticing my expression, laughed. "Yes, the mixture is not to my liking either, but sometimes, the cure is as painful as the illness, but it should help. The same concoction was administered to me by my grandmother back in the old country. It worked, for I was fit as a fiddle in mere days."

I began feeling particularly drowsy and hot at the same time. Certainly, it was the liquid. "Yes, you will feel sleepy," Endicott said with a queer smile. "It's part of the curative process, sleep is. It is only days 'til the arrival of Saint Nicholas. Let us wish for peace and the restoration of your health." It was the last thing I remembered before drifting off.

When I awoke, Endicott sat cross-legged in our tent, scribbling away furiously, aided by the flickering light of a lantern he had drug in. I knew I had dreamed, but could not recall them, as I know you have all experienced by the by. I do remember smiles coming from faces I could not make out. They were not frightening at all, but rather sweet and slight.

Groggily, I muttered, "Drink, I need drink." Desperate to moisten my mouth, I continued, "What time is it? What day is it?"

"Perhaps some tea without the elixir I added which put you to sleep? It is two days 'til Christmas. You slept for a day or so. How do you feel?"

I shifted my body slightly, and feeling no pain, replied, "Everything seems to work, and I have lost no limbs, so I would say I'm fine. I hope I don't go to coughing again. Why do my blankets hold wet?"

Endicott replied, "You had a fever that broke while you slept, so that explains the condition of your coverings. Although you say you feel fine, I would suggest you remain at rest until Christmas. While you slept, I toured the camp and no one and nothing is astir. Why, the general's family has arrived, which leads me to believe he plans no immediate action."

Endicott was right, at least for a short while. Christmas arrived, and I got out of the tent to stretch my legs and breathe in some cool air. With no cough erupting, I began feeling much better.

"Merry Christmas, Levon," Endicott said cheerily. "I'd offer you a smoke in celebration because, quite frankly, that is all I have to offer, but I would suggest you not partake, having only just recovered from your respiratory distress."

Glancing at him, I said, "Merry Christmas to you as well, Endicott, but what you say is true, so I decline your present, but not the spirit in which it was delivered."

That short while did indeed evaporate, and my black mood began fading as we were called into the ride once again by Stuart on the morning of December 26th, 1862. Stuart had plans to again disrupt the Yank's communication lines. I guess he felt like we had the Yankees back on their heels and it would do much good to continue their journey back to their country.

1800 strong, we crossed the Rappahannock in the afternoon and headed toward the Potomac. Being out in the air astride Spirit, and again embarking on another adventure, did much to enliven me. Endicott even spoke up about my apparent sharp return to health.

"Young man, it appears my brew has improved your health as it did mine when I was young. The wonder of nature's treatments. It provides us the means in which to heal ourselves. You would agree?" he said, trotting along next to me.

I laughed at his queerness and replied, "You know, Endicott, you have a rather strange way of saying things, but I suppose you are right. The tea you made from those herbs you found from God knows where has indeed cured my cough and cleared my head. I do thank you for that."

"It is well. Where do you expect Stuart to lead us now? I hope not into another great waste of human life."

"I really don't know, Endicott. I just blindly follow along, we all do. I leave the thinking to the generals, you know. I suppose the Yanks do too. We are really just like pawns in a huge chessboard being moved at the whim of others."

"You play the game, Levon? I have never seen you

play chess."

Chuckling, I said, "I play a little. But there's no time for it, plus, we don't even have a board."

"So true, so true," he said before growing quiet.

We camped for the night at Morrisville, Fauquier County.

Early the next morning, we splashed across the Potomac. The water hit my face with cold kisses of some clarity. I heard that Stuart's intentions were to strike the Telegraph Road at three separate points. While I stayed with Stuart and Fitz Lee, W.H.F. Lee and his men were directed to Dumfries, and Hampton to Occoquan. The next twenty miles were largely uneventful until encountering a wagon train on Telegraph Road just north of Chopawamsic Creek.

I was riding ahead, alone, acting as a scout. Up ahead, a wagon train with escorts approached, and frankly, it surprised me. I had not heard them, and so my talent as a scout had deserted me at that moment. My surprise left me rooted to the spot and I just stared at them. I heard the hiss of a bullet pass my ear while the vision of the dead on the battlefields of Sharpsburg and Fredericksburg dazzled my eyes. Shuddering, I shook my head to clear it, and pulled out the Navy colt. I wheeled Spirit around ready to race back and report to Stuart and Fitz Lee's command, but they were there right behind me!

I pulled the trigger and watched a Yankee horseman drop from his saddle, while troopers streamed by, casting looks of puzzlement at me. Stuart reined up to me and barked, "Go, Levon! Help them secure the train."

I listlessly prodded Spirit toward the captured train. Perhaps I hadn't had enough of the river splashed on my face to give me much clarity at all. By the time I reached the stretch of wagons, they were already secured by us, with the glum teamsters sitting on their seats, and the soldiers already disarmed. Now, I was fairly embarrassed of myself, and wished to correct Stuart's feel for me right then. I galloped about a mile further down the road and spied a heavily armed camp right there along Telegraph Road. I turned, double lickety-split, back toward Stuart. Arriving back in front of Stuart, I blurted out, "General, down the road there is indeed a large body of the enemy."

Stuart gave me a look that told me nothing, and said rather coolly, "Yes, I know. Some of the captured prisoners have told me as much. I fear their number is greater than ours, and entrenched, therefore, I will retire instead. I expect Hampton to bring even more captured wagons, which could slow us down."

With disdain, he continued, "That is all, fall in." That night, after skirmishing with the Yanks, we camped near Cole's Store. As Stuart's various brigades reunited, he sent the captured prisoners and wagons back toward the Rappahannock ahead of us.

Feeling rather sullen, I fell in the next morning on the attack at Burke's station which sits astride the Orange and Alexandria Railroad, a scant 15 miles from Washington.

This bold move caused me to think of Wilson. After all, it was in Washington that I had last seen him. During my last conversation with Chiswell, he had said he would try to get some information about my cousin, but I hadn't an occasion to speak with him since. Our surprise attack on the station allowed us to add to our captures, and we took possession of the telegraph office before they could sound an alarm.

I ambled over to the telegraph station, eager to get back in Stuart's good graces. Stuart stood in the office with a sly smile, listening to our enemy's frantic reports seeking our whereabouts. Still smiling, he ordered our brass pounder to tap out a taunting message to Union Quartermaster, Major General Meigs, which read,

"Quality of mules lately furnished me very poor, interferes seriously with movement of captured wagons. J.E.B. Stuart."

That completed, Stuart lost his smile and addressed me sternly. "Cut the wire, Levon." I quickly climbed the pole and severed the line with a knife. Without conference, we trotted toward Fairfax Courthouse, seeking its capture as well. Almost a mile out of town, our advance was fired upon by a volley of both infantry and artillery. Stuart broke off most of our column and led us on the turnpike between Fairfax Courthouse and Annandale to Vienna. After reaching Vienna, we veered westward to Frying Pan, reaching it at daybreak.

After a hard ride, what awaited all of us was rest and food. All of us except for Stuart, who had the chance for a dalliance with Laura Radcliffe, his sleighing partner from the previous year. We did finally cross back over the Rappahannock, celebrating with our prize of 200 prisoners, 200 horses and mules, and nearly twenty wagons loaded with supplies.

Much of the rest of the winter was spent on the heights overlooking Fredericksburg, in solitude with various forces rotating in and out of the area at Stuart's insistence to regain their strength. We had lost a few men, but an incredible amount of horseflesh, they was plumb wore out.

I generally stayed out of Stuart's path, and Endicott, sensing my hesitation, followed right along. Mosby sought me out in early January with a proposition.

Approaching me one crisp morning, Mosby hailed, "Levon, I would like some words with you. That alright?"

"Sure, Lieutenant Mosby, what is on your mind?"

"Lieutenant Mosby, is it? Please, John. There is no need for formality," he said with a rare show of mirth.

"Good morning, Mr. Mosby, sir," Endicott bellowed,

hoping to trumpet his presence.

"Good morning, Mr. Wales. I would beg your pardon, but I need to talk with Levon privately. Does that meet with your approval, sir?" Mosby said, more as an order than a question.

Feeling snubbed, Endicott answered curtly, "Of course, sir. I am but a guest here. I have other business to attend to in camp. Good day."

I glanced at him as he stalked away, knowing he didn't have any other damn business to attend to that I knew of.

"Levon, I need to ask you something," Mosby started. "I know I talked to you and your cousin about this before, but it now seems upon us."

"What's that?" I asked.

"I would like to ask you to join me in a somewhat unorthodox command. I have received approval from Stuart to act on my own with like-minded men to harass the enemy from behind their lines."

"I don't understand you one bit," I said.

"What I mean is, we would act as irregulars. Our operations would cover the counties south of the Potomac and along the western base of the Blueridge Mountains."

"Isn't that what we do now? What do you mean by irregulars? We wouldn't be part of the Confederate cavalry then?"

"Oh, we would be part of the cavalry, all right. We could operate independently of Stuart, for a time. We could disrupt the enemy demonstrations through surprise attacks, then blend back into the sympathetic families that live in Fauquier and Loudon counties."

"But I don't know anybody that lives in those counties. Besides, why me?"

"Blending in won't be a problem. The men who you would ride with could vouch for you. You do know the area well, it seems. But let me ask you a question. I was in that last raid around Dumfries. I thought I noticed you hesitate in the face of the wagon train, and Stuart upbraided you about it."

"What's upbraiding mean?"

"Okay, scolded you then. What was that about?" Mosby pressed.

"I...I don't know. I guess I just remembered the bloody messes at Sharpsburg and Fredericksburg. I don't know. It's just hard for me to stomach sometimes."

"Killing doesn't bother you that much, does it? I figure not, or you wouldn't be here. But what I'm asking you to do would take the wholesale slaughter out of your view. It seems to me you don't exactly cotton to the military life. Am I right?"

"Yeah, well, I guess you're right," I stammered.

"Precisely. Surprise attacks. Small amounts of the enemy. Military life doesn't exactly appeal to me, neither. I prefer scouting and vedette duty. I'm restless, and that just butts up against wasting away in camp. Levon, you ride like the devil and you are young. You must consider it. "

"I don't know, John. You said Stuart gave you his approval, for me?"

"Well, now, not directly. But I see no reason why he would disagree."

"What about Endicott?" I asked.

"What about the Englishman?"

"He is sort of in my charge."

"C'mon, now. Do you not think Stuart could find another watchdog for him?"

"I don't know, John. I'm in this war because of Stuart. I feel a great deal of loyalty toward him."

"I will give you time to decide. But don't allow blind allegiance to a man, even such a man as General Stuart, prevent you from acting on your real loyalty. Your real loyalty should be on the cause." Saying that, he wheeled and stalked off.

Now, rightly he made some sense. I did enjoy the raids, and they weren't slaughters at all. I knew it would be dangerous, but isn't that what war is all about anyway? He could call it blind allegiance to Stuart, and perhaps it was. But being with Stuart aided the cause, not subtracted from it, and sure, Stuart could find someone to be what Mosby called "a watchdog" for Endicott, but the queer Englishman, well, he had grown on me. At least I had time to ponder it, Mosby said so himself.

End of January, 1863, I think it was on the 28th, I chanced to dine with von Borcke, Adjutant General, Channing Price, Endicott, Stuart, acting as if all was forgotten, and Chiswell! Inside Stuart's tent we ate a hearty meal of cold bread and turkey, corn beef, and oysters. The food had been brought to camp by Price and Chiswell, who had both just returned from furloughs. I was eager to talk to Chiswell to see if he had any information on Cousin Wilson, but waited until after we ate. I didn't want to seem impolite.

I took the opportunity when Stuart stepped out of his tent and a banjo and fiddle commenced playing, to pull Chiswell out of the tent, as well.

"Chiswell, glad to see you," I said, clapping him on the back.

"Good to see you too, Levon. How are you?"

"Well, Chiswell, I was hoping you might have some word on my cousin. Is it so?"

"Funny you should ask. I have a message that Stringfellow was able to get to me. It was smuggled out. It was written by Sil Burrows, who you may know," he said with a smile.

Excited, I asked "What does it say?"

"Well, most curious, it is addressed to you," Chiswell said, handing a small parchment scroll to me.

Dear Levon,

I hope this letter finds you well. Franklin said you wanted information regarding Wilson and I have complied best as I am able. He is alive, but walks with a limp. I fear his leg did not mend properly after being broken. I'm sorry to say that it is the only good news I have. Now, I must be careful in talking to him too much because of my work, but he speaks badly of our cause and has gone to wearing a castoff Union uniform. He does have the run of the prison, and although he is treated with some rudeness by the guards, I believe they do trust him. He continues to exclaim, "I'm waiting." I don't know for who or what, if anything at all. I hope things will get better.

-Sil-

I quietly stared at the letter. Chiswell asked, "Everything is okay, Levon, considering?"

"Yes, considering," I said blankly.

Endicott, who had come out, seemed to notice my mood immediately. "Come on, my boy. Let us take leave and go back to our tent. Lieutenant Dabney, you will give our regards to the others for the fine repast?"

"Um, yes, certainly, good night," Chiswell said nervously. As Endicott and I headed back to our tent, I filled him in on the contents of Sil's letter. I previously spoke to him about Mosby's urgings.

Arriving back at our tent's opening, he pulled his pipe and pouch out and began packing it, while offering me a cheroot. He always leaves me wondering as to why he carries cigars when he smokes a pipe, but I decided to let it pass.

"So, you received news of your cousin's condition and Mosby wants you with him. What do you plan to do?"

"I would like to get to Wilson, but that seems all too impossible. I can't just go waltzing into the Yank's capitol and get him. I don't even know if he would come with me, if Sil's beliefs are correct."

"And Mosby?" Endicott asked.

"What he says does make some sense. But to join him lends me to operate and expect to be cared for by people I don't even know."

"But is it so different than now? You told me when you came to Stuart, you and Wilson did, and knew no one."

"It was different then. That seemed like the best thing to do under those circumstances, and at that time. Mosby is asking me to do something a little different, and to tell you the truth, I have friends here."

"Friends?"

"People I've become acquainted with. You, Chiswell..." I paused, taking a draw on the cigar.

"It is not like you are not, as you say, acquainted with Mosby."

"I know, I know. I have done things with him and he has helped me too, but..."

"But?"

"Mosby said that to follow Stuart would be more like following a blind allegiance to Stuart rather than the cause."

Endicott snorted. "Preposterous! Stuart has your cause deep in his heart. I have witnessed it, after all."

"He said that showing such regard for Stuart might take away from the true result. Of course, I don't believe it, but nevertheless, my attachment to Stuart and his command is absolute. I will not go. I have promised the general I would not leave. Not for anything!"

"So your next step is to be?"

"Mosby did mention the slaughter, and he is correct to believe that I'm affected by it. Who would not be? But I think I must find a way to cast it aside and work toward bringing it all to an end," I replied.

"Perhaps when the weather is better you can prove to yourself and Mosby that you should remain here and continue as you have."

Little did I know that Mosby had given me little time and already made my decision for me. Mosby was no longer at Fredericksburg.

The month of February passed slowly and listlessly, and I grew restless. I had grown tired of the snowball fights, and was eager to prove only to myself that I could fight.

Since Stuart was again gone, attending to the trial of a Henry Pate, and had not asked me to accompany him, I attached myself to Fitz Lee and his command at Culpepper Courthouse, dragging Endicott along with me.

Lee was aware of a Yankee attempt at crossing at Kelly's Ford after he had attacked them previously, and crossed back over the Rappahannock unmolested. I joined with the 2,000 troopers, where we galloped toward Brandy Station to the tune of "Boots and Saddles". We met the enemy at noon after they had forded the river. Lee, in conference with Stuart and Pelham, who had just arrived back, ordered a saber charge. Since I don't own a saber and never used one at all, I dismounted, joining a skirmish line of the 3rd Virginia. From a stand of trees, I pulled shot after shot from my carbine. Hell, I don't know if I hit anything, but kept sighting into the fog, awaiting a muzzle flash before shooting.

I watched waves of our cavalry surge into a mass of

Yankee cavalry, slashing and whirling together as if in a ballet. As we began faltering, or so it seemed to me, I remounted and joined the 3rd under Colonel Owen on an assault across the pasture land of the Wheatley farm.

I guided my mount through an opening in a rail fence as the ground before me kicked up dirt and wooden rails splintered from enemy bullets. I kept forward until coming to a stone wall that forced us all back. Their artillery began to pound into us, dropping several troopers around me. I turned back to see Pelham topple from his saddle after being struck by a fragmenting shell. I raced over and draped him over his saddle, as he was unconscious. Leading the wounded Pelham away, I saw Stuart, his face a mask of anger and grief. He knew Pelham was severely hurt. The fighting broke off as the night streaked in. Pelham never regained consciousness, and with the stroke of midnight, he passed. Stuart wept over his body, and kissing his forehead, whispered farewell. Stuart ordered everyone to wear black armbands in mourning. The heroes continued to fall.

TWENTY

Chancellorsville
April and May, 1863

They crossed the river. I first noticed the enemy movement while I was some distance from Stuart with some other scouts. Endicott I left behind with Stuart while performing my duties.

Mid-April, while riding Spirit some distance from the banks of the Rappahannock, I saw a long line of Yankee cavalry, complete with batteries, pack mules, and horses winding their way up the river from Falmouth. It was not at all curious to me that they would be on the move, for the lull in fighting had stretched for some time. It did strike me, though, as I watched them under a slight rain, that they seemed to be set for heavy fighting. You would ask me why I felt that. It was for the fact that they had so much artillery. Of course, it is not uncommon for cannons to accompany cavalry, for we seemed to always to be accompanied by the late Pelham's batteries, and almost all cavalry units on both sides had artillery, but, oh lord, the number of cannons. It seemed to me they were toting about 40 pieces, and pack mules and horses heavily laden with supplies. This wasn't just a raid, no sir.

I didn't head right back to Stuart, though. Perhaps I should have, but I know Stuart had received orders to gather information on just this, enemy movement. Trailing them, I watched as they attempted to cross the swollen Beverly Ford when the sky just opened up.

Sheets of rain and ice poured down, halting their crossing as the ford began to quickly fill and swell even more. I started my ride back to Stuart and was quickly surprised. There were Yankees everywhere! Not the ones I had been watching, but others, infantry and cavalry corps roaming freely about.

They came across other parts of the Rappahannock at Kelly's Ford and the Rapidan, from Germanna and Ely's Ford. They struck the Virginia Central Railroad at Trevilian Station, Louisa Courthouse, and the village of Columbia after crossing the North Anna River. I dodged their units for two or more days, never sleeping, but stealthily creeping among the pines heavy with snow. It seemed as if their cavalry, led by a General Stoneman, I later learned, was conducting raids of nuisance as if he had taken pages from Stuart's book.

I have to tell you that I nearly lost myself with all the dodging I was doing. I nearly stumbled into a fierce fight at a tavern near the edge of the wilderness of Spotsylvania. My skills told me that the enemy had massed there, for I knew they existed in the area. Surely the Yanks would not be as foolhardy to pitch battle in the Wilderness.

The Wilderness covers nearly 300 square miles of

scrub oak and second growth timber, being that the original timber had been chopped down as fuel for Catherine Furnace, the semi-abandoned iron foundry. Dizzy with a lack of sleep, dog-tired, and wet, I found Stuart at Culpepper Courthouse.

"General, we are cut off by Union cavalry behind at Wilderness Tavern."

"They are all around us in fact, Levon. I have opposed them at not only Brandy Station, but have also done my best to protect the Central Railroad, Gordonsville, and Wilderness Tavern. Since evening is upon us, we will set camp at Todd's Tavern. I don't believe what you saw was active movement but rather a feint meant to deceive us. At any rate, I'm going to headquarters to receive further orders. It is a fine job you have done."

I dismounted and took to caring for Spirit, for she was as tired as me. Stuart and some of his staff had been gone for no more than 30 minutes when his call for aid came. Stuart's party had come upon Yank cavalry in the bright moonlight and was in some danger. I quickly re-saddled Spirit and charged into the line of battle drawn by the 5th Virginia. Immediately, I was thrown into a hurricane. The enemy was behind us and in front of us, all at once, it seemed. I rode among the mass of horses, shooting indiscriminately, with my pistol hitting some but not dropping any. I couldn't see the color of the uniforms because the night, which had been lit by the moon, was now shaded by thick pines to one side of the road.

I grabbed a passing rider and he grabbed me as well, throwing fists. But neither of us fell from our mounts. I heard someone scream, "Don't shoot, don't shoot, we're friends." The horseman I was grappling with paused and I cracked the butt of my pistol upside his head and broke away. I swear as he fell from his horse, I thought I saw more than a touch of gray. I scampered away as did everyone else, and gave the road to Chancellorsville up to the invading Yankees.

So it came to be, on April 30th, the Yankee hordes had reunited, but so had we. We joined with Jackson's men on the Orange Plank Road southeast of Chancellorsville. Fitz Lee's men took position near Catherine Furnace. Again, I pondered the madness of fighting in the Wilderness. If there was an advantage, it surely would be ours since we knew what obstacles the Wilderness contained, but the Yanks, well, the Yanks would fight amid the unknown. So we nestled there in the underbrush while the Yankees built entrenchments just outside the grinning ghosts of the woods.

That day and into the next, the generals' strategies floated though the branches of timber buoyed by the smoke of cannon fire. Fitz Lee's scouts had found the right flank of the enemy "up in the air," which put Robert E Lee, Stonewall Jackson, and Stuart to plotting. I stood by, watching Chaplain Beverly Lacy, who had administered to the people of the area, and Lee's topographical engineer, Jed Hotchkiss, race back and forth, repeatedly going into quiet conversations with the generals. I was awakened by Chiswell early on the morning of May 2nd and told to report to Stuart. Being already dressed, I jumped out of my tent and hurried to Stuart's tent.

"Levon, come in, come in. I have need of your assistance. It seems that an alternative route through the Wilderness area has been found. Jackson's army is to proceed along a rough trail leading from Catherine Furnace to the Brock Road. We are to shield Jackson's movement as he proceeds."

Bewildered, I said, "Okay, General, but why are you

telling me this? I act under your command, so why tell me of your strategy?"

Stuart laughed loudly. "Oh, I'm not asking for your approval at all, Levon, but the proprietor of Catherine Furnace, Charles Welford, knows of this trail and has graciously offered his young son to serve as our guide."

Still unsure of what he was getting at, I asked, "Yes?"

"He is young, as are you. It has dawned on me that the youngster may be put at ease if he's accompanied by you. Being that you two are of similar age, and you, possessing the experiences of this war, may ease that task to which he is to undertake. So you are to ride alongside him. Is that understood?"

"Yes, General, completely!" I snapped off a salute.

"Good, we are to leave shortly. Make all preparations."

Trudging back to my tent, I couldn't help thinking that now I would be responsible for two. Not only Endicott, but this young man as well. Upon entering the tent, I found Endicott astir.

"Levon, what is going on?" Endicott asked while rubbing his eyes.

"We are to move out. I believe an attack is coming, and soon. I've been asked to accompany a young guide in the area on our march. Just come on along with me, for we will be with the main column, surely."

Packing up, I saw Chiswell approaching with the youngster in tow. Holding a candle aloft to light his way, he hollered, "Levon, you are to meet this boy, err, ah, man. Stuart has issued you his orders, correct?"

"He has, Chiswell."

With a sweeping gesture that was more dramatic than was really called for, Chiswell shouted, "Private Lewis, let me introduce you to young Welford, who will be our guide this morning."

I grabbed the seemingly awe struck boy's hand and simply said, "Pleased to meet you."

The boy mumbled, "Yes, sir."

For a few awkward moments we just studied each other. He was no more than twelve or so, I figured, not so close in age as Stuart had remarked. Mop-haired, wearing overalls and a drab overcoat, he just looked at me, wide-eyed.

I drew myself erect, trying to impress the boy that I was a battle-hardened soldier, which I wasn't at all.

Chiswell broke the silence by clearing his throat. "Ahem, well boys, let's get mounted up. Stonewall is arranging his brigades. I'm to believe that we leave before dawn."

The boy, Endicott, and I walked toward the horses' tethered lines. Welford almost immediately began to chatter.

"This is exciting. But I'm scared, too. You ever get scared?"

"Sure," I said. "Everyone does. I don't think you are a real person if you don't get scared."

"But it's exciting too, right? I mean, you're a soldier. Carrying a gun and all. Plus, you are around men like General's Jackson and Lee."

Endicott rolled his eyes. I replied, "Exciting I don't know about. Killing a man is not exciting, it's dreadful. I didn't carry any gun when I got in. Didn't want to."

He looked at me incredulously. "Didn't carry no gun? How come you're a soldier? All of the soldiers I've seen have guns."

"Oh, sure, I do now. You have to, but I didn't originally. Besides, I came on as a scout, still am, but I stupidly thought then that I would never have to defend myself with a rifle or pistol. I figured I would just outrun trouble on my horse."

Welford pointed at Spirit. "That horse there? She looks like a real strider, long legs and all."

"No, not Spirit here," I said, patting her on the neck. "But a horse much like her named Sol's Mistress."

"She get shot or sumthin'?" he asked.

"No, captured, she was," I replied glumly.

"Oh," was all he said as we mounted up and rode out. Fitz Lee's men fanned out as guards for Jackson's fast moving infantry and wagon trains.

Welford led us through a rough woodcutter's trail where the brush had been cut away, but the ground was spongy due to the recent rain and snow. Welford pressed for further information.

"I know I'm excited that I'm able to provide some service to so many of the South's greatest generals. You must be excited all the time. That right, Private Lewis?"

"Well, I don't know if excited is the word I would use, boy." I chuckled when I realized I had just called him boy. He wasn't really all that much younger than me. "It's a privilege, that's for sure. But, really, what drives us all is to aid the Confederate cause."

Again, he just said, "Oh." He prodded his horse's flanks.

"Watch this curve here," he whispered kind of low as we eased our horses into a trot. For the better part of the day, we wound through the Wilderness underbrush from Decker Farm, moving northwestward to Catherine Furnace, and then toward Todd's Tavern. I had to smile when I heard Stonewall shout out, "The Virginia Military Institute will be heard from today." My brother, Caleb, had followed Jackson right out of the gates of that Institute.

Near the crossing of Catherine Furnace and Brock Road, Welford, following Jackson's orders, guided us northwest. Now, I don't know as much about the

Wilderness as the young boy, or Jackson, apparently, yet it seemed to me to increase the distance between us and the Yankees. Alongside the great Stonewall, with no Stuart in sight, Fitz Lee rode up on his horse, greatly lathered by the ride.

"General Jackson, sir. To attack at where I believe your orders indicate would put us in the middle of their line rather than their end. Begging your pardon, General, but if you would accompany me to a farm, I can point out the benefits to us."

Stonewall gazed at me, and with a slight nod of his head, he, Fitz Lee, and I rode to the Brook Farm vantage point. Stonewall's face lit up upon reaching the vantage point. Clearly he agreed with Fitz Lee's impressions.

Stonewall turned to me and calmly said, "Young man, return to the head of the column and instruct the officer of the day to continue up the Brock road to its junction with the Orange Plank Road. Make haste, young man, make haste."

"Yes, General," I said, my voice shrill with excitement, and after snapping off a salute, galloped off.

I kicked Spirit's flanks repeatedly, urging her faster. It felt like the whole Wilderness was engulfed in the same excitement as me. We were to be placed no more than a mile from the enemy now! Arriving back at the column, I informed the officer of Jackson's orders while the young Welford and Endicott stared at me with eyes wide and mouths agape. It took several hours for the army to reassemble and take position among the pines surrounding the Luckett farm. Welford, Endicott, and me, we all dismounted and simply rested. Not a word was uttered between us. The Wilderness had gone quiet as if in slumber.

With evening creeping forward, Jackson's attack commenced. The spine tingling chorus of the Rebel yell coursed through the trees, and the infantry sprang on the unsuspecting Yankees. The three of us quickly mounted up, but only Endicott and I advanced. Apparently, the young Welford, unnerved by the tumult of battle, had dashed away.

Except for a misty arch that ended in the clearing, there was little to see. What could be seen was flight. The Yankees were being, well, destroyed, is all I can say.

Stuart was next to Jackson, and he saw me and Fitz Lee's men sitting idly by. After conferring with Jackson, Stuart led us to the heights overlooking Ely's Ford, a possible escape route for the Yankees.

Once at the heights, we all quickly dismounted. I grabbed my rifle from its scabbard.

Endicott was left to help with the horses as I scampered to the top of a small rise. All below me were the backs of our enemy, many on horseback, fleeing from the fight. A few artillery pieces pounded away at them.

Now, I don't think it's quite fair to shoot a man in the back, but an order being an order, I hefted the rifle to my shoulder. Slowly, I drew a bead and my hands began to shake. Pulling the trigger, I watched a man slump forward on this saddle and slide to the ground. I fired a few more times, not certain if I had hit anybody, and stopped altogether as darkness fell.

Endicott came forward and offered me his handkerchief to wipe my face, wet with sweat. Speaking softly, he said, "It would appear to be a Confederate victory, thanks in no small part to you and the young boy's aid to General Jackson."

With my voice cracking, I replied, "Part of the strategy of men greater than me, Endicott. I'm a piece on a chessboard to be moved at the whim of a knight."

"Poetically said, my young friend, but couldn't you be moved at the whim of a queen or king also?"

"But I serve Stuart, and he is a knight."

"Help me build a fire on which we may cook a meal."

After a meager meal, I stood and looked out over the ford. Small fires winked in the darkness, but few in the undergrowth, for obvious reasons. The pines groaned under the wind. Lone pops, and even full volleys of musketry, rang out in the darkness. Suddenly, the ground underfoot began rumbling and shaking.

Endicott, with a look of fright, screamed, "Levon, what is happening?"

There were no cannons around that would cause the ground to shake so, and I had not heard the pounding of their fire. I struggled to keep my footing on the pitching ground before losing the fight and crashing to the ground. Just as suddenly as it started, it stopped, and I heard a faint cackling laugh. It was just after 9:00 pm, May 2nd, 1863.

Uneasy, I was, and grew increasingly that way. An out of breath horseman rode up to Stuart and gasped, "General Stuart, I'm from General Hill's command. General Jackson has been wounded, as has General Hill, and he begs for your assumption of command. You are the only Major General West of Chancellorsville that hasn't been wounded."

In his usual calm demeanor, Stuart said, "Levon, you and Mr. Wales will accompany me. Make haste." Within minutes, we were racing along with Hill's aide through the woods to Orange Plank Road.

Stuart went into a hurried conference with a general I didn't know, someone said his name was Heth, and took command. He pulled back the army from the right along Orange Plank Road, which lay about half a mile from Chancellorsville. We waited for daylight, at least Wales and I did, while Stuart directed Jackson's artillery chief, Colonel Porter Alexander, to fire on a ridge that ran through Hazel Grove, and then ordered the infantry forward.

Again and again, they attacked a clearing called Fairview near the ridge, but were repeatedly beaten back. We were extremely close to bitter fighting, and I dodged unseen bullets. I pulled my pistol but had not used it. Stuart rode through the lines merrily singing, "Old Joe Hooker, get out of the Wilderness."

Stuart had his horse shot out from under him, but simply mounted another. Hazel Grove, and later, Fairview, crumpled under the relentless attacks, and the Yanks fled. Stuart ordered Alexander's artillery to the top of Hazel Grove and commenced firing at the brick dwelling, Chancellor House.

"Ahh, a conclusion to a fine afternoon," Stuart remarked while continuing to order assorted infantry brigades forward, seemingly at all points. The undergrowth of the Wilderness caught fire and ringed the Chancellor House, which was also ablaze. With the enemy scattered, we rode down with Stuart to the clearing where Chancellor House stood.

The air was alive with triumphant screaming mixed with the cries of the wounded caught in the burning undergrowth. Stuart seemed to me to be indifferent, content to bask in the glow of victory, but I couldn't just sit there and watch men burn to death.

I dismounted and ran over to the bodies caught in the underbrush. One Yankee soldier pleaded for my help through a foreign tongue that I could not understand. I didn't need to understand his language because his face said it all. I desperately looked for a way to get to him, but just like the clearing, he was surrounded by fire. I stood there helpless, peering into his sad eyes. Not a scream did he utter as the fire consumed him.

The screaming rose into a roar and I turned to see

why. Marse Lee himself came into the clearing. He being more compassionate than Stuart, at least at this point, ordered us to help the wounded regardless of what uniform they wore.

Lee continued to press the enemy toward the Rappahannock, and under Stuart's command, we pushed the enemy all the way back over the river on May 6th. We retired to new headquarters which overlooked Brandy Station and the Rappahannock River, slightly northeast of Culpepper Court House.

I must admit, once again, I was feeling overwhelmed with all the bloodshed, and sometimes, just the sheer savagery of it all. My very soul cried out for an end to it, but I realized with more than just a little despair, that this war was far from over. And while luck had been on my side so far, even as men next to me had fallen, I couldn't help but worry that, one day, it would finally be my turn.

I stared into the distance and longed for home as dread gripped me. My throat tightened at the thought that I might never see it again.

About the Author

The author was born and raised in southern California, and currently resides in Phoenix, Arizona, where he has lived since 1995. He holds a BA degree in Public Relations from San Jose State University. He has two adult children. Among his favorite hobbies are hiking, reading, going to the movies, and listening to classic rock music. Finally putting this series to paper has been a long time dream. He hopes you enjoy reading it as much as he enjoyed creating it!

Fighting Under the Stars and Bars ~ Book 1:
Everyone is certain this "little rebellion" will be over in less than a year. But it's not long before 18 year old Caleb Lewis begins to fear that just might not be the case. While attending the Virginia Military Institute under the tutelage of Colonel Jackson, the man who would become known as Stonewall Jackson, Caleb and some of the other cadets take to the field as what would come to be known as the Stonewall Brigade.

They are pushed beyond their limits, and battle after battle, they are plagued by exhaustion, hunger, lack of shelter to camp, and ragged clothes to protect against the elements. But their fierce loyalty to their leader, and their belief in succession, drives them on. When a great tragedy strikes, will they have what it takes to carry on?

Gray Becomes Black ~ Book 3 Available Late Fall 2018
The conclusion of the trilogy brings Levon and his brother, Caleb, together at Gettysburg. Amid the most vicious, deadliest battle yet, it's no longer a matter of winning the war, it's a fight for their very lives. With the odds wholly against them, Levon can only wonder who, if any, will be left standing when the smoke clears.

Special Thanks

Special thanks to the Wytheville Historical Society whose research lent to the authenticity of the book.

CPSIA information can be obtained
at www.ICGtesting.com
Printed in the USA
LVHW080743050722
722718LV00036B/1533